KT-526-921

JOHN MCNALLY

INFINITY DRAKE

THE SONS OF SCARLATTI

HarperCollins *Children's Books*

First published in hardback in Great Britain by HarperCollins *Children's Books* in 2014
This edition published in Great Britain by HarperCollins *Children's Books* in 2015
HarperCollins *Children's Books* is a division of HarperCollins*Publishers* Ltd,
1 London Bridge Street, London, SE1 9GF

The HarperCollins website address is: www.harpercollins.co.uk

1

Copyright © John McNally 2014

ISBN 978-00-0-752161-6

John McNally asserts the moral right to be identified as the author of the work.

Printed and bound in England by Clays Ltd, St Ives plc

Conditions of Sale
This book is sold subject to the condition that it shall not, by way of trade or
otherwise, be lent, re-sold, hired out or otherwise circulated without the publisher's prior
consent in any form, binding or cover other than that in which it is published
and without a similar condition including this condition being imposed on the
subsequent purchaser. All rights reserved.

MIX
Paper from
responsible sources
FSC C007454

FSC™ is a non-profit international organisation established to promote
the responsible management of the world's forests. Products carrying the
FSC label are independently certified to assure consumers that they come
from forests that are managed to meet the social, economic and
ecological needs of present and future generations,
and other controlled sources.

Find out more about HarperCollins and the environment at
www.harpercollins.co.uk/green

INFINITY DRAKE

THE SONS OF
SCARLATTI

CR'

000000995772

Books by John McNally

Infinity Drake: The Sons of Scarlatti
Infinity Drake: The Forbidden City

To my children Rose, Huw and Conrad,
with love everlasting and a third share of all royalties*

DUDLEY PUBLIC LIBRARIES	
000000995772	
£6.99	JF
15-Mar-2016	PETERS
JFP	

* conditions apply

FILE NO: GNTRC 9437549███████████████-OP/DRAKE~∞

TOP SECRET – MOST CLASSIFIED – RESTRICTION ULT9

FILE ABSTRACT: (.1) MULTIPLE POINT OF VIEW NARRATIVE ACCOUNT OF OPERATION
SCARLATTI BASED ON ████████████████ANALYSIS AND DEBRIEF INTERVIEWS WITH ALL
PARTICIPANTS. INTERVIEWS CONDUCTED AND EDITED BY ████████████████████████

SUPPORTED BY TECHNICAL DATA FROM GNTRC SOURCES ███████████████████

ACCOUNT INCLUDES: FULL OPERATIONAL DETAILS. DECISION-MAKING PATHWAYS.
███████████████████████ FULL PSYCHOLOGICAL/EMOTIONAL CONTEXT.

UPDATE –

FILE UPDATED████████████████(.2) TO REFLECT TESTIMONY AND INTERROGATION OF
██

RESTRICTED ACCESS: PRIME MINISTER/CABINET SECRETARY/SECRETARY OF STATE DEFENCE/
CHAIRMAN JOINT CHIEFS OF STAFF/CHAIRMAN GNTRC.

LIFETIME RESTRICTED ACCESS: A. ALLENBY/ ∞DRAKE.
RESTRICTED STUDY ACCESS (REDACTED VERSION: LEADERSHIP AND TACTICAL COMMAND LEVEL ULT9.

FILE MOST SECURE – NOT TO LEAVE REGISTRY

Else, if thou wilt not let my people go, behold, I will send swarms of flies upon thee, and upon thy servants, and upon thy people, and into thy houses: and the houses of the Egyptians shall be full of swarms of flies, and also the ground whereon they are.

Exodus, 8:21

Consider yourself lucky. So far.

Six-Legged Soldiers – Using Insects as Weapons of War,
Jeffrey A. Lockwood, OUP, 2008

PART
ONE

PART

ONE

ONE

"This is exactly what happened to Liz and Lionel when Kismet went missing in her GAP year…"

Finn's grandma stood in front of the Departures gate, and fussed.

"Grandma! He's in the building. He'll be here any minute," said Finn.

They were waiting for Uncle Al to turn up. He was supposed to be providing cover for Grandma while she took a well-earned break – flying to Oslo for a 'knitting cruise' around Scandinavia with another hundred or so grey-haired needlecraft enthusiasts.

Al had promised to show up at Grandma's the night before.

Then Al had promised to meet them at the airport, first thing.

Then Al had promised – just now, by phone – to meet them at the Departures gate.

But Al... well, Al was Al, and nothing was certain, and Grandma's way of coping with the distress her son caused her, from babe in arms to now, thirty-two years later, was to fill the world with a breathless stream of anxious chatter.

"...Kismet their eldest with the tattoos they had to fly out to Kinshasa cost them five thousand pounds silly thing had lost her phone it was the not knowing if she was dead or alive you can't imagine what that does to a parent – *where is he?* – I looked after their cat same bladder problems as Tiger..."

"*Last call for passenger Violet Allenby, Oslo flight 103, proceed immediately to gate 15*," announced the voice over the loudspeaker.

"...John very helpfully ran me into Woking young vet from New Zealand lovely girl wet food and herbal treatment..."

"Grandma! Please!"

"I can always catch the next one..."

"Noooo, Grandma!" Finn gyrated in frustration.

"Infinity!" she snapped. "*I am not moving an inch.*"

(Infinity. All Finn knew about his father – all he needed to know – was in his name. Who would name a child after a mathematical concept? "Exactly the sort of man you'd imagine," Finn's mother would say wistfully, claiming it had been all she could do to prevent him being named $E=mc^2$.)

"Al is *here*! I'll be *fine*!"

"He is not! One thing you can rely on is that you can never rely on Al. He says he's 'in the building', but that could mean anything. It could mean an imaginary building; it could mean a building on another continent, on another planet..."

"Grandma, get on the plane!"

"I have a duty of care. You are a *child*..."

"I'm *almost a teenager.*"

"...and if you *really* think, *if he thinks*, I'm going to abandon you to your fate in an airport full of germs, runaway trolleys and international terrorists..."

And then, thank goodness, from around the corner, looking like he'd just rolled out of bed, walked Al.

Six foot two and thin as a whip, part muscle, part bone, part wire, suede jacket and ancient cords worn to the point of oblivion, dark hair, darker eyes, designer glasses held together by tape, arm raised in surprised greeting as if he'd just wandered in and spotted them by chance.

"Alan! Where on earth have you been?"

"Ah...? I was in the middle of something." He thought this would do. "Why are you still here?"

Yap!

On a lead by Al's side bounced a delighted, knee-high mongrel (a kind of spaniel/hyperactive kangaroo cross, Finn always thought).

"What are you doing with Yo-yo? You can't bring dogs in here!"

"I saw him *tied him up outside.* He was *crying.*"

Officials across the concourse were already beginning to take notice.

"Marvellous! Now we'll all be arrested..." said Grandma.

"We've got to get her out of here," said Finn to Al.

With that, Al scooped Grandma up like she was a toddler, gave her a kiss on the cheek and put her down again, pointing in the right direction.

"For goodness' sake, I'm sixty-three!"

Finn wheeled her bag after her and together he and Al herded her through the Departures gate like a reluctant farm animal.

"Have you spoken to Mrs Jennings? She's agreed to check Finn in and out of school."

"Mrs Jennings and I speak all the time," confirmed Al.

"Go, Grandma!"

"You're lying!" she protested. "All the meals are in the freezer marked—"

"All the meals are in the freezer, all the knives and forks are in the drawers, there are doors and windows that allow access to the dwelling place..." interrupted Al.

"The keys!"

"...the keys to which are in Finn's pocket, which is a cloth appendage sewn into his trousers about so high. Go on, Mother! I can reheat lasagne and hold a high moral line for a week!"

"That I doubt very much!"

She was being urged through now by a red-faced airline official.

"Love you, Grandma, have a great time!"

"You too, darling, but do be careful. Al? Alan?"

"I promise, he'll be fine, go!"

As Grandma finally disappeared through passport control, Finn fell to his knees in relief, Yo-yo licking his face.

Al looked at Finn, puzzled, and said, "Did she say *school*?"

Fifteen minutes later, Grandma was in the air, and Finn and Al were gunning it out of Heathrow and on to the M25 in Al's 1969 silver grey De Tomaso Mangusta, the most extraordinary car ever hand-built in Italy, loud and low, a monster V8 coupe with perfect styling capable of 221bhp. Yo-yo howled and loved it. Finn *adored* it. Grandma thought the car ridiculous and a prime example of Al's financial irresponsibility.

"I've grown tired of pretty dresses and I can't think of anything better to waste it on," Al would tell her, something Finn knew was only partly true because more than once he'd found cheques from Al in Grandma's handbag, and they seemed huge. For no matter how unconventionally Al behaved, people still seemed to want a piece of him – corporations in need of a technical fix, pharmaceutical companies looking to reconstitute molecules, governments stuck with insoluble nuclear waste. They all came to Al.

He ran a small lab in the heart of London and was a 'sort of scientist': an atomic chemist with a wandering mind who found it difficult to fit into any one category – in science or life.

He was the only person, or so he claimed, to have been fired from the staff of the Universities of Cambridge, England, *and* Cambridge, Massachusetts, in the *same term* (for challenging the Standard Model of particle physics via the Tau Neutrino Paradox and for striking a right-wing economist with a steamed halibut during a buffet, respectively).

Al saw it as proof of moral fibre. Grandma saw it as proof of insanity and prayed it didn't run in the family. After bringing up two totally reckless children, she had resolved to wrap her only grandchild up in sixteen tonnes of cotton wool.

Finn already shared Al's bony, clumsy physique, but had sand-coloured hair that grew in several directions at once ("your father's"), and mad blue, deep-blue eyes ("your mother's") and now Grandma fretted that he'd inherited a tendency to have his "own views" about things too (rejecting all yellow food apart from custard, pointing out a teacher's "confrontational attitude" at a recent parents' evening and bringing up his "problems with religion" with a vicar, *during a funeral*).

Not that Finn wanted to upset anyone. He was just trying to stay one step ahead of boredom, which meant – as he pointed out on his Facebook profile – 'not being on the same planet as school'. He loved Grandma and made every effort not to cause her unnecessary suffering – avoiding dangerous sports, playground conflict and potentially lethal pastimes (while retaining the right to self-defence, of course. And who could resist making home-made fireworks? Or skateboarding into a neighbour's pool, or practising overhead kicks on concrete, or…).

When Finn was with Al though, there were no rules.

Other people's uncles played golf. Other people's uncles might give them ten pounds at Christmas. Al was happy to see every moment as an opportunity for discovery and entertainment and he *never said no.* Even Finn realised this might be crazy, but it made being with him a very exciting place to be.

"I'm training him up," Al would say whenever Grandma complained.

"What for?!" she would demand, terrified (for she knew he sometimes operated out of a secret world). Life, Finn supposed, trusting Al's training absolutely, for, if his uncle's head was in the clouds, his heart was always in the right place. Yes, he was erratic and unreliable, yes, he might have "a difficult relationship with stuff" (which included parking, losing things and an inability to tidy up), but he bridged the gap between everyday life and the way life ought to be – impulsive and instructive and full of things that blew up.

He dropped in every couple of weekends, sometimes staying for a week during the holidays, and he'd stayed the whole summer after Mum had died.

"You pack a bag?" Al snapped at him.

"Yep!"

"Got your passport, checked the date?"

"Yep!"

Yap! added Yo-yo.

"Get all the gear ready?"

"In the garage, all lined up."

"Weapons? You know they still have wolves?"

"M60 with grenade launch side-barrel."

"Hah! This is not Xbox, this is life or death – sunblock?"

"Sunblock, shades, tent, clothing, waterproofs, Swiss Army knife,

Mars bar, torch, lighter, hand-held GPS – I've even got a blow-up pillow."

"*Trust yourself*," had been one of his mother's Big Three Rules. "*You can't always rely on other people.*"

Finn's stuff weighed 6.5 kilograms packed into a natty dry bag.

He was ready for anything.

"I bet you didn't remember we were going till this morning! I bet you haven't even taken a shower!" Finn teased Al.

Al pretended to be appalled.

"Hey! I've got credit cards, a restaurant guide and half a tube of Pringles. Now let's load up and let rip."

DAY ONE 07:33 (BST). Hook Hall, Surrey, UK

A convoy of six cars pulled up silently outside Hook Hall.

They were expected. Little was said.

In one vehicle was Commander James Clayton-King (Harrow, Oxford, RN, MoD, SIS, G&T Chair.), known simply as King. Not the jolly King of nursery rhymes, but the cruel, commanding type. Pale skin, powerful jaw, bone-deep intelligence. He wasn't as menacing as his hooded eyes suggested, but he liked it suggested.

Two Security Service officers hopped out, one held open the door. From the cars behind, more senior figures emerged in similar fashion, including General Mount of the Joint Chiefs of Staff, three aides accompanying him.

They were led through the complex until they reached the Central Field Analysis Chamber (CFAC), a cathedral-sized, concrete-lined warehouse where researchers could recreate and control any climate or environment imaginable, from lunar desert to lush rainforest, and proceed to blow or blast or poison the jelly beans out of it simply to see what happened. In essence it was a giant test tube and one of only three such spaces in the world.[1]

They climbed a steel gantry to a reinforced glass and concrete control gallery that flanked the space. Others had already arrived: an eclectic mix of soldiers, scientists, engineers and thinkers.

A group of bespectacled experts from a research institute on Salisbury Plain clustered self-consciously. They looked like men who hadn't slept.

There were handshakes and nods, but no high fives. Tea and coffee were offered and refused. A selection of biscuits lay untouched.

The Global Non-governmental Threat Response Committee (popularly reduced to 'the G&T') was formed in October 2002 to respond to extraordinary threats to global security and the fabric of Western civilisation. It had fourteen expert members and a decision-making core of five including Commander King as its chairman. They had only been forced to meet three times over the last decade[2],

---

[1] The others being: Shenyang, China, and Brookhaven, USA.
[2] Following incidents of nuclear disaster in Japan, chemical blackmail in Iraq and terrorism aboard the International Space Station.

and they knew whatever they were here for it would be serious.

Deadly serious.

A technician reported: "Ready when you are, sir."

"Good. Seal the room," said Commander King.

He waited as doors were locked and blinds whirred down.

"Now… You may be wondering why you've been called here."

His voice was deep and used to command – controlled, no-nonsense and yet also theatrical.

"Well. One of our scientists is missing. And it *seems* he has released – this…"

The technician hit a key and up on the screen, in enormous scale, appeared an image…

DAY ONE 07:41 (BST). Willard's
Copse, Berkshire, UK

Kill kill kill kill kill kill kill kill kill…

TWO

"Lamp trap?" snapped Al.

"Check," said Finn.

"Nets?"

"Check."

"Traps?"

"Check."

"Pins?"

"Check."

"Jars?"

Yap!

"Idiot dog."

They were back at Grandma's rambling old house now, going through the gear Finn had got together for their trip.

"Ethyl acetate?"

"'The Agent of Death?'" mugged Finn. "Check."

"Cards and fixing spray?"

"Check! It's all here, let's go!"

Yap! agreed Yo-yo (particularly delighted as 'go' meant 'run about outside with Yo-yo'), leaping at Finn with such excitement that he knocked a shoebox full of plastic soldiers off a shelf and sent the lot skittering across the garage floor.

"Oh great," Finn said, having to pick them up one by one.

"There should be some fishing rods back here..." said Al, wading through a decade's worth of accumulated junk at the back of the garage.

Finn had been on a similar junk hunt on his first summer at Grandma's, which was how he'd discovered Al's boyhood bug-collecting gear behind a defunct Mini. He and Al had set up the lamp trap, a glowing, tent-like apparatus, in the back garden, and stayed up half the night collecting and cataloguing the multitude of insects drawn towards the light.

Grandma hadn't seen it as a proper way to mourn the passing of a mother, a sister, a daughter. But then they were male, and men were different when it came to emotions, especially powerful emotions, and if arranging dead insects helped them to cope then so be it. She also knew her daughter, wherever she was, would be looking down in approval at the two of them forming such an odd, unbreakable bond.

The second of Mum's Big Three Rules for Finn was: "*Be yourself.*"

Finn had never really figured out what that meant, but he'd ended up with 108 different species of native insects in various states of disrepair mounted on two A3 cards above the fireplace in his room.

Bombus lucorum, Bombus terrestris, Bombus lapidarius (bumblebees that sounded so good it made your mouth go funny); leafcutter, miner and carpenter bees; churchyard, mealworm and common oil beetles; big stags, small stags; seven-spot and eyed ladybirds; sawfly (you should see their wings), blowfly, housefly, horn fly; fantastic, impossible dragonflies and damsels (some in distress); moths upon moths – almost every type of hawk; and butterflies fit for an art gallery – tortoiseshell and fritillary, red admiral and Camberwell beauty, swallowtail and green-veined whites.

The writing on the labels was childish and some of the pins and mounts had been knocked off, but the samples themselves still looked fantastic. He knew everything about them; he'd read every book and article. He could recite all their names and characteristics.

Finn wondered if his interest was just natural or whether he was trying to force a connection back to his parents, both of whom had been scientists (he'd lost his father, Ethan, in a laboratory accident just after he was born, his mother more recently to cancer). Either way it felt right. And when Al asked him what he'd like to do on his 'week off' from Grandma, Finn immediately knew he wanted to add to the collection.

"Great idea. How about the blind insects of the Pyrenees?" said Al. "Freakish, eyeless *Ungeheuer* found in the deepest mountain caverns, evolved over twenty million years of total darkness!"

13

"The Pyrenees?"

"It's a mountain range between France and Spain."

"I know where it is, but Grandma…"

"Never tell Grandma anything; it only worries her and then you can't shut her up."

Before Finn knew it, the trip was on.

"Let's hit the road," said Al, reappearing from the back of the garage with two fishing rods and a jar of old tobacco pipes. "We've got to get to the ferry by three."

Finn snapped his fingers and Yo-yo sprang into the tiny back of the Mangusta, delighted because everything delighted Yo-yo. Bathtime. Being locked outside in the rain. Being shouted at. And right now – being taken to certain incarceration in kennels.

En route, Al called the secretary at Finn's school, Mrs Jennings, claiming, with a completely straight face, to be consultant dermatologist "Dr Xaphod Schmitten, that's X-A-P-H—", and that he was rushing Infinity Drake to his private clinic because of "an acute case of seborrhoeic dermatitis".

"It is absolutely vital to initiate wire-brushing." If everything went well, the boy would be discharged in a week, Al continued, though he might be totally bald, and if so what was the school policy on "the wearing of a headscarf and/or wig for medical reasons"? The secretary, alarmed, put him on hold to consult a higher authority, then came back on the line to ask if she could just take his name again. "Of course," said Al, "Herr Doktor

Xaphod Schmitten, that's X-A-P—" and then pretended to be cut off by poor reception.

"That ought to do it."

He screeched to a halt in front of the kennels.

"Ditch the mutt. Go."

Finn took a deep breath. "Come on, Yo-yo."

The dog sprang out of the back seat and followed Finn up to the kennels, excited by the other doggy noises and smells. Once shut inside his cage though, Yo-yo sat on his haunches and howled.

Mum had got him for Finn as soon as she realised she was ill. It was obvious therapy, but it had worked.

Finn touched his chest. Scratched the stone. Although he couldn't get his head round the concept of his mum's 'soul', he'd long ago decided that if there was such a thing then it lived in the stone that hung from a leather tie around his neck. It looked dull and ordinary, but in fact it was a rock called spharelite that his mum had always worn. When you scratched it – with your fingernail, with anything – it would literally glow. Triboluminescence it was called, but not even science could tell you quite how it worked, or why. Which was in part why Finn loved it. It was mysterious *and* it was scientific *and* it had been his mum's *and* it had a great name. If he ever had children, one of them was going to be called Spharelite Triboluminescence.

Finn reached in and gave Yo-yo's neck one last rub.

Yo-yo thought the cruel 'lock-up-your-dog' game was over and rolled on his back, offering his tummy to be tickled.

15

What an idiot.

It was at times like this that Finn remembered his mum's third and final Big Rule, delivered in her last days alive when she hadn't seemed like she was dying at all and had showered him with affection and practical instruction.

"If you're ever in doubt, work out what feels right in your heart of hearts then, whatever happens... *just keep going.*"

Al watched, appalled, as a minute later Finn marched out of the kennels – followed by Yo-yo.

"What...?"

Yap!

Finn got in the front, Yo-yo hopped in the back.

"Mum..." Finn started to say – and Al knew what was coming: "*Mum wouldn't just leave him like this.*"

"Why you little..."

It was an emotionally loaded, totally absurd unwritten rule between them that, if either Finn or Al invoked his mother, the other had to obey. The rule was stone crazy and wide open to abuse ("*My sister would've* loved *you to make me another cup of tea...*" "*My mother would have* loved FIFA 14 *on PSP...*"), but it was not one Finn ever felt he could revoke. It needed Al to be the grown-up and break the spell, to put an end to the madness, but that just wasn't Al.

So, six minutes later, they found themselves outside the church.

Christabel Coles, vicar of the Church of St James and St John in the village of Langmere, Bucks, had been fond of Finn ever since – in the middle of his mother's funeral, aged eleven – he held up his hand to bring the service to a halt and demanded to know *exactly* what a 'soul' was and *if* it did exist then *exactly* where was his mother right now? Christabel had paused, then said, "Good question," and sat down in her vestments, ignoring the packed congregation, to discuss it with him. It had been interesting, illuminating and inconclusive, though it had helped both of them to get through the day and they'd become great friends and indulged in many such conversations since, often in the company of this… blessed dog, which Christabel didn't have the heart to tell Finn she found among the most trying of all God's creatures.

Finn argued that he could no more leave Yo-yo locked in kennels "than you could lead rich men through the eye of a camel or whatever it is. Y'know, Christabel? Will you look after him? I'll come to church next week, honest…"

She caved in. "I'll do my best."

"Brilliant! Wet food in the morning, dry at night, and just give him a blanket to lie on. Oh and walk him when you can, but it's just as easy to let him wander."

"And don't kill it," added Al.

"But I will have to tell your grandmother about this!"

"Don't worry, Al will do that. He's in enough trouble as it is."

She watched Finn jump back in beside his unreasonably handsome uncle and gave a little sigh.

Al put his foot down and the Mangusta razzed off, Yo-yo chasing them halfway down the lane.

Trust yourself.

Be yourself.

Just keep going.

It wasn't much of a legacy, but it was all he had.

"Can we go on holiday now?" asked Finn.

"We can go on holiday now," replied Al.

The sun was shining and they were roaring through the English countryside in an Italian sports car, headed for the continent on a school day in possession of various bits of scientific equipment, a tent, two fishing rods, half a tube of Pringles and not a care in the world.

Could things be more perfect…?

The beast whipped at the flank of the sow badger again and again and again.

It was an attack so frenzied, venom leaked from the beast's abdomen, spattering the animal's hide.

The effects of the cold store and anaesthesia had left it sluggish most of the morning, but the moment it had locked its barbed extendable jaw into the badger flesh, rich blood overwhelmed the beast's senses and only one thing flashed through its crazed nervous system –

Kill kill kill kill kill kill…

Three Tyros[3] watched.

---

[3]   From the Latin for 'novice', or for 'one who is young and who learns'.

Two stood well back in Kevlar bodysuits. Fully masked.

The eldest, who couldn't have been more than sixteen, stood close by in just a hoody and jeans.

It was he who had positioned the badger, crippled but alive, on the north side of the wood. A farm animal would have served just as well, but in the remote chance a walker happened across the body, a dead cow might have given cause for concern and a phone call to a farmer, whereas a dead wild animal was just... nature.

He'd held the beast as it woke. He had touched it: him it would taste, but not attack.

He had released it carefully, directly on to the badger's side. Now he watched as it drank its fill.

After eight minutes, the beast unhooked its jaws. The sow badger was unconscious. In a few minutes she would be dead.

The beast, fat and drowsy with blood, felt an instinctive urge as its abdomen strained and cells divided and extended in a race to become full, viable eggs.

The Tyros withdrew, as planned, and split up without a word.

Nothing remained of the release operation but an electronic eye concealed in a nearby tree.

THREE

"Help-me-Mrs-Murphy – come to my aid!
You're gonna flip the pin on my love-grenade!
I-mean boom I-mean bust I-mean whom I-mean us!"

"I wrote that. I was in a band. Do you 'dig' that? No. Because you lack the life experience to appreciate the majesty of—"

"Do you see that helicopter?" interrupted Finn, looking back out of the window of the Mangusta.

"That what?"

Al believed in the to and fro of vigorous debate on long journeys and, as such, he and Finn had spent much of the morning arguing about wind turbines, football, whether Concorde could be revived and adapted to fly into space, whether snow was better than powered flight and, if the Nazis had taken over, which of Grandma's friends would have turned collaborator.

They were just starting on Al's assertion that "rock music is wasted on kids" when Finn first noticed the chopper.

He craned his neck to get a good look back up the road. Al tried to locate it in his mirrors.

The route was winding and the tree cover heavy, as they were on the edge of the New Forest, but unmistakably, less than a couple of hundred metres behind and above them, a helicopter was swinging back and forth, following the line of the road, getting lower and lower as it went.

"It's getting really low," said Finn. "What do you think they're doing?"

"I hope it's not your truant officer..." said Al, letting the joke trail off as he became more concerned.

The chopper was approaching fast now, almost skimming the tops of the trees. A couple of cars behind them had both slowed and pulled over.

Al carried on – the chopper didn't have police markings after all – but as they came over a ridge into more open country it closed in, violently large and loud, bringing itself right up alongside the Mangusta.

"What *are* they doing?" said Al.

Then a voice echoed out of a loudhailer on the chopper's belly.

"DR ALLENBY, PULL OVER."

"They *know you*?" squealed Finn, impressed.

Al slowed to a halt. The chopper went to land in the road ahead.

"What is this? What's going on?" said Finn.

Al paused for a moment. "I'm not sure, but at the very least it's bad manners."

He suddenly put his foot down. The car shot off. Then Al threw it into a screeching handbrake turn which spun them back the way they came. The V8 engine roared and Finn felt himself pushed back into the leather seat as the acceleration bit – there was no doubt about it, these cars were built to thrill.

"Why aren't we stopping?" Finn shouted.

"Might be agents of a foreign state... Might be an old girlfriend trying to kill me... But don't worry, we can lose them in the woods up here."

Was he joking? He must be joking. Then Finn noticed that Al's knuckles were white where he gripped the wheel. Finn hunkered down lower in his seat, heart hammering with excitement.

"Drive fast, Al."

"Check."

They were closing on the woods, but the chopper was almost upon them.

Again came the voice from the chopper's loudhailer: "PULL OVER, DR ALLENBY, BY ORDER OF COMMANDER KING."

Al cursed, slammed on the brakes and spun the Mangusta back to a halt at the side of the road, just short of the trees. The chopper descended gently on to the grass beside them.

Finn was transfixed. "Al...?" he started to ask, but his uncle, too furious to speak, just folded his arms and waited.

Further down the road two police 4 x 4s were approaching. Two men in Security Service suits leapt out of the chopper and made their way over as the engine powered down.

"Sir, you've got to come with—"

"Do thank the Commander," Al interrupted, "but tell him we're on holiday, tell him we're 'en route', and he'll have to get in touch next week, and tell him he doesn't need to bother with all this either. I'm on email, Facebook or even the telephone. Oh, and don't forget to tell him he'll have *to come crawling to me on his hands and knees* while you're at it..."

"Sir, I have been instructed to inform you the matter pertains to Project Boldklub."

Project Boldklub? Finn laughed. What a bizarre name. "Who's that? Some Viking?" He looked at Al.

Al's face was suddenly still and serious.

DAY ONE 12:38 (BST). Siberia, Russia

The Arctic fox confused it with a lemming at first, but the scent soon became richer and sweeter.

The temperature was 2°C. Summer. Bog and meltwater pools characterised the surface at this time of year, the illusion of thaw. As the fox drew in towards the scent, the salt and sweet notes increased, grew irresistible, sending his nervous system wild.

23

And then he saw something he didn't understand.

A man.

The man raised an arm. Fired. Then continued eating his hot dog.

The impact propelled the fox into a gully. As blood seeped through his crystal-white fur, a last survival instinct kicked in, and he curled and clamped his mouth round the wound.

A disc of congealed blood formed on the surface of the tundra. Insects and micro-organisms, adapted to the extreme environment, drew in to feed greedily upon it.

Fourteen metres beneath, in a vast insulated bunker and in simulated tropical luxury, David Anthony Pytor Kaparis lay in his iron lung[4] and waited.

The lung breathed in. The lung breathed out.

It encased him like a coffin, leaving only his head exposed, and that was all but enveloped by a cluster of automated mirrors and optical devices that allowed his gaze to roam free without troubling the muscles in his damaged neck. These mirrors and lenses swivelled and shifted constantly, bending and distorting reflections of his face so it appeared almost pixelated and an observer could never be sure where those eyes were going to pop up next. Eyes of black ice, sour and entombed.

Above him a panoramic screen array carried multiple data, news and intelligence feeds. Optical tracking meant he could manipulate it all at a glance – trawl the web, analyse data, model an idea, visit any place on earth, even (if looks could kill...) order a drone strike.

---

[4]   A negative pressure ventilator, a chamber into which pumps periodically increase and decrease air pressure in order to expand and contract the chest cavity.

The meeting in the CFAC at Hook Hall had been relayed to him in real time through a concealed 816-micron digital video camera built into his agent's spectacles. It was transmitting pictures first to a microprocessor sewn into the agent's scalp via an induction loop, then via tiny data-burst relays between specially adapted low-energy light bulbs fitted throughout the Hook Hall complex, and thereafter via the Scimitar Intelcomms 8648 satellite to Siberia. Transmission lag to Kaparis – 0.44 seconds.

It was an ingenious system.

His serotonin levels should've been satisfactory. Instead Kaparis was intensely irritated. The pictures from the live feed kept jumping because the agent constantly flicked the spectacles up and down. Despite the eighteen months of effort and detailed planning that had gone into this most complicated operation, no one had thought to supply the correct ophthalmic prescription.

1. *Was simply doing your job really so difficult?*
2. *Was it only him that cared about the details?*
3. *What must it be like to be ordinary?*

"Heywood?" *Kaparis said, summoning his butler in a cut-glass English accent.*

"Sir?"

"Establish who supplied the incorrect lenses for the camera spectacles."

"Yes, sir."

"Then have their eyes pulled out. And salted."

"Yes, sir."

Killing would be too much. It was important to keep a sense of proportion.

Onscreen, a helicopter hove into view. The image flicked again, taunting his leniency.

"And Heywood?"

"Sir?"

"Record the screams."

FOUR

DAY ONE 12:51 (BST). Hook Hall, Surrey

Finn's first view of Hook Hall was from above: a grand old country house with a formal garden, surrounded by a complex of ultra-modern buildings. Outside the largest of these buildings, as they came into land, Finn could see a clutch of officials and lab-coated scientists drawn towards the spot like ants to a dropped ice cream.

Al took off his helmet as they touched down and indicated Finn should do the same.

"We are *still* on holiday until I say so. OK?"

"If you say so!" Finn yelled back, still numb with exhilaration from the short flight and having already decided to just go with the bewildering flow. He stepped off the aircraft after Al and stumbled self-consciously through the rotor wash, half deaf, towards the small welcoming committee.

A shortish, fattish old man was first to greet them, overwhelmed apparently to be meeting –

"Dr Allenby! An honour! Professor Channing. I reviewed your paper on anti-concentric-kinesthesis."

"Wonderful. This is Finn," said Al.

"Hi!" said Finn.

"Is the resort this way?" Al asked.

"Ah…?" said the Professor, confused.

Huge road transporters packed with equipment were lined up outside the large building waiting to go through its hangar-sized doors.

"What an unusual hotel. Is there room service?" said Al.

"Er…"

"Finn likes chips, don't you, Finn?"

"Or potato wedges," Finn explained, unsure why this was relevant.

"We have a canteen…?" tried the Professor.

Al took in the line-up of trucks. "What's all this for? Are you having a pageant?"

By now Professor Channing was completely confused.

"No, it's… every centrifuge, laser and electromagnetic accelerator we can lay our hands on. This has just arrived from Harwell, part of the new Woolfson Accelerator, and…"

"Oh my goodness, I think I spot an old friend!" said Al, taking off down the line of transporters, Professor Channing trotting to keep up.

Finn's strong instinct was to keep out of the way, but Al pulled him along front and centre, determined to make a spectacle, leading everyone a merry dance as he searched among the trucks like a weekend shopper in the aisles of Ikea.

As they entered the Central Field Analysis Chamber, Finn felt like they were entering a game, the 'facility' level of a first-person shooter – concrete industrial construction, glass control booths, steel gantries and outsize scientific equipment: an outlandish vision of a not too distant future. The big difference here was that real human security personnel carried real guns: large, heavy and scary.

"Aha!" Al cried. "It's you, Fatty!"

Al seemed to be addressing a large vehicle. But, as they came round it, Finn saw what was inside. Huge quarter-sections of a giant metal doughnut, each the size of a cottage, were being manoeuvred off the transporter by an outsize forklift, a freak-show mirror of perfect polished steel on the inside, a mess of hydraulics and wiring on the outside, featuring domestic plumbing and gaffer tape – a dazzling piece of engineering that looked like it'd been knocked together in a shed: very Uncle Al.

Finn caught his distorted reflection on the perfect inner surface and remembered a night at home the year before when Al had appeared unexpectedly on the doorstep to demand Toad-in-the-Mustard-Hole from Grandma (the family comfort food). He had sworn and ranted at the table saying "they've mugged me" and "they have press-ganged Fatty". There was little indication who 'they' or

'Fatty' were, but a general hatred and distrust of anyone In Charge had come across before he'd drunk too much and fallen asleep in front of *Match of the Day*.

"Ah yes, the Fat Doughnut Accelerator you developed at Cambridge!" said Professor Channing.

"Stolen from me a year ago in the dead of night!" said Al.

"Ah… it was?"

Commander King appeared on the gantry above them like a materialising vampire.

Al pretended not to notice.

"Ripped from my still beating breast and shipped to the military by that perfidious, superior, mendacious, warmongering…"

"Dr Allenby."

"Ah… Lord Vader."

King allowed himself a minuscule, dry smile (no one else dared) and descended slowly. Finn hid behind Professor Channing.

"As I recall, we commissioned a preliminary study into possible defensive potential only after you had withdrawn cooperation, concealed the sequencing codes and thrown what my nanny used to call 'a wobbly'?"

"Because I said NO to weaponisation."

"But you were already working with the military?"

"Only with my guys – and we were having 'fun'. Didn't Nanny ever teach you to 'have fun', Commander?"

"Certainly not. She taught us Cleanliness, Godliness and to Ignore Naughty Boys."

"Then what are we doing here? Because I warn you, if you're on holiday too, there's no pool."

"We need you, Dr Allenby. If not your terrific sense of humour."

There was a cold connection between the two, the ghost of a mutual respect.

"So spill the beans," said Al.

Without even looking at Finn, King said: "Not in front of the children."

Uh-oh.

Finn shrank further behind Channing.

"They're perfectly normal human beings, just smaller and largely odourless. Say hello, Finn, you're frightening the King."

Finn emerged from cover.

"Hi. Sir. Finn. I mean, I'm Finn. Not sir. Not you, you're sir. I'm just…"

"Hello, Infinity, I am sorry we've interrupted your excursion. We have a canteen area. There's a television, some magazines. Why don't you go with Nigel and he'll show you the—"

"I think I'll stay and watch!"

(Canteen. Television. Nigel. Apart from an absurd facility for science and maths, Finn was average or hopeless at most other things, but he did have an Acute Sense of Dread – the one great advantage of being orphaned. *Just keep going.*)

King, not used to interruptions, raised an eyebrow.

"He thinks he'll stay and watch," confirmed Al, dragging Finn forward for a formal introduction.

"Meet my late sister's child, my sole heir, my DNA. I promised him an adventure and my mother a week of respite care – and that's exactly what they're going to get. Wherever I go, he goes."

Finn felt briefly at ease, proud even, till Al continued, "He may look like a scruffy, not particularly well-coordinated boy from a bog-standard comprehensive…"

"Hey! It's an *academy*. It has *academy status*."

"…but he's in the top set for science and maths and has been schooled by me in the wilder side of theoretical physics, rocketry and blowing things up. What's more, he has a soul a mile deep, a smile a mile wide and can be trusted absolutely."

Finn thought this might be overselling him a little, but still couldn't help tacking on, "And I've had two letters published in *Amateur Entomologist*. It's a specialist magazine."

"You surprise me," said King drily and took a step forward so that he and Al were eyeball to eyeball.

"This is an extraordinary situation, an aggregate threat to human life that demands a global response through the G&T *and the reconstitution of Boldklub…*"

Al whispered back, "*He already knows.*"

Commander King turned a shade of white not known in nature. A shade of murder.

Al slapped Finn on the back and drove him on up the gantry.

"*What do I know?*" Finn whispered.

"*Shut up and go with it,*" hissed Al.

Up in the control gallery, Finn no longer felt like he was in a video game. Up here it was more like the bridge of a spaceship in some movie. There were banks of computers and displays and an observation window that ran the length of the gallery and looked down across the vast CFAC below.

"Wow!"

Beyond the giant lorries that were depositing the accelerators and physics kit, Finn could see more trucks arriving, military green and brown. He could make out the tarpaulin-covered shapes of what he took to be vehicles, and maybe even a helicopter. Signs were appearing everywhere that warned ORDNANCE – EXTREME CARE – RESTRICTIONS APPLY.

Al headed straight for two soldiers – one huge, the other small and wizened – who had risen to greet him: the first like an old friend, the second with wary resignation.

"Kelly and Stubbs! My boys! The old team back together again!" laughed Al.

Captain Kelly wore an SAS badge and was a comic-book action hero: six foot six and one hundred kilos of scarred flesh and raw power. He poked Al's chest in mock accusation (nearly breaking his sternum) – "They let *you* back in?" – before following up with a laugh and a bear hug.

"And *Major* Leonard Stubbs! Sir!" gasped Al once he was free.

Stubbs grimaced and Kelly ruffled his hair.

"He's happy," insisted Kelly. "He's wagging his little tail."

With the physique and charm of a defeated tortoise, Engineer Stubbs was technically retired and past pensionable age, but, as a

33

minor genius with both mechanical and information systems *who could fix anything*, he'd been given an honorary commission at sixty and asked to stay on – which, considering he had never attracted a Mrs Stubbs, was a blessing all round. He clearly didn't do hugs or emotion, which of course made Al kiss him on both cheeks like a Frenchman.

"For goodness' sake…"

Al introduced Finn. "My nephew – Infinity Drake."

"Please, just Finn."

"I'm looking after him for a week. He's a short version of me without the looks, brains or char—"

"He always says that."

Stubbs sighed as if he knew exactly what Finn had to put up with.

"We can shoot him for you. Seriously," said Kelly, crushing Finn's fingers with his handshake.

"Ow!"

"Don't listen to anything these men say," said Al. "No one knows how they got in here."

"Seats," ordered Commander King.

Seats were duly taken. Technicians were setting up a series of digital projectors, fiddling with cables and tapping at keyboards.

As Al took his seat, Finn sat beside him and whispered, "By the way, Al?"

"Hmm?"

"What the hell is going on and why do all these people think you're some kind of—"

"It's just what I do. Sometimes."

"Just what you do?"

"The secret side. There have to be secrets, Finn, to protect the innocent."

"But how...? When...? Why didn't you tell me before?"

"When you were *eleven*? Come on. Who would tell an *eleven*-year-old something like that?"

This stumped Finn.

"Now go hide," said Al, nodding to a gap between two banks of computers, out of sight.

"Why?" Finn asked.

"Oh, you'll see," said Al.

Screens came online.

World leaders started to appear.

FIVE

"**M**r President."

    "Commander King."

"Prime Minister."

"King. Mr President."

"Prime Minister."

"*Guten Tag*, Frau Chancellor..."

King went through the introductory motions.

Finn thought, *I'm supposed to be in double geography right now.*

The President of the USA was in shirtsleeves – the Oval Office in the background familiar, if a little less tidy than in its TV incarnations. The British Prime Minister was in a large, book-lined room – not the smooth PM of news bulletins, but an alarmed posh little man. The German Chancellor settled herself into a reclaimed pine 'ergonomische stuhl' as the President of France came online from the gilt and ornate Élysée Palace.

"Is Allenby there?" said the US President.

Al leant into shot and waved so that the leaders of the free world could see him.

"Guys," said Al.

Guys? Finn thought.

"So. What have we got, Commander King?" asked Al.

The room fell silent. The lights dimmed.

"Slide," ordered King.

A digital projection lit up a wall-sized screen and showed… nothing.

Or at least nothing but a blank whiteness with a black dot in the middle.

King snapped, "Bring it up to scale."

The lens zoomed in on the dot and suddenly the creature exploded across the screen.

Projected to the size of a man, a vile black, yellow and red-flecked monster, fresh and newborn-slick from its final moult. Its exoskeleton was extended, exaggerated; its thorax like a clutch of girders; its head a felt and fang atrocity; its silver-black wings still plastered against its abdomen which, cruelly coloured, scaled and distended, hung bulbous from its thorax like a great droplet of buzz-fresh poison. And, at its end, an ugly cluster of three barbed, glossy harpoon stings.

Finn froze and the hairs on the back of his neck prickled. For a moment he tasted his own fear. The fear of death he sometimes got when he thought about his mother. A sense of something terrible, unstoppable and unknowable. He gulped it back.

A mouse click and the next image flashed up. A rear shot of the insect with a better view of the array of stings emerging from the bulbous abdomen.

Click. The underside, amour-plated and beetle-black. *How does this thing fly?* Finn thought.

Click. In the next image, the answer: silver-black wings fully extended, as long as a dragonfly's, but broader.

Wow.

Click. The head and mouthparts, feelers and proboscis. Finn felt his stomach turn. He didn't want to look, yet couldn't tear his eyes away.

Click. The egg pouch and reproductive organ.

The six legs.

The black and yellow and red-tinged whole, like some vile bullet that in flight must look like... Who only knew what.

And the sound? thought Finn. What evil bass buzz would those wings make?

Al watched, face frozen, King pleasantly surprised to observe that even he was stilled by the sight.

"Meet Scarlatti," said King. "Named after the eighteenth-century Italian composer noted for writing five hundred and fifty-five piano sonatas, because it registers a score of five hundred and fifty-five on the Porton Scale: that used to measure the lethal potential of weaponised organisms. A single Scarlatti could theoretically kill five hundred and fifty-five human beings."

"*Sacré bleu...*" said the French President, without a hint of irony.

"During the Cold War, all sides developed and produced biological weapons. One of the main branches of study at our research institute at Porton Down was entomology, the study of insects, and how they could be adapted to carry and spread disease. In 1983 a geneticist accidentally developed a whole new genotype of insect by exposing the embryo of a highly engineered smallpox-carrying wasp – phenotype Vespula cruoris – to gamma radiation. The result was... Scarlatti."

An old video recording came up onscreen of live Scarlattis being studied in a laboratory.

"Scarlatti is an asexual self-multiplier that, given a sufficient supply of simple protein – the body of a dead mammal say – can lay up to fifty eggs. It's pesticide resistant, seventy-five millimetres long (the size of a hummingbird or a human thumb) and is all but physically indestructible. It nurtures supplies of a unique and fatal strain of smallpox in the poison sacs of its abdomen. Accelerated development means a single egg can become a viable flying insect in four days. Therefore a single insect can produce a fifty-strong swarm in four days. And swarm they do – given how much protein is required during their nymph, or rapid hemimetabolic, phase. Each swarm produces many new colonies, each swarming every four days, and so on ad infinitum. Or until the supply of protein dries up."

Finn could taste something sickening.

He means people by 'the supply of protein'. He means... us.

Onscreen, the video turned nasty. White mice were introduced to the test chamber and seized upon by frenzied Scarlattis. They seemed to relish the kill, whipping their stings into the poor creatures long after they were disabled or dead.

"This hideous project was immediately discontinued, the remaining nymphs first being frozen and then incinerated at the end of the Cold War under the Biological Weapons Convention.

"However, two specimens remained. One was sent to the United States under the Hixton-Fardale Shared Research Agreement, and has presumably been destroyed.. A second was secretly frozen and stored at Porton Down by the government of the day 'just in case' or, as we like to put it more formally, for 'Reasons of National Security'."

Commander King allowed his eyelids to close so as to avoid the righteous glares of the other committee members. Then he took a deep breath.

"One of our Porton Down research fellows, a Dr Cooper-Hastings, seems to have lost all reason, found a way to access the secure cold store and… has released the last remaining Scarlatti."

There were gasps.

"He did *what*?" asked the US President.

King turned to his screen. "Dr Cooper-Hastings released the specimen into the atmosphere, sir."

A staff-card mugshot of a middle-aged scientist flashed up. Thick glasses. Dull eyes.

"He stayed late at work, leaving at 10pm. A search was initiated six minutes later when an algorithm discovered an access control code override on his staff card. An empty cryogenic support cylinder was eventually found outside his abandoned car at 03:32 this morning near the village of Hazelbrook, thirty-six miles north of here."

A map of Hazelbrook flashed up onscreen and a photo of the abandoned car.

"The area around the village has been declared a biohazard zone and evacuated. We're conducting a full investigation and every available officer from every agency is involved in the manhunt for Cooper-Hastings."

"Cut to the chase. What exactly are we talking about here – worst case?" asked the US President.

King and Professor Channing exchanged looks. The Professor stood up to deliver the bad news.

"Worst case: we estimate that with a first swarm in four days national contamination will be total within four to six weeks, continental within three months, global-temperate within six months."

"Global-temperate?" repeated the US President.

"Nearly all of Western Europe, a good two-thirds of North America, Africa, Asia, the Middle East, most of South America, Australia. Only cold air and altitude offer any protection. In total, two-thirds of the land mass of the earth."

There was a pause.

"Nearly six billion people," said King.

Dr Miles Cooper-Hastings opened his eyes. They stung. Blackness and stars swam before him. His throat was so dry he half retched to bring forth some saliva. He could see nothing, but he could feel his head pressed up against something wooden. He was freezing. For a waking moment of pure terror, he wondered if he was buried alive. But, as his body repulsed and kicked out at these thoughts, the lid of the sea chest he had been locked in for eight hours or so leapt up as far as its lock and clasp would allow and for a split second let in a strip of daylight.

He kicked out again. He saw light flash again. And he realised he could taste the freezing sea.

"Where is it?" Cooper-Hastings yelled into the blackness, fear filling his lungs. "What have you done?"

SIX

"**O**n day one the Scarlatti lays its eggs," said King. "On day two the nymphs hatch and grow. On day three the nymphs develop distinct body sections and the wings separate – shedding their skin several times. By the start of day four – after their final moult – they can swarm."

The danger was spelt out in a fan graph that showed a range of possible development outcomes if the Scarlatti had located a 'host protein' overnight. The blood-red line of development started tight on day one and by day four spread to cover the entire graph.

"Four days. We're already halfway through day one and we daren't risk day four," said King.

He turned away from the graph and back to his guests.

"So far, so bad. What matters is what we do now," he said.

43

There was an air of stunned disbelief in the control gallery and around the world.

Seated beside the US President, General Jackman – the grizzly bear Chairman of the US Joint Chiefs of Staff and the world's most powerful soldier – punctured the silence:

"Create hell. Flood the area with chemicals. Go nuclear."

"Thank you, General Jackman. The problem is – scale," explained King.

On a projected map he drew a rough semicircle east of the village of Hazelbrook.

"Last night's turbulent air could have taken it twenty miles north and east, which means an area that covers roughly a third of London."

"Nuke London…?" said someone, appalled.

"Or," King said before a hubbub could break out, "following on from discussions with the scientists this morning, there *may* be another way."

With a quick glance at Al, King turned to the corner of the gallery.

"Entomologists, would you oblige us?"

Channing beckoned a pair of entomologists from Porton Down into camera view, part of the group that had been there since early morning. A grey, middle-aged man with a much younger, sharper colleague.

"Professor Lomax and Dr Spiro were colleagues of Dr Cooper-Hastings at Porton Down."

Lomax wore a suit under his lab coat, Spiro a T-shirt and jeans.

"Professor Channing? The hypothesis, please."

Finn remembered his mum explaining that hypothesis was a term scientists used to describe an idea so they didn't sound common.

"Pheromones," Channing began, pushing back his glasses as if addressing a learned symposium, "are tiny distinct chemical signals that all living things emit."

"'Phero' from the Greek for 'to carry'," Professor Lomax helpfully explained, "'mone' from 'hormone' or—"

Dr Spiro cut across them with the urgency the occasion demanded.

"If we can trace the Scarlatti's pheromones then we can catch it before its first swarm. We could locate it, find its nest and destroy a much, much smaller area."

"Possibly," interjected Lomax, glaring. But Spiro continued.

"The '83 data is categorical. Scarlatti pheromones are very distinct – the result of atomic mutation almost certainly – and emitted in very large quantities, with receptor sensitivity heightened by a super-developed swarm instinct. These insects will do anything to be with their own kind. Anything."

"Thank you, Dr Spiro, I did produce much of that data…" muttered Lomax.

But how? How would you trace the pheromones? Finn wanted to yell, wriggling in his hidey-hole and finding it difficult to keep his mouth shut. King sensed it and shot an eyebrow his way.

"How?" asked Al obligingly. "How would you begin to define and then detect the appropriate molecules, let alone—"

"With another member of the same species!" Professor Channing

45

announced, striking a blow for the over-fifties by jumping in before young Dr Spiro.

Al looked across at Finn. He raised his eyebrows at him: "Plausible?"

Finn shrugged back a *Why not?*

"*Non!*" said the French Conseiller Scientifique. "You would have to replicate Scarlatti. If Scarlatti is a random atomic mutation, you could never replicate it *exactement.* Never. *C'est impossible!*"

"Unless, of course, there *is* still a second sample left in existence?" mused Commander King, letting the cynical words hang in the air.

"*Ach*, the American one?" said the German Chancellor. "Destroyed, *nein?*"

"Like we destroyed ours?" said the British Prime Minister.

All eyes turned to the US President.

"Retained for 'Reasons of National Security' you mean?" said Commander King, enjoying the moment. "Where would it be, I wonder? The Fort Detrick facility outside Washington? One might look in warehouse nine, aisle eight, section two S."

"Find out," the President snapped at someone off-screen, furious that King should so easily reel off a US state secret. General Jackman bristled.

"Forget it. Even if it is there," said the US Chief Scientist, a silver-haired woman on the President's other side, "you'd never be able to get a viable tracking device on to something that small."

King smiled. Inside.

"Any thoughts? Dr Allenby?"

Al pushed himself out of his seat and walked over to the giant image of the Scarlatti, deep in thought. He turned back to Spiro. "You're sure they'll read each other's pheromones over great distances?"

"Over miles, definitely," said Spiro.

"More than ten?"

"Reasonable probability," said Spiro.

"Really…" Lomax sighed. "More than 'reasonable' at ten, unlikely beyond twenty."

"Can we anchor a tracking device on to that thorax?"

Spiro and Lomax looked puzzled.

Al changed tack.

"Theoretically, if we could drill into it, or glue it on to, say, this cross member here?" He pointed out a girder-like section of the armoured thorax that flattened at the centre.

"Theoretically? Yes," said Spiro. "This is cellulose material without nerve endings."

"You would have to 'theoretically' be extremely careful then," said Lomax, attempting sarcasm. "The thorax plates move against each other to allow greater flexibility than in other wasp species. It's a weak point so the joints between the plates are packed with nerve endings."

Al checked his watch, a Rolex adapted to his own design to incorporate a Geiger counter, pressure gauge and half a dozen other tiny instruments (the secret gift from a grateful nation), and turned things over in his mind. *Tick tick tick tick tick.*

"Well, Allenby? Will you revisit Project Boldklub?" said the Prime Minister.

47

Most people in the meeting didn't have a clue what he was talking about. The name Boldklub was obscure, being short for Akademisk Boldklub, the football club that Niels Bohr, the father of subatomic physics, once played for.

Al looked at King, suspicious. King studied his nails.

"We've faced down one chemical and two nuclear Armageddons in the recent past. I don't see why we can't pull together as a team to deal with this."

King looked back up at Al.

The world waited. Al looked over at Finn.

And from his hiding place Finn studied the Scarlatti. The colours, the grotesque armour, the clutch of stings, the distorted feelers and proboscis… everything about it gave off a sense of anger and suffering. In a perverse way Finn felt sorry for it. Yet within a few months this thing could wipe out *six billion* people. Everyone he knew, as well as the four he loved (Grandma, Al, Yo-yo and sometimes Christabel), plus everyone that filled his day, from everyone he watched on telly to everyone he travelled to school with. All gone. Like his mum.

Finn was fascinated, locked on.

"Oh… go on then," said Al at last.

"What? Go on what?" barked General Jackman from the US.

Al seemed to snap awake. "We haven't got much time. I suppose I'd better explain."

He picked up an iPad linked to an interactive whiteboard and started to draw.

SEVEN

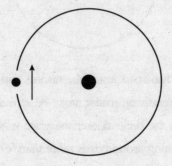

Al looked up, as if to a classroom of kids.

"Anyone know what this is?"

"It's an atom," said General Mount, irritated by Al's playful tone.

"Is this a physics class?" asked the American President.

"Yep. Everyone needs to get a handle on this. It is indeed an atom," said Al. "Which one?"

Hydrogen! Finn wanted to say, itching to put his hand up.

"Hydrogen," muttered the US Chief Scientist.

"Good, a hydrogen atom, nice and simple: a nucleus in the centre and one electron spinning around, with a constant spatial relationship between the nucleus and the electron – this distance, this distance right here." Al drew a dotted red line between the dot at the centre and the dot on the outside.

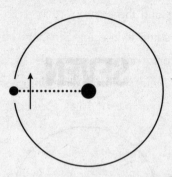

He then tapped the two spots again, the nucleus and the electron. "Now these two dots are something, matter, *stuff*," he explained, "but this –" he waved around inside the circle all over the place – "is *absolutely nothing.*"

"Me, you, everything around us is more than 99.9 per cent nothing, because every single one of the atoms we're constructed from is more than 99.9 per cent nothing, with only a tiny bit of actual atomic *stuff*. Everyone got that?"

Al looked up at the world leaders, then glanced across at Finn, to make sure they were all still with him; with furrowed brows and a big grin respectively, they were.

"I will never understand this," said the British Prime Minister.

"There's a whole quantum dark energy/dark matter thing we could go into, but it's better to think of it as a beautiful mystery. Think of atoms as being balloons rather than building blocks, balloons filled with nothingness and a tiny nucleus."

"*Bravo*," said the French President. "But this not catch flies."

"Not yet, no. But my Big Idea, known to a select few as Boldklub, was –" he pointed again to the red dotted line denoting the distance between the nucleus and the electron – "to see if we could create a magnetic field that could reduce this distance and—"

And before Al could say the next word a neural synapse fired at the speed of light in Finn's brain and a conclusion so fantastic occurred it smashed any last compunction to stay quiet.

"You're going to *SHRINK* stuff?"

Everyone turned. Finn's eyes were as wide as wonder.

Lit from below by the iPad, and looking 999 per cent mad scientist, Al pointed straight at him. "Ta-da!"

"WHAT?"

"What did he say?"

"*Shrink* stuff?"

"*C'est impossible!*"

"Mein Gott, was that *a child*?"

Commander King let his eyelids drop in momentary exasperation. This really was all he needed.

"That's my nephew," said Al proudly.

"Young Infinity is here contingent upon Dr Allenby's cooperation," King declared. "We really must move on…"

Heads were shaking, voices rising, English, American, French,

51

German – all demanding answers, all offended by such an absurd suggestion, at being caught out by a child.

Finn didn't give a damn. He was staring at Al in open-mouthed wonder.

"Shrink? Is that really what the boy said?"

"This is flat out impossible," the US Chief Scientist advised her President.

Al overheard. "No! *Possible* –" he insisted, adding a much smaller atom to his diagram – "by exploiting a chain reaction at the quantum level, you can create a new type of magnetic field, a 'hot area' within which all matter can be reduced, sucking the electron right up tight against the nucleus."

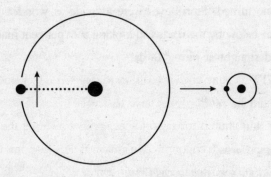

"That is totally absurd!" the US Chief Scientist responded.

Voices immediately started to rise again.

The entomologists were stunned.

Finn's mind was spinning. He wanted to ask a million questions. He wanted to understand every impossible detail. He wanted to know about the who and the why and the how. He wanted to know it all and yet somehow, right now, it was all so much to try and take in and he was just thinking: *I Want A Go.*

He walked straight up to his uncle through the babble, looked into his eyes and asked in wonder and for a second time, just to make sure, "You're going to shrink stuff. You're going to shrink some soldiers and get this thing?"

"Yes I am," said Al, delighted with Finn, who then all but burst with questions.

"Won't you still be the same weight when you're tiny as when you're full size?"

"No, because there's a proportionate shrinking of dark matter..."

"Will you be really dense and super tough?"

"Theoretically, no, though of course power-to-mass ratios are different and gravity won't break you so easily..."

"Will bacteria and diseases be able to eat you, like, really easily, like flesh-eating bugs chewing off your face and arms and ears and nose and— Hey! Will you be able to smell?"

"The rule of thumb for nano-to-normal interaction at the molecular level is that complex compounds don't interact, though atoms and simple molecules do, so you can relax about contracting the Ebola virus..."

They were having to raise their voices as the meeting was all but out of control, until the chilling opening bars of 'The Phantom of the Opera' emerged from Al's jacket.

It was the ringtone he had assigned to one very special caller. For the first time, Al looked scared. He checked the time again – nearly two o'clock – and began to panic.

"Shush! *Shut uuuuuup!* SHUT UP!" he shouted at the room.

The room gradually fell silent as everyone looked at Al, frozen in terror. Once again Finn got there before everyone else.

"Grandma!"

"Is his *Grossmutti* there too?" the German Chancellor asked.

"Nobody say *a word!*" insisted Al.

The leaders of the free world, along with their best and brightest, followed orders and "shut up" as Al interrupted The Phantom and took the call.

"Hey! Mum! How's Oslo? I know I promised, I'm sorry, I lost track of time... No, don't call the police, we're fine! That's ridiculous... Have you transferred to the ship?"

With his outstretched arm, he indicated that everyone could relax a little; he had the situation under control.

"He's fine, he's right here, he can tell you himself... oh, school? School's clo— canteen! No! School canteen's closed, they were sent home for lunch – no food. Wasp infestation. Astonishing... No, he's fine! Here..." He put his hand over the mouthpiece and handed it to Finn, whispering, "Speak! Just tell her everything's fine."

"I can't lie to Grandma," Finn tried to insist. "I promised Mum I'd..."

"I order you to lie to your grandmother!" snapped the Prime Minister in a loud whisper.

Al looked at the Prime Minister like he had no idea what he was getting into.

Finn took the phone and accidentally pressed the 'speaker' button on the touchscreen so that everybody got the benefit of – "Grandma?"

"Do you need me to come back? I've unpacked but we're still in port…" came her voice.

"No, no, I'm fine, everything's fine."

"What a lot of nonsense about the canteen! Tell him to take you straight back right now!"

"We're going! We're just getting in the car."

"He will starve you to death! Neglect… Did he do any vegetables?"

"What…? Yes."

The watching experts and world leaders – who had grandmothers of their own – were nodding him along.

"Exactly which vegetables?"

Finn's mind went blank. There was a terrible, panicked silence.

"Broccoli?" mouthed the US President.

"Broccoli! And… just broccoli. What's your food like? What's the ship like?"

"Food is tepid, the cabin is cramped and I have to share a bathroom, but there's a lovely woman from Godalming on our corridor who, would you believe it, went to the same boarding school as Jennifer – second cousin Jennifer not Jennifer from the Hartford Pottery who I don't think you know her grandson wants to be a solicitor it's good to have ambitions but as I told her not a solicitor Jennifer not at twelve… anyway I—"

"Grandma, I think we'd better go or we'll be late."

"Oh… all right, dear. Please don't trust Al, he's already missed one call."

55

"OK, Grandma, love you, bye!"

"And keep safe!"

Finn killed the call and everyone breathed a huge sigh of relief.

The Prime Minister gave an order to someone off-screen. "Get on to the Norwegians. Upgrade Mrs Allenby's cabin and get her, and the woman from Godalming who knows Jennifer, on to the Captain's table. Now."

"Would someone please explain to me what the hell is going on?" said the US President.

DAY ONE 14:13 (BST). Siberia

Deep in the Siberian permafrost, 2,546 miles away, east by northeast, Kaparis watched the scene via his agent's spectacles.

Everything was going according to plan. They were falling into his trap.

1. *The beast was at large.*
2. *The 'pheromone hypothesis' had been successfully introduced by his agent at the meeting.*
3. *Boldklub had been established as the only viable response.*

Kaparis was where he liked to be: in control. And yet... he was overwhelmed.

The boy.

Kaparis stared.

"My goodness, he looks like his father."

The lung breathed in. The lung breathed out. And for a moment his heart swelled with nostalgia as he was transported back nearly twenty years to a Cambridge University of scarves and bicycles, lectures and tutorials, girls to fall in love with and limitless early promise... before, inevitably, his mind went to his moment of glory.

Why Does Grass Grow In Clumps?

A General Theory on the Development of Super-organisms

A lecture by D.A.P. Kaparis

St Stephen's Hall, 10am, Wed 4th May 1993

And to how it was stolen from him.

In front of everybody.

In front of her.

And, as quickly as it had swollen, Kaparis's heart emptied of blood and once more beat acid revenge.

"Our proposal," said King, "is this – one: shrink a tracking device and fit it to the American Scarlatti and release it to find its missing clone.

"Two: shrink an attack helicopter and its crew..."

Eyes popped around the world.

57

"...all their equipment, including all tracking, transport, communications and weaponry..."

"Woah! Shrink people! Weapons?"

"...to the scale 150 to 1..." continued King.

"One hundred and fifty times!?"

"...and three..."

"Hang fire! Why not just shrink the tracking device and track the thing? Why shrink people?" asked General Jackman.

"Without going into too much classified detail," said Al, "it's to do with changes in waveform when you collapse the electromagnetic spectrum. A nano-transmitter produces a nano-signal that can only be picked up on a nano-receiver with a very limited range, perhaps 800 metres at the most. You can't just amplify the signal in the normal sense. That's why we'll need a hunter crew at nano-level as well. Their transport can be fitted with a tiny 'full-scale' radio for communication, although again it will have a very limited range and we can't bank on constant contact."

The General looked like his brain ached.

King continued. "And three: the crew are to pursue the second Scarlatti to the first, then destroy both adults and any eggs or nymphs they find."

"Whatever else it is, this whole scheme is crazy! At the very least untested. The risks to any participants must surely be suicidal," said the American Chief Scientist, shaking her head.

"We have to measure the risks against what's at stake, and against the only viable alternative," said King.

"Which is?" asked the German Chancellor.

"Go nuclear. Displace a million people. Lay waste to part of London for generations to come."

There was a long pause.

Finn suddenly realised something and looked back at the map that King had marked up earlier. The area of destruction included the village of Langmere.

"Grandma's?" Finn said.

"I know," said Al. "It's personal."

The US President was incredulous.

"And who's going to take on this mission?"

"Given the unknown physiological risks, we propose just a three-man team led by Captain Kelly from our informal military cohort. Captain Kelly and Engineer Stubbs – both with nano-experience – plus a pilot."

"Wait! Nano-experience? You've done this *before*?" asked Finn.

"Roll the film," said Al.

Up on the screen appeared some scrappy, hand-held digital footage of a goat on a lead. At the other end of the lead was Al. Both looked like they'd been partying for three days straight. A time code ticked over along the bottom.

Captain Kelly walked into shot and spray-painted 'Good luck' on the goat's hide.

The image cut to the Fat Doughnut Accelerator operating with a loud hum. Outside, Engineer Stubbs sat at a desk crammed with laptops. Al tethered the goat in the centre of the Fat Doughnut.

The time code jumped forward a few minutes to a more distant shot of the accelerator. The camera zoomed in on the goat as it became increasingly disturbed. Wheeling around its tether until... the screen went suddenly and completely white.

The camera pulled out to reveal the Fat Doughnut now contained a ball of perfect, intense white light. It seemed to ripple and spin for a few seconds before it faded, leaving behind a party of blinking observers and... no goat.

Al ran into the centre of the Fat Doughnut. On hands and knees he searched for something. Kelly and Stubbs crowded in.

Very carefully, Al picked something up. The camera zoomed in on his hand. Trying to focus. All blurry, unfocused skin tone. And then – finally, shakily – in the rivulets of Al's skin, in the lifeline, stood a rather confused, silently-bleating, 4.5mm goat.

"Me next," said Kelly off-camera. "I'm next!"

"Hey! Who did all the work?" protested Stubbs.

"Back away!"

The argument raged. The goat didn't join in. It was all way over its head.

DAY ONE 14:19 (BST). Willard's
Copse, Berkshire

Lay lay lay lay...

Smallpox had laid waste to the badger and left its corpse a wretched thing, barely identifiable, pustulated and leaking the gall the Scarlatti found so conducive.

For fifteen hours more the Scarlatti would continue to produce fat white eggs from its abdomen, straining to evacuate them, planting each one carefully in the decaying flesh, its insides a furnace of reproduction.

In each egg a primitive nymph was forming. In less than six hours, such was the furious rate of growth, the first of them would begin to consume the remaining contents of its egg sac before bursting out to feast upon the corpse in turn.

Someone whispered something in the US President's ear. He made his decision and nodded.

"You want our Scarlatti, you got it," he said simply.

"And further accelerator capacity from CERN, Monsieur le Président? Frau Chancellor?"

"*Oui.*"

"*Ja.*"

Commander James Clayton-King loved it when a plan came together.

Then the American President raised a finger. "One condition. We supply the pilot. I want a man onboard."

King raised an eyebrow in protest.

There was another whisper in the President's ear.

"Make that a woman."

DAY ONE 15:17 (BST). Andrews Air Force Base, Maryland, USA

A Variant T Lockheed Martin F-22 Raptor taxied out of the restricted M3 hangar.

Delta Salazar knew nothing yet of the mission she was being asked to undertake, only that it was priority number one: transit to RAF Northolt outside London at maximum speed, refuelling in mid-air twice over the Atlantic. With afterburners engaged and almost no payload, her cruising speed would be well in excess of Mach 2. Deep in the heart of the $150-million fifth-generation stealth fighter, in the empty weapons bay, wrapped in an 'indestructible' transport crate, was a single small frozen phial.

Control had cleared the skies.

Delta loved Aviator shades, beating men at anything and strafing ground targets with 44mm cannon. She also *love love loved* to fly.

In fact, the only thing she loved more was her little sister Carla, but that was not the sort of thing that she would say out loud in the (Classified) M3 Wing of the US Air Force.

"Clear for take-off," said Control.

With an easy touch, Delta fully engaged the twin F119-PW-100 turbofan engines producing 35,000lbs of thrust that shot the aircraft off the runway and into a steep climb.

Her mother had been an alcoholic and she'd spent most of her childhood neglected, finding escape only in video games (starting with *Splinter Cell* back in 2002). In 2004 the USAF had started looking for recruits with exceptional hand-eye coordination in the online gaming community. They noticed the data spike around Delta's tag and traced it to a state children's home in Philadelphia where they found a fierce, scruffy, skinny thirteen-year-old who intensely distrusted authority, having been separated from her baby sister when taken into care. She tested off the scale.

The USAF put her into a top-secret training programme, arranged an appropriate adoption for Carla, with visitation rights, and gave Delta the chance to excel. She was triple-A rated on six different aircraft and had won two Air Force Distinguised Service Medals and a Medal of Honour. She was twenty-three years old – even if she looked an Indie rock nineteen.

At 20,000 feet she banked east off the American continent. She could never get used to how great this felt.

"Badass…" she sighed.

"I heard that, Salazar," snapped Control.

She laughed and rocketed off across the Atlantic.

EIGHT

DAY TWO 02:46 (BST). Hook Hall,
Surrey

Just over eleven hours later, at the climax of what must have been
an astonishing briefing, and in the midst of the organised chaos
of all that was going on in and around the CFAC, Finn witnessed
the moment Flight Lieutenant Salazar finally stopped chewing her
gum.

Her eyes were still hidden behind her Aviator shades (despite it
being the middle of the night), her boots were still on the desk and
she still carried an air of youthful insouciance, but... the chewing
had stopped. This was the biggest reaction they'd had from her since
her arrival.

"We need your decision in the next hour. Lieutenant? Do you understand the proposition?" Al said.

Nothing.

Finn looked at Al. *He's not handling this very well*, he thought. The Lieutenant seemed to have unsettled Al somehow. He was trying to be clipped and cool, but was coming across as nervous and edgy. The silence crackled.

"They're going to shrink you!" said Finn, trying to lighten the atmosphere.

Still nothing.

Using his thumb and forefinger to illustrate actual size, Kelly tried to translate into militarese.

"Listen up! You're going to be shrunk to 12 millimetres, put in a 110-millimetre Apache chopper, then pursue and terminate an apocalyptic bug with extreme prejudice. You copy?"

"I copy… Just let me suck it up," Delta responded.

(She could have been more specific and told them what it felt like: that the idea was so crazy it had caused a temporary gap in the game code of her reality and that she needed to download a patch,[5] but she had learned never to discuss her feelings with fellow soldiers. Besides which, where was she supposed to find the patch?)

Al blinked. Finn smiled. Kelly laughed.

"She'll be fine," said Kelly. "Move on."

*   *   *

---

[5] A piece of software designed to fix problems or update a computer program or its supporting data.

With the main briefings out of the way, Kelly, Stubbs and Salazar were handed over to a medical team itching to study the 'before and after' effects of 'atomic collapse' on the human body (they could smell a Nobel Prize).

Al expected them to be poked, prodded and drained of various fluids in the usual manner, but when he was recalled to the crew area, he was informed that the process had ground to a halt during a 'psychiatric evaluation'.

Each crew member had been asked to construct a solid sphere out of a number of irregular-shaped blocks. Delta had just sat there (evidently still hanging with the concept). Stubbs had got started, but then fell asleep like a granddad doing a Christmas jigsaw, and Kelly got a member of the medical team in a headlock and forced him to eat one of the pieces.

"You have a voluntary mute, an old man suffering from depression and an idiot alpha male with the emotional sophistication of an earthworm," said the lady chief psychologist.

Al said, "The young woman is just *seriously* cool, Stubbs just needs tea and biscuits and Kelly was at Cambridge with me – he's only part Neanderthal. They're all perfectly normal."

"Dr Allenby, there's no way I can pass any of these people fit for active service."

"Fit for service?" laughed Al as he was dragged away to a crisis in Array Engineering. "They ride at dawn. Just make sure the pilot signs up – do whatever you have to do."

By the time Al and Finn returned, the psychologist had the

crew members sitting in a circle.

"If you could take one special personal item with you, what would that be?" the psychologist asked Delta. "Flight Lieutenant?"

Delta chewed her gum.

"OK. How about we move on to you, Leonard?" said the psychologist.

"I'll need my tablets," said Stubbs.

The psychologist gave him a hard stare.

"No, Leonard, we're talking about a special *personal* item that…"

Finn, having spent a lot of time with grief counsellors, knew the drill and decided to be helpful to hurry things along.

"She means like a teddy bear or a wedding ring or something."

"I never married," Stubbs said glumly. "Who would want me? Married to the job. Not much of a looker. And I haven't seen Teddy since the orphanage burnt down in 1962."

There was a moment of silence as Captain Kelly fought to suppress a snigger, but failed, setting Al off. They were soon hysterical. Stubbs glared and shook his head. Not for the first time Finn wondered what the little old man was doing on such a mission.

"Ignore them," Stubbs advised the psychologist. "Rise above it."

"Captain Kelly!" the psychologist snapped in a tone of admonishment. "When you've quite finished… what item would you like to take?"

Kelly stopped himself laughing and gave Stubbs a playful squeeze on the knee to show there were no hard feelings.

"Ow!"

"Apologies. I just want my Minimi[6] and maybe a couple of M27s[7]," the technicalities of which he then explained at length to the confused psychologist, the confusion added to by Stubbs explaining at the same time that he really had to take his mobile workshop with him (a Pinzgauer all-terrain truck adapted to his own specifications), otherwise, frankly, what was the point in him bothering to come at all?

In the meantime, behind her shades, Delta constructed her own patch:

```
0382*<this mission was about the craziest
   most suicidal thing she'd ever
   heard**<beyond combat***<beyond major
   league gaming****<beyond weird
0383*<awesome
0384*<but what about Carla*<<? **<She must
   be briefed before every combat mission
0385*<not possible. *<<operational security
   too tight **<concept too incredible
0386*<breach of Sisters' Pact of Truth
0387*<bummer**<[Nil]*<<[Nil]*<<<[Nil]...
0388*<on the other hand*<<[Nil]*<<<[Nil]
   **<Carla was now twelve*<<?*<<?
```

---

[6] Aka the M249 – the world's favourite light machine gun, fire rate and reliability first class.

[7] A new US weapon between a sub and light machine gun.

```
0389*<they had less and less in common
  *<<she wasn't a gamer *<<<she was no
  longer interested in mission briefings
  but only::**<> "Tell me a story"<>
0390*<all she wanted was <>"stories"<>
  *<<stories to read *<<< to watch *<<<<
  to believe
0391*<whatever else **<<this would be one
  hell of a story
0392*<breach pact**<accept mission***<QED
0393(*<Reboot>*(.)
```

Delta shot forward, lifted her shades, picked up the pieces of the
sphere puzzle that had been abandoned earlier and snapped it together
in two seconds flat. With a flick of her wrist, she then set it spinning
like a planet, and they all watched as it described a perfect orbit of
the tabletop.

"I think we're done here, ma'am," Delta told the psychologist.

Kelly started laughing again. The psychologist walked out of the
room. Al just stared at Delta, entranced. Finn prodded him.

"Can… can we take it you accept the mission, Flight Lieutenant…
Ms Salazar?" asked Al (in that upper-class Brit way, as if he might
be asking someone to marry him, thought Delta).

"You point. I'll shoot. Let's roll," she said, flipping down her
shades and putting her feet up again.

Cool, thought Finn.

Al tripped over as he was led off to the next meeting and couldn't help staring back at her.

Embarrassing, thought Finn.

NINE

It was nearing dawn as King watched the fully armed Apache helicopter being lowered by crane into the centre of the accelerator.

In the time lapse of his memory, the chaos had peaked at around 4am and was ebbing fast. The lifting gear and forklifts had cleared, and the new Large Accelerator looked as if it had always been there.

The original pieces of Al's Fat Doughnut had been repositioned and adapted to form four equidistant parts of a much bigger ring of particle accelerators. The nano-dimensional field – or 'hot area' – at the centre would be about the size of a classroom and demand so

71

much power it would draw on the national grids of both the UK and France.

Allenby would be controlling it all from a specially constructed command pod – his cockpit – on the floor of the CFAC.

A formidable range of military hardware was lined up on a conveyor system that ran the length of the CFAC, with more supplies in the loading bay waiting to go on – all of which would have to be fed into the hot area in three minutes flat.

Speed was of the essence. As soon as reduction was complete, the nano-dimensional crew and their nano-equipment would be transported, along with the Beta Scarlatti (the new American Scarlatti being named this to distinguish it from the original Alpha Scarlatti), to the release site thirty-six miles north in a full-scale Merlin transport helicopter – which currently waited on the tarmac outside the CFAC.

Given that a minimum of twenty-four hours would be needed to evacuate the population at large should the mission fail, the team would have a mission window of less than twelve hours before the authorities had to go public and declare a state of emergency. As no one could say for certain if the Large Accelerator would be ready to rescale the crew immediately the mission was complete, a refrigerated container with a two-week supply of food and water also waited in the loading bay to be reduced as a precaution.[8]

Worryingly little progress had been made in the search for Dr

---

[8]   Although nano-humans theoretically could consume normal food and water, their digestive systems would be able to process and absorb less than 10 per cent of it.

Cooper-Hastings. Every contact had been questioned and every possible lead followed up; every international security organisation was on alert. But they'd turned up nothing. Dr Cooper-Hastings was an unremarkable scientist who lived alone. The assumption had to be that he had gone quietly bananas and released the Scarlatti during some kind of breakdown. For King this was too simple. As zero hour approached, he had doubled the security presence onsite as well as tripled all electronic surveillance.

King looked down from the gantry and saw young Finn hurry to and fro, busy and integral, now joining the entomologists making their way to the reanimation suite.

It had become his opinion over the course of the night that Finn was the most important person on the project, not just as kin and comfort for Allenby, but as sounding board, test bed and "asker of bloody awkward questions" throughout – his tireless good humour and sense of adventure a tonic to all.

His plea to join the entomology team had been something of a classic. When Professor Lomax had pointed out his lack of correct qualifications, Finn had said, "Yeah, but there's this friend of mine at school, Hudson, who can't go on school trips over, say, twelve hours because he can't go for a poo on any toilet but his own – he doesn't say so, but there's a note from his mum in the register – so he's always left behind, and yet he's the only kid really interested in glacial geology or the *Horrible Histories* show or stuff like that. Instead everyone else goes and all they do is mess about."

Professor Lomax's face had been a picture of confusion and distaste.

73

Young Dr Spiro had touched knuckles with Finn in a gesture that King believed was meant to denote 'respect'.

The only glitch had been Finn's scheduled 9pm 'call to Grandma' (her monitoring regime was admirably simple: she expected reports morning, noon and night) during which she had asked to say goodnight to the dog. Finn had claimed the animal was "out chasing bats" which was far from acceptable. A team had to be scrambled and despatched to the vicarage in Langmere where the dog was briefly kidnapped and secret recordings made of its barks, snuffles and other noises for the requested call back. The vicar, a Christabel Coles, remained glued to *Celebrity Come Dine With Me* throughout.

Upstairs in the control gallery, dignitaries and politicians were arriving from across the globe, in person or onscreen.

Downstairs the excitement was about to begin.

Shortly King would have to go up and make polite conversation, answer pointed questions.

He almost wished he was twelve years old.

DAY TWO 05:46 (BST). Hook Hall, Surrey

A dry, translucent husk. A sudden movement within. The husk cracks to reveal a wet, thousand-celled eye.

The fight for life had begun.

Through heavily gloved hands and behind the thick glass of an isolation tank, Dr Spiro worked on the nascent Beta Scarlatti, with Finn in support holding a heat lamp, and Al right on the shoulders of both. Using tweezers and other instruments, Spiro picked away the husk that had been the Scarlatti's final skin at the nymph stage. Tiny 400mA electric shocks sent through instruments were bringing the Scarlatti back to life after thirty years in cold storage.

Professor Lomax glowered at them over his glasses from the sterile transfer trolley. The trolley was essentially a life-support system for the Scarlatti, one that would keep it isolated as well as subdued, allowing Lomax to glue the nano-scale tracking device on to exactly the right thorax plate following miniaturisation.

Beyond, other scientists and technicians fanned out. Those gathered in the control gallery watched onscreen.

Waiting for the newborn Scarlatti was a titanium harness – a sausage-shaped cage – that would muzzle the beast's wings and stings to allow the attachment of the miniaturised tracking device to its thorax.

Once harnessed, the Beta would be transferred to the loading bay ready to receive the nano tracking device the moment it was available – all achieved via airlocks to prevent the Beta's hypersensitive nervous system getting a hostile fix on any crew scent. They wanted it focused on the Alpha Scarlatti's pheromones and nothing else.[9]

Slowly, the giant insect began to wake. Deceptively slowly.

---

[9] Modern studies suggest the sense of smell works via the detection of 'quantum vibration' rather than direct molecular interaction, thus nano-scents can be detected at macro level and vice versa.

75

Just below the nascent Scarlatti's squirming head, Spiro used the tweezers to split open the rest of the husk...

SNAP!

"Ahhhh!" screamed Spiro.

The creature seemed to explode in his hand – whipping its huge tail clean through its dead outer layer. Bursting out. Vile and wet. A cluster of scales and stings – poisonous yellows and reds glistening through black. The clatter as it unstuck and buzzed its silver-black wings for the first time...

WWKWZZZWZWZWWKZWZWKZ

"Will someone please get a grip," hissed Professor Lomax.

Dr Spiro was stunned. Finn dropped the heat lamp and grabbed the flipping, writhing Beta. He felt it struggle against his thick glove like a frenzied rat. Finn held on and waited for Spiro to jump back in. But Spiro seemed to need a moment to recover. Finn looked across at him. Up close, his eyes were strangely speckled, blinking sporadically behind his glasses. More like a computer trying to reboot than a person reacting in surprise.

Finn wondered if he should yell for Al to take over, but Spiro just as quickly snapped out of it, pinning down the Beta Scarlatti with the tweezers. Between them they manipulated the beast into the titanium harness, carefully closing the topside release mechanism so as not to nip the monster's furious wings.

It was like a nightmare cigar – silver, live and absolutely lethal.

Spiro fed it through an airtight duct to the smaller tank on Professor Lomax's sterile trolley. Finally, a small grey atomiser unit on the outside of the trolley was switched on to produce a mild anaesthetic steam that would keep the beast subdued until release.

When it was all over, Spiro was relieved but also angry with himself. Again Finn noticed he seemed to be blinking strangely. Maybe he was just nervous. Finn wanted to tell him it was OK, nobody would mind, but it was not the sort of thing a kid could say.

"Congratulations," Professor Lomax said instead, with heavy sarcasm, "a triumph."

What an odd couple, Finn thought as they walked off in opposite directions, Lomax pushing the trolley through to the loading bay.

"That's what happens if you hang around entomologists too long," Al warned Finn. "You develop…"

"Oversensitive antennae?" said Finn.

"No. A sting," said Al.

The conversation was interrupted as the first countdown alarm sounded.

BEEEEEEEEEEEP. "T-MINUS TEN."

Ten minutes to zero hour.

DAY TWO 05:50 (BST), Hook Hall, Surrey

Everyone moved at once – Al so quickly that Finn had to jog to keep up.

They made their way into the centre of the CFAC where they both climbed up to Al's cockpit command pod. It was crammed with control computers and sat just in front of the Large Accelerator. Finn's final job was to bring down the perspex dome of the pod and shut Al in.

"Are you going to watch from down here with the Bug Club, or up top with the Bigwigs?" Al asked.

The politicians and honoured guests would be watching the action in the control gallery with Commander King. Most of the scientists would be opposite in the laboratories along the north side of the CFAC. They were already jostling for position, noses pressed up against the glass, spectacles clashing.

"I'll stick with the Bug Club." There was a great view down into the Large Accelerator. "Think it's going to work?" asked Finn.

"The chances of disaster are always between one in three and evens."

That didn't sound too promising, but Finn knew everyone had done all they could. All they needed now was... luck.

He touched the stone at his chest, then pulled the leather tie from round his neck.

"Take it, for luck," said Finn, handing the lump of spharelite over to Al.

"Luck? I'm a man of reason."

"*My mother would insist*," said Finn.

Al grabbed his head and gave it an affectionate knuckling. "Oh, ye of little faith..." but took the stone all the same.

"You're not going to sneak on the mission without me, are you?" asked Finn, the thought suddenly occurring to him.

"I'm the only one who knows how to drive this thing. And frankly, do you think me, you and your friend Hudson who can't move his bowels would be a better choice than trained killers like Kelly and Ms Salazar?" He looked over to where Salazar and the crew were being laid out on trolleys ready to be anaesthetised.

"My name's not Frankly," said Finn, "and hers is not Ms Salazar, it's Delta, and can you stop staring at her like that? It's *so* embarrassing."

"Hey!" said Al and knuckled him again a little harder. "I am not staring!"

The five-minute alarm sounded.

"Promise you'll let me have a go at this one day?" said Finn.

"No, but I do promise we'll get to the Pyrenees for a full week in the summer, and *as guests of the President of France.* Imagine the catering."

Finn brought the lid down and secured it over Al, who grinned and gave him the thumbs up.

He was the picture of absolute happiness.

TEN

Finn knew he should be excited as he walked back to the labs.

Instead he felt suddenly tired, really tired, and he could think of only one word. "Summer," Al had said. "We'll get to the Pyrenees for a full week in the *summer.*"

There was a concept in quantum physics that Al had tried to explain to Finn that he just couldn't get his head around, and yet it seemed to be true, called the Uncertainty Principle. It meant the more you could know about the position of a particle, the less you know about its momentum, and vice versa; or, as Finn figured it, the more you knew what you wanted, the less you could have it.

The last eighteen hours or so had been extraordinary, brilliant, engaging, exciting and important: and in a few short minutes it would be over. It was ungrateful, he knew, but he had a gut full of that awful end-of-holidays feeling. Summer was an age away. He could see himself back at school and sense the empty weeks stretching ahead.

Who would ever believe this had happened? Would it remain a total secret? Almost certainly. Grown-ups had so many secrets.

If only he could keep something, thought Finn, some souvenir to remind him, proof to himself if no one else. That miniature goat would be neat. Or maybe he could add the Scarlatti itself to his collection? Imagine showing that off...

Then he thought of the next best thing.

DAY TWO 05:58 (BST). Siberia

After seventeen hours of effort and agony, the Arctic fox had finally managed to drag his broken body over the frozen tundra and back into his lair. He was exhausted, but he was home.

At last he could rest for however long the wound might take to heal. Or he could die.

Deep beneath, Kaparis watched Finn hurry back to the laboratories.

Deep beneath, Kaparis watched Allenby grinning in his pod.

Since 19:43 the previous evening, he'd had access to the entire CCTV

and surveillance system of Hook Hall, the heart of which now lay, not in Surrey or anywhere in England, but with a fourteen-year-old girl, another one of his Tyros, Li Jun – half blind and hunched over her keyboards and screens in the communications wing of Kaparis's bunker, less than fifty metres away.

She had emerged from his seminary aged just nine. She still barely spoke, but her work – Kaparis had to admit as he watched King making tense small talk with a member of the royal family in the control gallery – was perfection.

DAY TWO 05:59 (BST). Hook Hall, Surrey

Outside dawn had broken.

The labs that looked directly on to the CFAC were crowded with the exhausted scientists, engineers and technicians who had built the accelerator, who had designed and put together the whole extraordinary mission.

Politicians and scientists were gathered in the control gallery. The atmosphere was tense and expectant.

One by one the crew were given a short-duration anaesthetic. (Delta's last thought as she passed out, looking up at Al in the cockpit, was a cross between *I hope he knows what he's doing* and *problematic boyfriend material.*) Then, one by one, they were wheeled on to the conveyor. Already in place at the centre of the accelerator was the helicopter; on the conveyor waited Stubbs's workshop truck, a fuel tanker and now the crew. The rest of the supplies to be shrunk waited in the loading bay, and just the other side of the loading-bay doors waited the trolley containing the imprisoned Beta Scarlatti.

Finn knew this was his last opportunity.

Leaving the crowd of technicians and scientists at the big Lab One windows, he slipped away and headed back through the now deserted corridors and laboratories to Lab Four where the entomology team had been based.

His plan was simple. To pocket the empty Beta Scarlatti husk.

He walked into the deserted lab and there was the husk in the corner of the chamber, just as he expected. Like an exploded purse, the shed skin sat there, just waiting to be taken home and mounted on a piece of A3 card, its Latin name printed on a slip beneath. It was the size of a small pine cone and was bound to provoke wonder. In his friend Hudson at least.

Finn was just looking around for something to put it in when he noticed a brand-new box containing sterile gloves that would be the perfect size, and remembered they'd thrown the old box away earlier. It was when he opened the bin to find the old box that he saw it.

The small grey atomiser unit.

The small grey atomiser unit that was supposed to be on the back of the trolley providing anaesthetising steam to the Scarlatti.

What was it still doing here? He'd better check the trolley and warn someone.

83

Finn didn't quite know what conclusion to jump to. Had there been a change of plan? What was the atomiser unit doing in here? He had to tell someone. Half dreading he might get in trouble, he hit an alarm button beside the door.

But no alarms sounded. No lights flashed. He hit it again. Nothing.

Finn jogged back down the empty corridors towards the doors which faced the CFAC loading bay. There was the trolley. There was the Beta Scarlatti safely onboard.

There was young Dr Spiro.

Al's speech from the cockpit was short.

"This is history, or we are. Let's go."

With that, he threw a switch and power dipped all over Europe.

With a surge in noise, the accelerator started up and began to find its va-va-voom.

Al started to manipulate the input interface and up the power. He wore earplugs and shades.

Upstairs, even through the control gallery's thick safety glass, the noise was extraordinary.

In the accelerator great arcs of lightning spun themselves into a blur, like electric candyfloss.

"The atomiser! I found it back in the lab!" yelled Finn at Dr Spiro over the sound of the accelerator just the other side of the loading-bay doors.

"It's been replaced!" Spiro shouted back. He seemed to be excited, glowing almost.

Finn looked down. The slot on the back of the trolley where the atomiser should have been now contained something else. Like a lump of clay or playdough. Some wires were coming out of it. Finn didn't get it at first, couldn't process what it might be, just that it definitely wasn't an atomiser unit. All was noise and confusion.

And then, in Spiro's hand, he saw a grey cover, just like the outside of the atomiser box. Just the right size to fit over the lump of clay. Still without joining the dots, but feeling something was very wrong, Finn hit the alarm at the loading-bay doors.

It was difficult to hear, but again nothing sounded, no lights flashed. Then Finn saw something that really threw him.

Dr Spiro wasn't wearing any shoes.

They were just behind the trolley. Both heels were askew. In fact, the heels seemed to be chambers, open and empty. *The playdough has come out of his shoes*, thought Finn absurdly. In a microsecond, a series of fearful connections flashed through his brain and he arrived at an even more absurd conclusion.

While everyone else was watching the display, Spiro was putting a bomb on the trolley. There was plastic explosive in the shoes.

"*The boy has seen the shoes. Deal with him*," said a voice only Spiro could hear.

Spiro became very calm and still. As if in a trance.

Just turn, thought Finn.

Just walk away.

Just tell someone as fast as you can.

Better still...

85

RUN.

The door back into Lab One was right there. He was less than ten metres from it. There were more than two dozen scientists and technicians just the other side, crowded at the window, marvelling at the Large Accelerator as it spun liquid lightning round its core.

All he had to do was make it through the door and scream.

But all he felt was the pain of the kick Spiro delivered to his ankle as he turned, and the floor rushing up to meet him as he fell.

The air was blasted out of him as he hit the deck, then again as Spiro followed up with a kick straight into his solar plexus. For a moment he could neither breathe nor scream.

He tried to roll and wriggle and claw his way towards the lab doors. But Spiro was up and over him in a heartbeat. Finn fought for breath, for life. But Spiro was crushing his chest with his weight now, his face a cruel gargoyle.

Finn used every last ounce of his strength to bring his leg hard up and over, as if performing one of his much-practised overhead kicks, and his knee met the back of Spiro's skull with what felt like the force of a cannonball. For a fraction of a moment Spiro was stunned and off balance.

It was all Finn needed. He bucked his body out from under Spiro, tipping him over.

Finn scrambled towards the lab door. He could see movement through the glass panel. He was going to reach it. He was going to collide with it and burst through and raise the alarm...

But, before he could make it, Spiro snapped out a leg that connected with Finn's ankle. Almost as Finn hit the floor, Spiro was over him and spraying something from a small phial directly into his face.

Finn felt himself drop from consciousness like a stone.

Good. Now get rid of the body. The refrigerated supply container is just the other side of the loading-bay doors.

And as Finn fell – and felt himself being dragged away – he thought no matter how hard you tried to understand things, no matter how old you got or how clever or how wise, there was always another layer of mystery.

And then all was black.

In the Large Accelerator cockpit Al, delighted with all he had created, took a simple blue memory stick from his pocket and inserted it into a USB slot in the control terminal. A new window flashed up before him. It was time to enter the crucial sequencing code, known to him alone. He rattled it into the keyboard, whispering to himself the snatch of poetry that he used as a mnemonic to recall it. It did its work. The flashes of spun lightning now became a continuous arc.

00:00:10
00:00:09
00:00:08
00:00:07
00:00:06
00:00:05
00:00:04

00:00:03
00:00:02

The accelerator was at squealing pitch.

00:00:01

Everybody was at the glass.

00:00:00

The CFAC became an extraordinary, blinding white light...

...that formed into a huge ball of solid spinning whiteness that consumed the centre of the accelerator and swallowed whole the Apache helicopter.

One and all looked on in awe.

The conveyor started up, the loading-bay doors opened and a supply crew ran into the CFAC in protective suits.

First to be fed into the light was Stubbs's truck, jerking as it slid forward and breached the vortex, six square metres and more than three tonnes of steel swallowed whole. One by one other items followed, ammunition, fuel tanker... the crew.

The conveyor was reloaded, the vortex kept spinning and items kept feeding in. The supply pallets. A jeep. The food supply container.

The accelerator began to power down and the ball of white lightning suddenly faded.

The assembled scientists and personages pressed their faces against the glass, trying to see.

The lockdown lifted. The control gallery doors automatically unbolted.

Al descended the cockpit ladder four rungs at a time and hit the CFAC.

In a moment he was inside the accelerator – the apparently empty accelerator – but there in the middle was what looked like a collection of children's toys.

A specially assigned nano-dimensional evac team immediately moved in to pack the tiny objects into their transport containers – adapted aluminium camera cases – and carry them out to the full-sized Merlin transport helicopter that *chackachacka*-ed in preparation for take-off outside the hangar, ready to fly north.

And, as Al backed away to let them work, he could hear something above the sound of the helicopter, something muffled and emanating from the control gallery and labs.

Applause.

PART
TWO

PART
TWO

ELEVEN

The ten-tonne Merlin transport helicopter was halfway through its flight at GO plus 00:15.12.77 at an altitude of a thousand feet and with a speed just approaching 110 knots when a 250g charge of fifth-generation plastic explosive – equivalent to 10lbs of TNT – detonated at a point just inside loading-bay door 2.

The bomb ripped open the fuselage and whiplashed the substructure and airframe such that centrifugal rotor force could no longer be contained. Within 0.789 seconds, the airframe failed, the main rotor bearings sheared and the aircraft disintegrated, its component parts falling to earth in a cloud of aviation fuel which quickly ignited.

Local radio received a call from a resident of Little Downs, Surrey, a vicar. The vicar, in shock and using the language of the *Six O'Clock*

News, reported a "huge explosion" and "wreckage strewn over a wide area" and then was suddenly, and inexplicably, cut off.

Please God, no, thought Al.

The implications and possibilities ricocheted round his mind.

The control gallery was still in stunned silence. Triumph had turned in an instant to disaster.

What fools they had been, thought Commander King beside him.

"*Got visual. Crash site in flames,*" issued a radio comms from the first chase team to get a decent view of the crash site. "*Edge of woodland about two kilometres northwest of the B235. No road access.*"

"It's over…" muttered General Mount. "It's all over."

"Let's wait till the recovery teams have reported, General," ordered King, with clipped sang-froid, trying to regroup.

Professor Lomax reported shortly after take-off that he'd found the atomiser unit in the entomology lab. He had raised the alarm. They should have grounded the flight immediately. Instead they asked Lomax to double-check that the unit he'd found was definitely the one that was supposed to be onboard the Merlin.

By the time he'd confirmed this, it was too late.

A team had scoured the surveillance AV and found nothing but obviously doctored 'vanilla' images of an empty CFAC complex. The last recorded 'real' images showed Finn leaving Lab One and heading towards Lab Four. It was at the same time the accelerator was at its most spectacular and distracting. Why had Finn left? What had happened? No one could find out.

Because no one could find Finn.

The CCTV effectively went blank for seven minutes, until Dr Spiro suddenly popped up onscreen with the trolley to help attach the miniaturised tracking device to the Beta Scarlatti.

Now it seemed Dr Spiro was missing too. As a frantic search got under way, Al tried to put it all together, fighting a losing battle with his worst fears. He remembered asking Spiro, "Is Finn still in the lab?" while they were watching the sleeping nano-crew, their equipment, plus the Beta Scarlatti locked in its trolley, being packed into aluminium transport cases and loaded on to the full-sized Merlin helicopter for the short flight to the release site. He had expected him to be by Spiro's side. "He's with the Commander," Spiro had said. He had lied.

The last image that could be found of Spiro on CCTV showed him swiping himself out of the lab complex just before the transport chopper took off.

"That door should not be open to anyone," said King. "Whoever our enemy is, they're in the system, they're in the CCTV, they're even in the coding for the door locks."

Finn wanted to wake. He felt hot, urgent pain.

He wondered what kind of nightmare he was in and tried to tip himself out of it, to force his eyes open as he had as a young child

95

when he had realised he was dreaming. But back and back it came. Pain at the back of his head. Blackness. A shaky otherworldly feeling that he was floating outside of life, but not part of it. He drifted in and out of this, semi-conscious, for... seconds...? Minutes...?

Then suddenly he wanted to be sick. He retched but produced nothing but a blinding intensification of pain. He finally opened his eyes properly and realised that this was it – this was awake – and it really did hurt this much.

As Finn came fully to – as fully as the pain would allow – all he knew for sure was that he must get up.

He was buried under something. His head trapped by... rocks? But he was wet too, and he could smell... tomatoes? He shifted and pushed at whatever it was. Tin cans gave way and tumbled around him. Food. He was buried under tins of food.

He breathed air – cool, yes, better than the stifling air he had been breathing, but corrupt. Smoke. He pushed back the mess of tins and leaking ration packs and found himself upside down in what he realised must be the refrigerated shipping container, the food store.

It all came back to him at once, like water sloshing back into an empty vessel: Al... the holiday... Scarlatti... Boldklub... Spiro...

His ears were ringing and his mouth felt dumb and numb, blocked, as if full of grit. He retched again. In the distance he could hear... voices? Burning?

For a microsecond he thought, *Fire... warm...* and could have laid back down and accepted it. But something stirred in him, something deep inside, and he knew he must try and get out even if it felt hopeless.

Just keep going.

He shifted. The shipping container was upside down and at an angle and it took him a few moments to orient himself.

He tried to take in the half-light ahead. He could smell smoke, sick oil smoke. Blocking the entrance to the container was a heavy curtain of green canvas. He wobbled towards the thick curtain. He pushed and it gave way to reveal more smoke and the crackling sound of fire, but also a flash of daylight. Finn squinted into the smoke and light until he got used to it and opened his eyes further. The whole area above the container seemed to be covered in green canvas, like a collapsed circus tent. The container lay in the dirt on its side, he could see now. He staggered on, heading for the light.

The sound of burning and the smoke were becoming more intense. The canvas ended at a point where it had been sewn into a massive seam. As he finally made it out into daylight, out from under the canvas, he saw it.

A bloodied thing the size of a beached whale. Flesh but not flesh. Too vast and fantastic for flesh. Great rolls and creases of it. Pale and lined and pitted. Curved. Cupped. As Finn stepped back and his senses fought to make some kind of sense of it, some kind of form, his heart pounded... and he realised what it was.

A hand. A human hand. Finn stood stunned before it for a moment, his rebooting brain unable to process the scale. He tried

97

to blink and wake himself up all over again. But still it was there. Filling the void. A hundred and fifty times the size it should be. Fingernails strangest of all, like slabs of stone, stratified and textured and several centimetres thick, their edges and cuticles pitted and jagged with dinner plates of flaking scale and skin hanging here and there. Dirt too. Clumps of dirt and drying blood in the grooves and swirls of the mattress-thick skin on the fingertips. He turned...

...and realised that the great mound – the mountain – behind him, above him was a body, the circus tent of canvas his clothing. His uniform. It was the body of one of the airmen, one of the crew of the full-size Merlin transport helicopter.

Finn's mind spun, his heart thumped, the world expanding, exploding around him.

I am me and I am not me...

A noise came out of him. A primal exclamation. It had happened – the most extraordinary, unimaginable, ridiculous thing had happened. He had never felt more helpless, more nothing... or more new. He felt shock itself, and a change of being, as great in sense as when his mum died – the difference between her being there and not being there, between her presence and absence.

I am me and I am not me, Finn thought, looking around in awe at the massive, macro world around him. After their fight Spiro must have shoved him, unconscious, into the food store in the loading bay...

I am me and I am not me... I am nano...
BANG!

A cinder popped nearby, shooting over his head, a live red spit.

He moved away from the hand and staggered on. Trying to take in everything. Trying to make sense of it. There was dirt underfoot. Fresh and flat. He was in a clearing – gouged out by the impact? – but surrounding it were towers of meadow grass as thick and lush as rainforest, some of it burning. Far above were trees – the edge of a wood, he guessed – debris burning in the branches.

The further he backed away from the hand, the body, the more certain Finn was that the airman was still alive, if badly injured. There was no movement in the hand, but Finn could see the great mass of the abdomen rise and fall as he breathed. But Finn could not save him. He needed to get away. He must get away. The smoke was getting thicker. He could only see a few centimetres ahead.

For a minute or so he was swamped in smoke again, then a breeze fanned the fires, but cleared the smoke briefly and he saw – lying smashed open in the jungle of grasses – the top of what could have been a large aluminium house of what must be…

…the transport container for the crew.

He looked back. The refrigerated shipping container he had been in was trapped beneath the airman. It must have been flung loose from its box on impact. How had he survived?

His head was still fogged. Never mind. *Just keep going.*

If he was alive, maybe the others were alive too, especially if they were in the padded container.

He tried to scramble through the jungle of lush, thick grasses to reach it, but soon found them impassable. Instead he scrambled up and on top of the thicker stems – stronger and more substantial that he expected, like densely planted saplings – collapsing them across each other as he progressed, forming a scramble net of sorts to the edge of the box.

The flames were getting nearer now, the fire in the grasses taking hold, starting to suck in oxygen and feed itself.

Finn looked down into the box and could see the top layer of protective padding had been lost, as had his food store container and two pallets of ammunition and supplies – now scattered like confetti…

…but there, still lashed in place in the foam, were the Apache helicopter, fuel truck and… the crew, all lined up.

None of them moving a muscle.

TWELVE

CRACKACRACKACRACKA – scattered ammunition started to cook in the burning grass.

Finn, perched on the edge of the container, had a choice. He could try and make it through the undergrowth and outrun the fire, or risk seeing if the crew were alive and if they could get out together. This would be his last chance.

Finn jumped down into the foam container.[10]

He landed awkwardly, his body jolting on impact, but at least the foam was easy to scramble over. Soft play. As soon as he got close enough to the crew, he realised they were alive, and Kelly and Stubbs were already coming round. From the briefings, Finn knew that each

---

[10]   See citation (i) Queen's Gallantry Medal (civilian), Appendix A.

carried a hypodermic on their chest filled with an antidote to the anaesthetic they'd been given.

He went to Kelly first, plucked the hypo pack off his chest and ripped it open. He hesitated. He had no idea what he should be doing with it, but he guessed he'd better jab it in Kelly's arm and press the plunger. He did so.

Kelly snapped awake, cried out and threw Finn off.

"Yaaaaahhhghhh!"

Wild-eyed and panicked, Kelly ripped up through his strapping with a knife. He was flipped out of his foam niche and about to throw the knife before Finn yelled, "STOP!"

Kelly paused. In the smoke. In the foam. Looking at the boy. The boy with a bloodied face... Things started to flood back.

"Finn...?"

Stubbs groaned behind him. Kelly snapped his head round to take in the others. Finn said, "You're nano! You've got to wake up! We've got to go! It's on fire! Something's gone wrong!"

Kelly looked through the smoke at the impossible, exploded, expanded scene – going through all that Finn had said – realising that the hill beyond was not a hill at all, but the injured airman. A colossus.

"What the hell!?" was all Kelly could think to say through his shock.

"I know..." was all Finn could think of saying back.

The fire was getting more intense.

"We've got to wake them!" said Finn, pushing back past him to rip open the hypodermic pack on Delta. Kelly followed suit on Stubbs. Delta snarled and struggled as she came to, but then sat there and took it all in with them… the bewildering, cosmic shift in scale. The nano-shock. And the burning.

Kelly realised something more as he came to. He grabbed Finn, alarmed. "Finn, what are you doing here? You're not supposed to be here!"

"I don't know. I think Dr Spiro pushed me in with the food. He was putting a bomb on the trolley…"

Kelly fought to understand. Finn hardly did himself. The crew were bewildered and still in nano-shock. They needed time to take everything in, time for the drugs to wear off – time they didn't have.

"It's burning! We've got to get out!" Finn yelled at Kelly to snap him out of it. Kelly stared.

So Finn slapped his massive face. For a moment he thought Kelly would hit him back, but instead he finally shook his head and exploded into life.

"Get up! UP! STUBBS – check the kit and comms! SALAZAR – pre-flight!"

"KK!" shouted Delta.

Pre-flight?

Kelly ran towards the helicopter and started to cut through the rubberised ties that anchored it in place – those that had held after the box broke open on impact.

Delta came back to life as she plugged herself into the cabin of the Apache, senses returning to optimum as she fired it up. She loved these machines. Helicopters were 'dynamically unstable' by design. Nothing could suit her more perfectly.

"Bring it on," she ordered the engines.

"Bother," said Stubbs, wobbling to his feet to take in the wreck of his mobile workshop. "Hell." He picked out a toolbox and motioned for Finn to help him with it. Together they tried to drag it across the foam to the chopper, but it was so heavy it was hopeless. Kelly ran over and picked it up like it was nothing.

Stubbs handed Finn some smaller tools and he staggered to the Apache with them instead. Choking. The smoke was thick and black now.

The Apache's engines had already started to whine, its rotors to turn.

"We know what we're here for! Let's get this thing in the air!" ordered Kelly.

Finn helped grab ammo and other supplies from the remaining pallet, but when Kelly kicked open the stow holds there clearly wasn't going to be room for everything alongside their weapons and water supply.

Kelly threw Stubbs into the cab then shouted to Finn, "Grab a couple of handfuls of food, ammo and meds, and that's it!"

Finn did so while Kelly hacked away at the foam embedding the Apache's three wheels.

Sweat was pouring off them in the heat. The noise of the chopper was deafening, its increasing downdraught attracting and feeding the flames creeping towards them.

"Get in!" Kelly said. Finn jumped into the cabin and scrambled up beside Delta on the top two seats. Kelly dived into the lower seats next to Stubbs – just as the foam padding in the box caught fire and began to melt, flare and burn.

"GO!" yelled Kelly, slamming the door.

"We're not there yet!" said Delta, eyes glued to the red-to-green power indicator above her head. Willing it higher.

The supply pallet was being consumed. Bullets crackled around them. Finn could feel his heart beating faster and faster. The fuel truck was next. Foam-fuelled flames swept round it.

"FLY!!" Kelly urged the machine.

"Give me some revs, you hunk of junk!!" Delta instructed the power indicator.

Once settled, and having unwrapped and inserted a boiled sweet to stop his ears from popping, Stubbs simply reached up with an aged, crooked finger, opened a maintenance panel and flipped a switch marked 'Ex. Override. Vap'.[11]

BANG!

The whole craft seemed to jolt forward, and the power bar shot from red into green.

"*GOOOO!*" yelled Finn.

"GONE!" reported Delta, and hauled up the stick.

The Apache roared and pulled away from planet earth, the foam

---

[11] A decarbonising maintenance procedure for use ONLY when the engine is unlit otherwise it ignites unburnt fuel and gas in the rear turbines causing an unstable turbo effect.

packing releasing the wheels with an uneven jolt – just as the fuel truck EXPLODED...

...so that they were catapulted and shot up and backwards inside the expanding conflagration into hell. Finn screamed. Kelly gritted his teeth. Stubbs sucked his boiled sweet.

Delta, back in her element, rode the aircraft like a rodeo steer as it reeled from the explosion, banking out of both the backflip and expanding fireball and sending the aircraft horizontal out of the flame instead of flipping back over to crash to earth. Finally she restored equilibrium in free air so that they found themselves hovering in the clear five macro-metres or so above the crash site, over the burning wreckage.

Finn allowed himself a mad, strangled laugh.

Delta allowed herself a chewing gum, flicking one out of a pack and catching it in her mouth.

Stubbs started switching things on. Beneath them lay a scene of carnage: a great flaming, formless mess, a huge splash of fire and shattered fuselage strewn over an area the size of a football pitch. They hung above it, barely the size of a baby bird – but still alive.

"Sabotage," said Kelly, surveying the scene.

And then, above the sound of the rotors, the popping ammo and burning wreckage...

Beep... Beep... Beep... Beep... Beep... Beep... Beep...

THIRTEEN

"It's still down there," said Stubbs.

"What is?" said Finn.

"The Beta Scarlatti."

Delta hit the radio using the agreed call signs Finn had come up with in the briefings: Ronaldo for control, Messi for the mission.

"Come in, Ronaldo! Come in, Ronaldo! This is Messi! Do you read me, Ronaldo? Over!"

Nothing.

"They won't respond. Unless they're right on top of us, we're out of range[12]," said Stubbs. "We are alone."

---

[12] A tiny – but macro-scale – radio transmitter had been attached to the miniaturised helicopter's underside in order for it to communicate via normal radio waves with circling macro-search aircraft. Its broadcast range was extremely limited.

"Thank you, Happy Smurf," said Kelly.

Beep... Beep... Beep... Beep... Beep... Beep... Beep...

"We still have the Beta signal!" said Finn, excited.

"Probably dead," said Stubbs.

"It must be alive if it's still broadcasting," said Finn.

"Well, that's what we're here for. Find it!" ordered Kelly.

Beep... Beep... Beep... Beep... Beep... Beep... Beep...

Stubbs tutted, put on a pair of spectacles and squinted at the green dot on the tracking screen, guiding Delta on to the signal. "East a few metres – macro-metres not nano-metres – this thing doesn't know the difference."

They banked back over the east side of the wreckage and descended. As they did so, the body of the injured airman was revealed through the smoke, parachute half open and trailing behind him.

"He must have tried to jump out with us before we hit the ground," said Delta.

"The fire's spreading the other way. They'll find him. He'll make it," said Kelly.

Finn looked away, praying Kelly was right and the flames wouldn't get that far. In doing so, he spotted a cigar shape.

"There!"

Almost directly below them, free of its shattered transportation trolley but still locked in its muzzle-ended titanium harness – which must have saved it from the blast – was the Beta Scarlatti. Flames licked as it buzzed and fizzed and fought for its terrible life, the attached nano-transmitter – a white stripe across its belly – beeping away, oblivious.

"It's going to fry," said Stubbs. "If it hasn't already."

"Can we pick it up?" Kelly asked Delta.

"We're overloaded."

They watched the flames lick nearer.

"Take her down! I know how to open it!" said Finn.

"Impossible. Unstable air," said Stubbs.

Kelly looked at Delta. "Salazar?"

"Watch me," she said.

"Take her down and get ready to run!" ordered Kelly, opening the door.

The Beta Scarlatti caught the scent of the crew. Getting stronger. Getting closer. In its forebrain the four scents became fused with the agony and confusion of its struggle.

The whole harness throbbed as it tried to vibrate its way out of its metal sarcophagus. It thought one thing.

Kill...

Venom oozed from its abdomen and sizzled against the scalding metal.

Kelly lashed a line to the weapons hardpoint on the fuselage as Delta, teeth gritted, lowered the Apache into the snarling conflagration, the rotor wash beating back the flames, yet fanning them at the same time.

Stubbs read the instruments and called out guidance as Delta kept the aircraft as steady as a rock in the roasting, turbulent air.

"Three nano-metres! Another two! That's it!"

The line secure, Kelly ducked back to hook an arm round Finn. "Kid! Can you do this?"

Any fear Finn felt – and he knew he should – was drowning in excitement. He nodded.

"Remember he's family!" warned Stubbs.

"I'll look after him," said Kelly, and before Finn knew what was happening Kelly had swung them both out on the line to drop the two metres or so on to the harness – right on top of the trapped and furious beast.

Finn felt a shocking heat assail him, drawing the air from his lungs and singeing his skin.

They jumped down off the harness and for a moment Finn found himself face to face with the Scarlatti – eye to thousand-celled eye – and again he realised exactly how small he was now. The beast dwarfed them, twice Finn's 9mm height on its side and six times his length. Trunk-like antennae flexed out of the muzzle end of the harness to taste him, but shrank back as they hit the heat, furious and confused, burning and dying.

Kelly shouted, "Finn! Where is it?" through the noise and downdraught.

Finn found the release catch halfway down the harness and mimed the action of yanking it up to show Kelly what to do. The flames were nearly upon them. Kelly nodded, and shoved Finn back up on the harness, motioning him back in the chopper.

Delta held it steady as Finn pulled himself back in.

Below, Kelly wrapped the line up to the Apache as many times round his arm as he could, then reached down and hooked the end round the release catch on the harness. He nodded up at Delta.

"THREE, TWO, ONE – GO!"

"Oh, glory..." said Stubbs.

Delta hauled on the stick.

The Apache and Kelly shot upwards...

...the harness sprang open...

...and the furious winged leviathan escaped its tomb like a bat out of hell.

WWKWZZZWZWZWWKZWZWKZWZWKKZWZWZWZWKKZ-WWWKWZZ!

The Apache shot out of the flames, centimetres ahead of the beast.

Crazed with anger, in mad flight, the Scarlatti dwarfed them, filling the glass canopy and blotting out the light, massive *thwack-a-thwack-a* wings creating turbulent air, nearly beating out their rotors. Delta twisted and twirled the Apache to evade. Again Finn clung on as she turned the aircraft on its side and made horizontal.

"Kelly!" shouted Finn.

"What's his position?" asked Delta.

"He's still there!" shouted Finn who caught a glimpse of him – hanging on.

111

"So is that ridiculous organism!" Stubbs added uselessly, as the Scarlatti spun to attack them, bringing its vile abdomen screaming towards them, stings first, bulging with venom.

"Tell him to hang on," said Delta and hauled again on the stick. She threw the Apache into an about-turn. Kelly, swinging beneath, screamed, his shoulder almost dislocated by the force of the escape.

"Shoot it! We'll have to destroy it!" shouted Stubbs.

"Not yet. Got an idea. Going down," Delta said.

"Back down?" cried Finn.

She plunged the nose of the aircraft towards earth... right back into the flames.

The Apache reached speeds in the dive equivalent to 220mph. Finn watched the Scarlatti track it every millimetre of the way, its great eye filling one of the rear-window panels and glaring at him.

Kill...

They hit the flames. Delta banked sharply through pure fire. Beneath them, Kelly screamed once more.

She held them in the conflagration as long as she dared: one second... two... then banked up and out again – downwind.

The Scarlatti was gone. The flames were too much. They'd lost it.

"Get us clear!" they heard Kelly shout.

Delta took them a few macro-metres across the meadow, as low as she dared above the level of the grasses, swinging round the clumps of nettles, thistles and white-crowned cow parsley twenty storeys high.

Beep... Beep... Beep... Beep... Beep... Beep... Beep...

The tracker showed the Scarlatti still moving – still alive – but getting closer then more distant, closer and more distant.

"It's going round in circles!" said Stubbs.

"Put us down!" shouted Kelly beneath them.

They landed on, of all things, a dried cowpat, which turned out to be the perfect size, shape and consistency for the job. Delta lowered Kelly on to the surface and landed right beside him.

Kelly – miraculously, thought Finn – was still conscious.

Stubbs clambered down and checked him over, Finn getting out to try and help too. Kelly's skin was burnt a mottled red and he'd lost most of his hair and eyebrows. Stubbs gave him an injection of some kind. Kelly looked up.

"You OK?" he asked Finn.

Finn couldn't believe the burnt, bleeding man would be concerned for him. He nodded.

Inside, Delta repeated her communications mantra: "Come in, Ronaldo. Come in, Ronaldo. This is Messi. Do you read me, Ronaldo? Over."

Nothing.

Finn opened a bottle of water which Kelly gulped back.

"Thanks. You did good. Quite a sight close up, wasn't it?" Kelly grinned.

Finn grinned back. "Its eye was bigger than me!"

"Were you scared?"

"Nah. There's a kid at school looks at me just like that."

Kelly laughed. "Just give me his name when we get out of this mes— WATCH OUT!"

Suddenly Kelly shoved Finn aside and reached for his sidearm.[13] Finn spun round.

Through the jungle of grasses – movement.

A black ant popped out of thin air in the grass ahead of them and Finn's heart all but stopped. It was liquid gloss-black, of indescribable geometric beauty, the size of a wolf and moving at great speed in a series of flicking limbs. The ant stopped maybe ten nanometres ahead of them and tasted the air with two huge serrated mouthparts, antennae swishing, thinking – *What are these new things, threat or food?*

Finn was rapt. A black ant, in the wild, in massive form. Totally stunning. Totally crazy. He wanted to walk over to it, to touch it, to ask it questions.

Kelly didn't wait for answers.

BANG.

Finn jumped out of his skin. The ant's armour shattered like crockery as the bullet ripped through it. Finn couldn't believe it. A life, electric and immediate – the most amazing thing he'd ever seen – just gone. Shaking, he stepped forward and picked up a leg section, shiny black, light and strong, like a piece of cycle frame.

He wanted to protest. He wanted to scream, but the shock of it – and the bullet still ringing in his ears – meant that no sound emerged when he opened his mouth.

[13] .357 Magnum.

"Back in the cabin!" said Kelly, getting to his feet and pulling him back, unsentimental.

"But... but..."

"That's an order."

Kelly lifted Finn bodily back into the aircraft and he found himself sitting up next to Delta with a souvenir ant shin in his hand. He offered her a look. She just chewed her gum.

Stubbs was already back in the cabin monitoring the Scarlatti's position.

Beep... Beep... Beep... Beep... Beep... Beep... Beep...

Delta slapped shut the maintenance panel he'd flipped earlier to activate his improvised turbo.

"Nice trick back there, old man."

"Playing around with these since before you were born, young lady," grumbled Stubbs.

Kelly hauled himself into the Apache and started to slather his burns with a white goo from one of the medi-pacs.

"It's heading west, 250 macro-metres," Stubbs reported.

"We got nothing on the radio," said Delta.

"They've got to be right on top of us to receive a signal – and the range on the Scarlatti tracking transmitter is less than 800 macro-metres. If they don't get here in the next minute, we've lost it," said Stubbs.

"It must have our scent – we can't get too close. We've got to stay downwind," said Finn.

"Beta now 400 macro-metres west," reported Stubbs.

"If they don't find us in the wreckage, they'll realise what we've done. They'll radio sweep for us, systematically, just like they said in the briefings," said Kelly.

"How long will it take them to sift the wreckage?" said Delta. "We might be miles away."

"It'll take days to cover that much ground," said Stubbs. "Could we leave the boy here with a radio to make contact?"

"We can't leave him, he's a kid," said Kelly.

"There are no macro-radios anyway, just the one under the Apache," said Delta.

"Flares?" suggested Stubbs.

Finn butted in, irritated. "I'm going with you! I know the mission. I know the science. I know the insects. And I know my uncle. He'll find us. They'll sweep for us. *He won't let us down* and I won't let you down either."

They looked at him.

"D'you shoot?" asked Delta with American simplicity.

"On *Call of Duty*," said Finn.

Beneath her Aviator shades, Finn could tell, she rolled her eyes.

Beep... Beep... Beep... Beep... Beep... Beep... Beep...

"Signal's getting weaker... 700 metres west-northwest," said Stubbs.

"Come in, Ronaldo. Come in, Ronaldo. This is Messi. Do you read me, Ronaldo? Over."

"Is it a straight line 700 metres?" asked Finn.

"More or less."

"Then it's probably locked on to the Alpha already."

"We're losing the signal," said Stubbs.

Kelly looked at Finn, weighed him up and winked a lashless eye.

"He's in. Let's go."

Delta hauled on the stick.

FOURTEEN

As soon as they realised what had happened, King gave the order to shut down all digital and computer systems and switch to analogue procedures. Hook Hall had been seriously compromised. Boldklub had been seriously compromised. The Western world had been seriously compromised. The immediate countryside would soon be crawling with security personnel. All local roads would have to be closed and roadblocks established at major junctions further afield; all ports and airports would be notified. Anybody in a uniform in the south of England would be out searching for Spiro within the hour. At the very least they were dealing with a highly sophisticated criminal network. Who were they? What on earth was their intent?

King felt – briefly – clueless. A terrible feeling only broken when Al headed out of the control gallery, determined on a course of action. Any action. King pursued him on to the gantry down to the CFAC.

"Where do you think you're going? You're exhausted and in shock," he insisted. "You can't disappear. Whoever's behind this will target you."

"Let's find them first. Worry about that later."

King grabbed his shoulder to stop him.

"Until we know exactly how far Hook Hall and internal security have been compromised, we have to assume that you're in grave danger. The likelihood is that everything and everybody was destroyed in the crash, and if your nephew Infinity was onboard…"

"Not yet! *We don't know that yet.* The witness thinks he saw a parachute. Now where's my car?"

Right on cue, the De Tomaso Mangusta rasped round a corner into the CFAC and screeched to a halt in front of them. On Al's command, one of the technicians had retrieved it from an underground car park.

"If you want to help me find out what the hell's going on, get in," Al said, throwing himself into the driver's seat and revving the Mangusta like a boy racer. Obligingly, it rattled out a high-octane smoker's cough.

Commander King reluctantly dropped into the passenger seat.

The Mangusta took off.

Kaparis received radio-signal confirmation of the 'total destruction' of the transport aircraft shortly before Commander King ordered the complete shutdown of all electronic surveillance and communication systems.

An almost detectable ripple of pride ran through the eighty-eight staff at the bunker.

Kaparis didn't share it.

The one thing he could never fully understand was the irrational, emotional impulse in weak people and its often chaotic effects. Clearly some such had caused the Drake child to behave the way he had in ignoring the accelerator and returning to Lab Four like that.

Spiro at least had acted ruthlessly according to instruction and the operation had been saved, with the considerable bonus that the Drake boy had been destroyed.

It should have been an unexpected joy and yet… Kaparis felt a vague dissatisfaction. It was a rushed death. There had been no time to savour it. Worst of all, the boy didn't know it was happening, and what was sweetest about revenge was its demonstrative execution.

There would be more, of course. The operation was still on track.

The only negative consequence of the morning's events was that they were locked out of the Hook Hall surveillance apparatus for the time being, and Spiro was no longer in position.

Kaparis considered this potential loss.

Spiro was a protégé from Kaparis's Zurich days. He had turned out well under careful tutelage. After proving his worth in the development of NRP[14], he had become the inspiration for the whole Tyro programme.

Spiro had performed brilliantly at extreme distance and over a protracted period, and had attained his primary objective. He would never allow himself to be captured alive. He was an exemplar. A direct expression of the Will of Kaparis...

...and because of the Drake boy he might be lost.

"Massage!" he ordered, to calm himself down. Heywood obliged and flicked a switch.

Within the iron lung, electrical impulses fired through Kaparis's paralysed body, keeping his nerveless musculature in peak condition. Although he could not feel the clenching and twitching, he was able to experience the consequent flow of 'feel–good' exercise endorphins – one of the many tiny pieces of evidence that suggested the nerve damage from his catastrophic spinal injury had not been as complete as first feared.

Which gave him, together with the riches and 'human resources' at his disposal, a godlike sense of boundless possibility.

Maybe things weren't that bad after all, Kaparis thought.

"What news from the Atlantic Front?" he asked.

---

[14] Neuro-Retinal Programming – an accelerated learning and personality control process whereby a probe, inserted directly through the eye, connects to the optic nerve and delivers information (specialist knowledge, emotional association, ideology, etc.) straight to the brain's cerebral cortex, and therefore the subconscious mind.

Cooper-Hastings watched the red LED light blink off.

He hung his head.

"Again?" asked the small guard.

The taller guard with the scar took the camera off the tripod and presented it to the blond-haired, ice-hearted teenage boy who'd been Cooper-Hastings' tormenter.

The boy watched the video playback.

Through his shame and pain, Cooper-Hastings could hear himself begin to speak the ridiculous words.

The smaller guard waited for the verdict from the teenager on the latest performance. He got it in a clipped German accent.

"The cut above the eye is still visible. Lower resolution. AGAIN, Herr Doktor," the blond boy ordered, and handed the camera back.

The red LED came on. Cooper-Hastings looked into the lens.

FIFTEEN

The Apache rose and, despite it all, despite the carnage and the shock, despite the loss of contact and the thought of what Al must be going through...

Finn's heart filled with pure excitement.

They took off, banking again over the crash site and heading off into the morning sun across the meadow, whizzing surreally over carpets of opening wildflowers and strong, succulent grasses, the colours blinding on such a scale, skirting the edge of the wood, dipping to track the Scarlatti signal along a hedgerow, swinging back and forth through the tallest clumps of wild grasses and weeds, seed heads puffing open in their wake, rising to hurdle occasional knots of barbed wire and hedgerow, and even a startled mink.

It was simply breathtaking. A tidal wave of astonishing detail revealed at the equivalent of 135mph; too much to take in and make sense of, so that all but pure sensation was suspended.

As they cut low across the next meadow, skimming over a gigantic hippie blanket of daisies and buttercups, silence and wonder possessed them. Finn couldn't have spoken even if he'd wanted to. There was a lump in his throat. The further they skimmed, it seemed to Finn, the further they entered a fantastic new world, a dimension always present yet unrevealed, of nature and colour and extraordinary detail.

Whenever he had asked his mum about his dad, she had told Finn to think of him not in heaven or in a grave, but as a part of everything, every ray of sunshine, every breeze and every birdsong. This is the way he tried to think of them both, and he'd never felt closer to that everything than he did now.

"This is… unreal," he heard himself say eventually, regretting it. But the others, too, were pinned to their seats.

"Drunks and children tell the truth," said Kelly.

"Man, this is uber," said Delta, slaloming the aircraft through the unfolding pasture.

Only Stubbs remained immune, glued to the tracking screen.

Beep… Beep… Beep… Beep… Beep… Beep… Beep…

"Still heading west-northwest, 750 macro…"

"Thing's fast," said Delta.

"Why aren't we closing?" asked Kelly.

"Crosswinds. Headwinds. Only takes the slightest breeze – that's why we're hugging the ground," said Delta.

"There's a stream – would that be more sheltered?" Finn asked.

Instead of ignoring a suggestion from a child, Delta simply assessed it and nodded.

She took the Apache further down the meadow to sweep along the course of the stream – a dappled black sunshine highway, the rotor wash whipping up a spray in their wake, spooked sticklebacks leaping like dolphins, and then – to a collective gasp – a kingfisher darting into the water ahead of them with such speed and grace, such a blaze of beauty and colour, on such a scale it made even Stubbs's heart leap.

Disturbed, he looked straight back down at his screen.

Beep... Beep... Beep... Beep... Beep... Beep... Beep...

"720 macro-metres..."

The Alpha Scarlatti took flight for the first time since the sun had risen. The decaying badger was generating enough heat now to have allowed the Alpha to take to the air even during the night – which had been mild anyway.

It had spent the first hour of morning nurturing and farming, crawling among its eggs, tasting the outer membrane of each one to check the health of the developing nymph within.

Thirteen of the eggs had been stillborn, were unfertilised, or had been too weak to survive the night. The Scarlatti consumed them.

Now it patrolled. The smell of the dead badger was attracting scavengers, large and small. There was a chance they would disturb or even consume the eggs themselves before they had fully incubated.

Crows were the boldest, and those that had reached the site had been stung, three of their shiny black-sack corpses surrounding the site, serving as a warning to others – crows, foxes, rats.

Now the wicked buzz of its wings, as it patrolled in a thirty-metre radius around the site, would sound further warning.

Airborne it was safe. Airborne it could better bring death.

It gained height and emitted a gush of poisonous musk and pheromone.

The swarm instinct had filled the senses of the Beta for more than two hours, tracing a pheromone trail so slight it teased and enflamed. But then this instinct was overtaken by another.

To feed.

The Beta had suffered in the heat, in the trap, burning half of its stored energy in its mad attempts to escape. The initial flight had all but exhausted it.

It landed on a week-old lamb, whipped at it three or four times with its lethal stings and felt the little creature skitter then sink beneath it. It nosed through the soft wool to seek out the warm skin beneath, then sank its razor-barbed jaws deep into the flesh.

Hot, sugary blood gushed out.

Feeeeeeeed...

"We're closing! Take her down slowly. We're right on it."

"How close?"

"Less than thirty macro."

"Anybody getting visual?"

"Not you, Stubbs! You watch the screen and the moment you see that dot move – scream," said Kelly.

"There!" said Finn, spotting the lamb on its side.

Delta let the Apache drift in closer in 'whisper' mode and they zoomed in with the scope and got a visual of the back end of the Scarlatti nuzzling the dead creature's neck.

"How long will it feed, Finn?" asked Kelly.

"Up to twenty minutes, then it'll rest for the same," said Finn, who'd not only paid attention during the Lomax briefings, but had read a summary of one of the research papers.

They flew further up the field and Delta chose the base of an electricity pylon to land on. The grasses around the concrete slab were like tall, swaying trees and, as they came in to land, Finn thought the aluminium pylon – which sank into the concrete at an angle, covered in white oxides and yellow lichens – looked like an ancient temple in a jungle clearing.

They powered down. The Scarlatti wouldn't be able to fly more than 400 macro-metres in the time it would take them to restart the aircraft and get airborne.

"Come in, Ronaldo. Come in, Ronaldo. This is Messi, do you read me, Ronaldo? Over…"

Kelly got out to check the small arms in the stow holds while

127

Delta checked the Apache for damage with a series of carefully aimed kicks and made a fuel assessment. Stubbs opened a map and took out a compass.

"What are you doing?" said Finn.

"Don't you know how to use a map and compass? Aren't you related to Sir Francis Drake, the great explorer?"

"Don't think so."

Stubbs rolled his eyes. Then, using the compass to represent the chopper, he flew their path across the map, the needle never wavering from north.

"GPS won't work down here, but… nothing can budge the earth's magnetic field. Once you have that and a simple magnetised needle, *you can conquer the world.* The Phoenicians had the stars, the Chinese had the needle, the Greeks had the maths, but it was the Portuguese who put it all together and they had the entire planet," Stubbs said in a trance, holding up an imaginary planet. He would have rambled on all day, as happily as Finn would have listened, but Delta and Kelly returned to confer.

"We got through a lot of juice with the aerobatics, but we've got maybe six hours left. If there's any weight we can dump, let's dump it," said Delta.

"In the hold we've got two Minimis, three M27s and a heap of ammo," said Kelly. "Let's keep one of each and dump half the amm—"

His hindbrain suddenly registered movement in the rocks behind Delta and he shouted, "Salazar! Six o'clock!"

She ducked. Kelly snatched up an M27 and fired.

DRRRRRRRT! DRRRRT!

Finn hit the ground in shock, ears ringing.

The bullets split clean in two what looked like a bright red beach ball.

Too loud! was all Finn could think at first.

As Kelly was processing what had just happened, a great grey creature the size of a walrus rose from behind the foot of the pylon. Again he fired.

DRRRRRRRT!

Armoured sections shattered and scattered, and yellow insect mush filled the air.

"Hold your fire!" shouted Finn, jumping up and waving his arms as another slow grey form rose over the edge of the concrete.

As the last scraps of grey shell floated to earth, Finn wanted to grab Kelly. Why would anyone fire at such amazing creatures? Didn't he realise how special this was? How outstanding? How awesome?

Instead he spluttered, "What! What did... did you *do*?"

"We're operational. We're here for one bug and one bug only. Everything else is an environmental threat," said Kelly.

"They wouldn't do anything! They didn't attack! The big grey things are only woodlice – they're vegetarians! They'll run a mile! And the red things are just velvet mites: they'll never catch you! You can just kick them away. Al would want us to photograph and document and..."

Kelly raised a finger to stop him.

"Your uncle is a friend of mine. He wants you back asap and in one piece. If you want to Save the Whale, you've got to make the call – otherwise I shoot first, ask questions later," he said, casually restowing the gun.

"I... I will!" Finn tried to say. Obligingly a velvet mite the size of a cushion sidled up, bright red, furry and stupid all over. Finn side-footed it – *poomf* – and they watched it curl up and bounce away.

"OK..." said Kelly, rethinking and turning back to Delta. "Let's keep most of the ammo and just dump one of the Minimis."

Finn followed the bouncing velvet mite across the concrete slab to cool off, though he could hardly stay sore for long. Ahead of him in the rocks – in fact in the grit and chippings – he could see half a dozen other mites, plus springtail bugs, all about knee-high, basking on the surface. They were motionless, like plastic sculptures, but as he walked towards them they shifted as one: the springtails, sensing danger, pinged away in series, propelled six or seven nano-metres into the air, while the dumber mites shuffled aside or curled into protective balls.

Wow, thought Finn.

Clinging to the top of the grasses at the edge of the slab, like monkeys up a tree, Finn could also see forest bugs and lacewings. And when he looked up further into the blue sky he saw any number of flying insects criss-crossing the air above him – mostly too fast to identify. He wanted to reach out and touch them all. He wanted to catch them, he wanted to explore and connect with this unconsidered wilderness.

"Kid? Anything dangerous?"

"Not yet. There's just so much of it. Look at those forest bugs."

Kelly took in the little shield-backed critters jumping from grass tip to grass tip and had to admit they were, "Kind of freaky."

Finn held out his arm and whistled.

"What are you doing?"

"Just wondering…" said Finn.

Kelly watched, stunned, as a lacewing dropped from the jungle to land heavily upon Finn's arm. It was the size of a peacock and shot out a tongue to taste Kelly, just like a dog, before flicking open its wings and hopping off again, obviously displeased.

"Do I taste that bad?" said Kelly.

Finn laughed and Kelly clapped him on the back, knocking the air from his lungs.

"About before, Stubbs said I was an 'ignoramus', and maybe I am too hard sometimes. But I've got to do right by you, and the mission. You understand?"

Finn realised he was trying to apologise, to be friends. He looked at Kelly. The man was the size of a monster and probably wasn't used to kids. Just danger. And he was trying.

"Course," said Finn.

They turned to walk back to the aircraft. More at ease.

"Can you imagine what Al would do to you if you left me behind?" said Finn.

"He'd torture me with acid and razor blades," said Kelly.

"Or cook you in one of his curries. Have you ever had one of those?"

"I wouldn't stand a chance."

Finn and the crew shared out brown mealy slabs from a single ration pack and scoffed the lot with plenty of water, as per instructions. The diet was designed for combat operations, to provide high energy and hydration. It tasted like the most boring cereal bar ever created, but Finn's body told him to eat.

"We've got ten more ration packs. Thirty litres of drinking water. Six hours' flight on an economy setting," Kelly summarised.

"And we're stuck in the middle of nowhere with a lethal organism and an average height of twelve millimetres," Stubbs pointed out. "It might be rational at this point to go home."

He would have gone on, but in the blink of an eye – less – a black and vile-looking fly-like critter, skinny and armoured, snapped down out of the sky a few nano-metres in front of them.

Everybody turned to Finn, waiting for him to make the call.

But he couldn't. The moment he'd seen it, a lump of high-energy bar had lodged in his trachea. Alarms were going off in his ears and lights were flashing in his brain: hunting wasp – a little over two nano-metres tall with a wicked wingspan double that and a sting the size of a carving knife.

The wasp tasted the air. Interested. Very interested. Finn went purple as he struggled to gesture and speak.

"Finn?" Kelly asked, then saw the colour of his face and slapped him on the back.

Finn expelled the lump. "Fire!" he gasped in an exaggerated falsetto.

DRRRRRRRRT! fired Kelly, in lightning response. The insect shattered.

"Sorry. Hunting wasp," Finn explained as he recovered and what was left of the creature fell to earth. "Very, very dangerous."

"Precisely," said Stubbs. "It might be rational at this point to return to the crash site and alert the authorities. We could plot the current course of the Beta, establish contact, then return to pick up the trail again."

"In time for your nap?" accused Kelly.

"Forty years' experience… ignore me," sighed Stubbs.

"We got ownage. We can't let up," said Delta.

"'Ownage'?" said Stubbs.

"It's gamer speak for we're in a good position," translated Finn. Delta glanced at him. Impressed.

"She's right," said Kelly. "All that matters is the mission. We track the Scarlatti, we find the nest and we annihilate it. *Then* we worry about making contact with a patrol."

"*If* they set up patrols…" said Stubbs.

"Al will set up something," said Finn, certain of that at least.

"They don't always do what your Uncle Al wants them to do, in our experience," said Stubbs.

"Why not?" asked Finn.

"Shut up, Stubbs. He's too smart, that's all," said Kelly.

"Causes too much trouble. He drinks in the laboratory, makes unreasonable demands and once, at a conference in Geneva, he got some ladies to hang me upside down off a hotel balcony."

Before Stubbs could add further evidence of Al's moral decay, a red ant flicked up on to the concrete.

"Fire!" snapped Finn.

DRRRRRRRRT!

The red ant flew in several directions at once.

"Watch out for reds," warned Finn, making his call. "Bad ant, bad sting, bad attitude."

"Got it. Anything else?"

"Has lots of friends..."

Six red ants appeared over the concrete ridge at once, sting-tipped abdomens twitching, armour flashing in the sun, making them look as angry as they probably felt, given what had just happened to their pal. It was in its way an awesome sight, if you happened to like crouching, twitching killers the colour of hell and the size of German shepherds.

They all seemed to move at once.

DRRRRRRRRT! DRRRRRRRRRRT! DRRRRRRT! DRRRRRRRT!

Finn, freaked, picked up a Minimi and promptly put it down again: it weighed a ton. He picked up an M27 instead. It was heavy too, heavy and dull and cold in his small hands, a million miles from an Xbox controller, and he hadn't a clue where to find the safety catch.

The reds were popping up all over now, an army emerging over a ridge.

"Where the hell are they all coming from?" said Kelly.

"We must be near their nest," Finn said.

"But how do they know we're here?"

"Alarm pheromone," said Finn. "Sends them into an attack frenzy."

The Beta stirred. It had fed, and now was resting, regenerating – semi-animate, semiconscious – when it was dragged back into full sentience by an intense burst of swarm pheromone on the air... the swarm must be signalling, must be sensing it in turn.

Roused, it issued back a burst of its own, then tasted something else on the breeze as it shifted and backed up.

Kill...

DRRRRRRRRRRRRRT!

The reds kept coming, now from the other side of the slab too. Kelly and Delta fired back to back as Stubbs scrambled in to start up the Apache engines.

DRRRRRRRRRRRRRT!

When, just to make matters worse...

Beep... Beep... Beep... Beep... Beep...

"It's on the move again," Stubbs shouted, firing up the auxiliary power. "Finn, can you check the bearing?"

Finn clambered into the cabin and checked the monitor.

"Seventy metres…"

DRRRRRRRRRRRRRT!

"Sixty-five metres… oh crap."

"What?"

"I think it's headed our way," said Finn.

Beep… Beep… Beep… Beep… Beep…

SIXTEEN

DAY TWO 08:58 (BST). Hook Hall,
Surrey

The recovery teams had divided the crash site into a search grid even as the last of the flames were being extinguished.

A four-man team in special protective suits and with magnifying optics then moved into each of the twenty-metre-square sections to search through the ash and debris, parting each blade of grass and examining every grain of debris as if in a lab.

Al and King arrived twelve minutes into the search, the Mangusta ripping across the open field, Al insensible to the venerable vehicle's underside and suspension. King emerged pale and shaken from the experience.

Much had been totally destroyed. Ash and oil and the occasional chunk of superstructure covered the bulk of the site. Both pilots had died (Flying Officer James Garwood, Flight Lieutenant Jane Lachild).

The team reported that so far no nano-bodies had been recovered at all – but the fire was likely to have done a lot more damage, indeed to have obliterated everything at the nano scale. "Any organic matter will have been instantly consumed." They weren't just looking for a needle in a haystack, but a miniaturised needle in its charred remains.

"We've found the aluminium transport cases, open and burnt out, away from the main fuselage. We think they must have been taken out by the airman who parachuted out, landing fifteen metres or so beyond the main impact. Although his chute didn't fully deploy, it did just enough to slow his descent. He was still unconscious."

"Where is he now?"

"On his way to hospital. Critical."

"Could they have got out of those boxes?"

"It's impossible to say."

"What about the equipment? Is that still there?"

"There are a lot of nano-metal fragments that we'll have to piece together and reconstruct in order to find out if anything is missing. We're talking hours."

"Hours we don't have," said Al, taking in the devastated scene. All around was blackness and the smell of aviation fuel. *Any organic matter will have been instantly consumed.* He could hardly bear the thought. His throat tight, he whispered, "Finn…"

King stepped in and ordered, "Make time. Throw everyone at it, then let's get it all back to the hall and go through it."

"In! NOW!" shouted Kelly, blasting at yet another wave of ants to cover Delta's dash back to the Apache.

DRRRRRRRRRT!

"Scarlatti position?" asked Delta, as she clambered over Stubbs to hit her seat.

"Fifty-five metres. Come on!"

Kelly backed in, blasting at the reds through the open door. Delta fired up the engines.

"Come on, come on..." Finn urged the aircraft, eyes glued like Delta's to the available power indicator as it climbed from red towards green.

DRRRRRRRRRRRT!

Kelly gave a final burst and slammed the door shut. The rotor wash was strong enough to blow back further red ants, but still they were on the ground and the Scarlatti was closing in.

"Thirty metres... twenty-five..." reported Stubbs.

Delta growled at the power indicator. "Stubbs! Do your thing!" she called.

"Can't. Not twice. Certain blade damage," said Stubbs.

Then Finn saw it. The Beta. A speck in the sky at first. But closing fast.

Fast and furious.

Delta gritted her teeth as the last red bar lit and edged to green. "GO!" screamed Finn.

Delta tipped the aircraft forward and drove it fast across the top of the grass as the beast closed in. As soon as she had enough momentum, she instructed, "Hold something," and threw the world upside down.

Finn clung on, heart beating and leaping round his chest like a jackrabbit. If he gripped the seatbelt straps any harder, his fingers would snap. Delta had just thrown the Apache round a full 360 loop. The Scarlatti was still there. She skimmed the top of the pasture in an attempt to outmanoeuvre it among the clumps and hummocks. When this didn't shift it either, she corkscrewed another full 360 to try and confuse it. Under any other circumstances, it would have been the best rollercoaster ride ever.

But again, as they levelled out, the beast was right on their tail – *kzzwkzzkzkwkwkwkzzzwwkwwkzzwkzzkzkwkwkw* – centimetres away, the only saving grace being that when it curled its abdomen ready to strike it increased drag and lost speed.

"You won't be able to keep this up all day," Stubbs observed. "The airframe will hold. The rotors will hold. The swash plates and engine mounts won't."

"You want to put some money on that?" said Delta, rolling the aircraft again, producing new screams from the engine.

"No. I want to go home and take a nice hot bath," Stubbs added helpfully.

The thought – hot/cold – flashed through Finn's brain and he yelled: "UP! GO UP!"

"Up? Great," said Delta.

"UP! Into cold air. It won't like the cold. Its blood has to stay at forty-five degrees to fly. It's colder up there, right?"

Delta took 0.006 seconds to think it through and hauled on the collective pitch lever, putting them into as rapid a climb as the machine could manage, trying to balance out increasing ascent and decreasing speed, Kelly calling out the danger as Stubbs called out the altitude.

"It's getting closer... it's getting closer..."

"Altitude 50... 70... 125 macro-metres... You should lose 1.5 centigrade every 100—"

"I know the stats!"

"It's still gaining," said Kelly.

"Altitude 150 macro," said Stubbs.

WkzzkzkwkwkwkzzzwwkwwkzzWZZKKZKZWKZZZZZ

Delta levelled out to regain speed and stretch ahead of the Beta Scarlatti a fraction.

Finn looked back out of the vent window – there it was, a carnival freak, evil incarnate, burning fury, giant eyes boring into his, locked on just as they had been in the flames.

Kill...

"Just keep going!"

When they reached 300 macro-metres, because of the wind chill, they began to notice the cold.

Almost imperceptibly at first, the Scarlatti started to slow and drop back.

At 500 macro they lost visual contact altogether.

At 800 macro they were beginning to freeze.

"Talk to me, Stubbs!" said Delta.

Beep... Beep... Beep... Beep... Beep...

"It's... falling away."

Finn was frozen. They had climbed what seemed to him an impossible distance above the earth.

"It's turning..."

Kelly was slapping and thumping his upper arms to try and get some warm blood into them. Delta's hands were locked on the controls.

Beep... Beep... Beep... Beep... Beep...

"It's picked up the westerly course again... descending fast now," said Stubbs.

"Yes! Yes!" said Finn.

"Follow it down and whack up the heating," said Kelly.

"Taking her down."

"Turn off the engine," said Stubbs, "we've just burnt a quarter of the remaining fuel."

"Check."

They started to warm up again as Delta took them on autorotation almost silently back to earth.

She looked across at Finn, pushed up her shades and inspected him (he was roughly the same age as Carla, roughly the same size and colouring, roughly as smart even).

"Good call, Noob[15]," she said.

Finn raised an eyebrow, recognising the gamer slang, and deciding to take it as a compliment.

"What do you play?" he asked.

"Few shooters, few drivers," said Delta.

"You don't look like a gamer," he said. "You don't look like a soldier either. You look like you're in a band."

"Well, you look like a noob, Noob."

She restarted the engine as they approached the ground and they powered forward after the Beta, which had returned to its persistent southwesterly course.

"We're back and locked on. Well done, boy wonder," said Kelly. "Chip off the Allenby block."

They swept down towards a field of mustard in flower, a perfect, endless plain of canary yellow, and Finn glowed inside in a way the others could not begin to imagine – feeling part of a family, feeling part of this unlikely crew.

[15] In gaming slang, a new, naive, easy-to-kill player.

SEVENTEEN

The admired Commander James Clayton-King had not slept properly for thirty-six hours and had never been under such pressure, or such scrutiny.

The various parties involved in the Boldklub project were being brought together for an emergency briefing and to start turning contingency plans into action.

Everyone wanted answers.

About the helicopter crash and the failure of the mission.

About identifying the enemy.

About security.

About 'time wasted on crackpot schemes' (favourite phrase of the Deputy Prime Minister).

About the containment of the Boldklub secret.

About plans for mass population evacuation and resettlement.

About the potential destruction of a significant chunk of suburban London and the southeast of England: some 60,000 homes, shops, offices, factories, ancient monuments and buildings, motorways, fields and farms, baronial estates – the marks of 4,000 years or so of human activity and habitation.

He had to prepare for the potential tsunami of panic and political fallout if it got anywhere near that far.

He had to deal with increasingly irate and anxious world leaders.

And he still had to deal with the Scarlatti outbreak, with trying to save the world.

But worst of all he had to deal with Al.

And the curse of hope.

Down in the labs Al watched the tiny charred metal remains of Engineer Stubbs's Pinzgauer truck being painstakingly reassembled by a team from the Air Accidents Investigation Branch, using tweezers, glue and magnifying glasses.

The Pinzgauer was one of the four pieces of nano-hardware found thus far in the wreckage at the crash site. The best preserved of these was the food container which had largely been protected from the fire by the body of the airman. No nano-human remains, youth or adult, had been found. There was also no sign of the Apache.

The chief crash investigator had warned, "The foam in the carry case could have burnt at a high enough temperature to consume metal," – the effects of intense heat on nano-materials being as yet a complete unknown. But, while there was no sign of the Apache...

Hope.

Back up in the control gallery, the mood was grim. The Presidents of the US and France, together with their advisors, were blunt and critical.

"I fail to see how, in all the planning and investigation, that malicious act of sabotage was overlooked."

"The irrational is always overlooked. You cannot assume everything, you cannot protect against every possible occurrence," said King.

"But do you have *any* idea what's going on here?" asked the US President onscreen.

"We're certain about the course of events to this point."

"But we're nowhere near finding out who did it – or why," noted General Mount to King's right. Solemn.

King turned to address the world leader feeds from London, Paris, Washington and Berlin. A list he knew would soon have to be extended.

"Not yet. 'Dr Spiro' was appointed at Porton Down more than a year ago. His cover identity and academic record were a sophisticated cocktail of identity fraud and forgery; his character and security references obtained through blackmail and bribery. Who would have the resources, the will, to pull off something this big? This professional? And what do they want? The Italian and Russian mafias are crippled by infighting. Celestial[16] are in pieces and frankly not up to this. No fragment remains of PICUS[17] or the Knights Templar[18]. And nothing suggests another state is involved, so we're looking at an as yet unidentified criminal network."

"*Exactement* the General's point. They are 'unknown'," said the French President.

"Which brings me to mine," said King. "Whoever these people are, if they can do this to *me*, they can do this to anybody, and they've probably infiltrated your most sensitive institutions too. There must be other operatives out there, we just don't know who they are yet."

There was a moment of uncomfortable digestion.

King saw his chance.

"We propose – given the very small chance the crew survived and continued their mission – to sweep for radio communications in a widening circumference around the crash site for as long as possible."

"How long exactly?" asked the US President.

"The Scarlatti will not leave its young until their final moult, which won't be until tomorrow morning at the earliest. We propose to continue the search for at least the next six hours in orde—"

"*Six hours?* You've got to move half a million people!"

"At the same time the evacuation can be planned for, and preparations for area destruction can be advanced."

[16]   [REDACTED]
[17]   [REDACTED]
[18]   [REDACTED]

"We should start the evacuation now. Why wait?" asked the British Prime Minister.

"As we said, there is a small chance that the crew—"

"There isn't a chance in hell!" The US General Jackman lost his cool and stood up. "If they were alive then why haven't they contacted you?"

Al marched in from the labs to answer this one.

"If they had a fix on the Beta Scarlatti, they would have had to stay on it: they couldn't double back and risk losing the trail. They are following our orders to prosecute the mission *at all costs* and we have to give them twenty-four hours, their original mission time, before we do anything drastic. So far there is no nano-chopper, there are no nano-corpses…"

"Because they were all consumed by fire! Delaying the evacuation increases the risk for us all!" complained the German Chancellor.

"Your fears are not a proof in science. Far from it," said Al.

"We're not in a laboratory, we're at war!" snapped General Jackman from Washington.

"Hey! I did my part. I delivered for you! All of you!" Al said, turning round and looking every screen in the eye. "Now they get their chance to deliver too!"

"OK, gentlemen! 'Chillax', as my ten-year-old would say," ordered the British Prime Minister. "King, are you reasonably confident you can organise an evacuation in twelve hours?"

"Absolutely certain," said King, insulted.

"And do you think there is any realistic prospect these poor wretches survived? Because, if there isn't, General Jackman is right: we should not waste a moment searching for them."

Commander James Clayton-King calculated. The world leaders watched him. The teams in the gallery watched him. Al watched him.

"On balance... at this point..."

Come on, King, thought Al.

"It doesn't look good..."

King held the moment, suffocating hope, then released it again.

"...however," he continued, "if by some miracle they are still alive, there's still the chance they can reach the Alpha Scarlatti and complete the mission. In which case we can avoid displacing half a million people and burning out the heart of England. I think the delay of a handful of hours is a risk we can take."

Al breathed a sigh of relief.

"Horseshit," said General Jackman.

"Thank you, Linden," said the President.

"The crew has till 06:00 hours tomorrow. The original mission time," demanded Al.

"We're carrying all the risk we can handle," said King. "We'll reconvene at 18:00 hours BST for an update and if necessary to coordinate the evacuation and plan for the nuclear option."

"But—"

"Six hours. No longer," warned the US President.

King glanced at Al. "Agreed."

Al walked out of the room before he punched someone.

The meeting broke up with no sense of resolution, just a continuation of anxiety.

Beep... Beep... Beep... Beep... Beep...

"Two degrees west... sixty-five macro... Another two west... sixty-four..." went Stubbs in monkish incantation, reeling off the tracking data for Delta to follow, as he'd done all afternoon.

Delta responded and guided the Apache across a field of young green wheat, skimming the top of the ears that bobbed and waved in patterned unison in the afternoon breeze. They seemed to Finn like hands in countless millions reaching up at them.

They had covered nearly twelve miles and burnt three-quarters of their fuel tracking the Beta across open country. Now the tracking pattern had changed and the Beta had swung due north towards an ancient wood.

They were right on the western edge of the predicted search area, not ten miles from Langmere. Most of the modelling in Hook Hall had assumed the Scarlatti would drift east with the prevailing wind. Clearly that hadn't happened. Finn prayed that they'd disregard their models and extend their search this far.

As soon as they crossed the boundary wall at the edge of the field and entered the woods, they passed out of the sunshine they'd bathed in all day and into the relative darkness of the wood. Delta took off her shades so her eyes could adjust. The canopy of native broadleaf trees was thick with rampant early summer growth; below all was cool, damp and calm. It had been a gardeners' May of sunshine and showers, great for plant life, birdlife... and for every last spider and insect.

Beep... Beep... Beep... Beep... Beep...

"Fifty metres... Another two degrees east... forty-five metres... forty— Wait, I think it's stopped."

Delta turned to Finn. "Noob?"

"It's either feeding or... it's found something."

"The Alpha?" said Kelly.

Finn didn't dare respond. He didn't want to jinx it.

"Let's take her up and come down real slow on it," suggested Kelly.

"And stay downwind whatever happens," said Finn.

Delta hovered over a stream that split the wood and held the chopper and compass steady, looking down at the surface of the water. After a couple of ripples, she deduced the exact direction of the breeze.

"Still westerly. Is the Beta still stationary, Stubbs?"

"Forty macro-metres. Hasn't moved."

"Then take us round the northeast," said Kelly.

Stubbs navigated the tiny craft through the wood, beautiful and still to the normal eye, but to Finn, at the nano-level, alive with activity, like a dystopian city, full of chaos, noise and strange flying objects.

He leant forward and all but pressed his face up against the glass canopy to try and take it all in. He had to. Gnats and midges whizzed in circles, but with so little weight and force the helicopter's blades scythed through them, creating such a fine mist of red-yellow innards that Delta had to use the windscreen wipers to clear off the glass. The air was thick with nature's detritus: flaking, floating plant debris, clouds of tree pollen, excrement dumped by grubs and caterpillars in the canopy. Bees dodged and bulleted back and forth to their hives, urgent and loud. Most spectacular of all, damsel and dragonflies sped past along the banks of the stream, stopping dead to hang stationary, magnificent creatures in highlighter blues and greens, almost the same size as the Apache, but many, many times more beautiful.

Beep... Beep... Beep... Beep... Beep...

"Another ten macro then swing back due west. That's it… thirty… twenty…"

"Go high."

"Climbing."

Delta took the chopper high into the canopy, rollercoastering in and out of branches, clipping swathes of swaying green.

As they closed in on the signal, she slowed and descended.

Beep... Beep... Beep... Beep... Beep...

"Ten macro due west…"

They crept down through the canopy.

"Anybody got visual?"

And then Finn saw it.

"There!"

"What is it?"

"Dead stuff."

It was as if it had all been laid out for some bizarre cult. A ring of death. In the centre lay the sow badger, now bloated through decomposition, and surrounding it a festering circle of dead crows, two foxes, half a dozen rats and one no-doubt-much-loved domestic cat.

"Woah..."

"That has to be it, Noob?" said Delta.

"Does it match the signal?" asked Kelly.

"Exactly," said Stubbs.

"Then it's the nest," said Finn. "I think we made it."

"Scope," ordered Delta.

Stubbs called up the scope function on the main screen and operated a powerful lens beneath the main fire position on the aircraft's nose. They watched as he used a joystick to zero in on the sow badger.

As Stubbs tracked the flanks, Finn again spotted something.

Two things.

The Alpha and Beta Scarlattis, writhing and dancing in the guts of the corpse.

"Oh my God..." said Delta.

It had worked.

They took a moment. Of disbelief. Of pride.

EIGHTEEN

Swarm... swarm... swarm... swarm... swarm...

The twin Scarlattis, Alpha and Beta, danced round and round each other in frenzy, in joyous reunion, wings clattering and straining, hormones and pheromones and musk pouring out. Bodies twitching and flicking, senses alive, biting and even stinging each other in joy.

Swarm... swarm... swarm... swarm... swarm...

In the corpse the newly hatched nymphs could taste it too and wriggled their nascent wings, desperate to join them, desperate to be free.

DAY TWO 15:02 (BST). Siberia

Kaparis had decided to let the authorities 'stew' for a while. He had picked up plenty of tertiary evidence of increased military activity in east Surrey and other signs of blind panic in the environs of Hook Hall, including a huge and steady increase in sensitive diplomatic communications around the world. Now, having watched the UK's Trident nuclear submarine fleet put to sea from its base in Faslane, Kaparis decided it was time to 'put them out of their misery' and launch Phase 2.

"Get me Stefan," he ordered.

Stefan was the oldest and most trusted Tyro in the field.

Aged between twelve and seventeen, the Tyros were Kaparis's proxy selves, children of every race, creed and colour, brilliantly educated via NRP in everything from quantum mechanics to unarmed combat, often specialist in one area; ruthless, cunning and, above all, totally loyal and obedient.

And, to the outside world, just children. Nondescript teens. Invisible. All that linked them was the 'speckled iris' scarring of their eyes, a result of repeated NRP work. But who would ever notice?

Following his paralysis, Kaparis had scoured the orphanages and charity hospitals of the world, rigorously testing the brightest, selecting, adopting and developing a select few into a 'higher state of being', in his seminary in an abandoned monastery in the Carpathian Mountains.

Few entered and only thirteen had emerged alive so far (NRP drove unsuitable subjects insane).

The comms link to the Atlantic could be bitty during a heavy sea, but Stefan's blond head soon flicked up onscreen.

"I think 'Go', Stefan, don't you?"

The blond boy bowed.

DAY TWO 15:18 (BST). Hook Hall, Surrey

Al stared listlessly at a plate of scrambled eggs. He knew he had to eat something, otherwise he'd be consumed by the acid in his stomach, but he didn't feel like it.

He'd had the wreckage from the Merlin sifted, checked and rechecked, and there was still absolutely no sign of the nano-crew or the Apache helicopter or, indeed, of any unidentified organic remains. This was positive. This was a straw, and he clung to it.

However, the search was getting nowhere. Trying to cover nearly fifty square miles when the signal range for the crew was only a few tens of macro-metres was a mammoth task. They'd flown a series of aircraft in a grid pattern across the area and come up with nothing. They were continuing to use a shifted grid, but with the same result, and the number of low-flying aircraft they had out searching was itself becoming dangerous.

He forced a mouthful of eggs into his mouth just as King appeared and sat down next to him.

He swallowed the mouthful, and asked King, "Anything?" – reflexively, as he'd been doing all day.

"Nothing," King replied – ditto.

King held out a battered schoolboy mobile. Finn's. Al had been avoiding it.

"This keeps going off in a desk draw in the gallery. Children should not have phones. Your mother keeps calling."

Al took the chipped and stickered handset, his heart contracting for a moment. He had promised Finn a new one. But who could ever want to replace a thing so precious?

Six missed calls from his mother and a mangled predictive text:

whoro6 areyou? All in commune ocado. Alldya.
Furryus. Call.

Al and Finn had established a 'call anytime' relationship as part of their coping strategy. At first, when Finn was still at junior school, there would be tears and anger, nearly always at teatime. Over time this had evolved into long talks about nothing in particular. Then, as wounds began to heal, it became more infrequent. How Al wished he could call him now.

He opened the keypad, and proceeded to lie to his mother.

All OK. Al has lost phone. At Harvester in Cookham.
Going into cinema now. Knit for Britain. Fxxx

Al pressed Send. His heart squeezed again and he felt he was beginning to tip over some kind of edge when, "Commander King?"

King and Al looked up to see a nervous-looking intelligence officer standing before them.

"We think we may have something."

Thirty seconds later, King and Al were back in the control gallery staring at the main screen.

"We think it's Dr Cooper-Hastings, sir. Just posted on an obscure Chinese social network. Our search algorithms picked it up."

Finally they're breaking cover, thought King.

A poor quality still of Dr Cooper-Hastings appeared on the screen, grainy, and in the grimly familiar style of a terrorist martyrdom video.

Professor Channing was shocked.

"Is that Cooper-Hastings?" said Al.

"It's him…" Channing said sadly.

"Play it," ordered King.

Cooper-Hastings looked into the camera. He was determined, disgusted even, as he spoke. He rocked back and forth, his voice rough from lack of sleep.

"*You will know by now what we have done. The organism is quite safe and breeding fast.*"

Cooper-Hastings' face was replaced by a video feed from a static camera. It showed a dead badger in light undergrowth, slowly zooming in on its belly to reveal the Alpha Scarlatti moving this way and that, tending its eggs.

"*We will provide you with its location should you meet our demands.*

"*First, pack the Cambridge Fat Doughnut Accelerator into two shipping containers and have them placed freestanding on the deck of the container ship* Oceania Express *which has just unloaded at Felixstowe.*

"*Second, by 06:00 hours have said ship steam towards the tip of the Jutland peninsular, there to await further instruction. Its cargo must remain unaltered, the ship unmonitored and unmanned by security personnel. We shall know from within your operation if you deviate from this one iota.*

"*Third, Dr Allenby will provide us with the Boldklub sequencing codes which we strongly suspect exist on a small blue USB storage device kept on his person.*

"*Our intentions are entirely peaceful and benign. We believe such technology cannot be trusted to nation states or mediocrities in public employment; it is much better in the hands of trusted, exceptional individuals.*

"*Post your official response as a comment on this blog. The Scarlatti nymphs will reach maturation at some time between 06:00 hours and 12:00 tomorrow. If you have not fully acceded to our demands by then...*

"*...we will let nature take its course.*"

In the shock and then the brief hubbub that followed – as heads of state were informed, as Security Service staff rushed to get the host site blocked and to find out whatever they could about how, where and when the video was uploaded, as the general level of panic rose – Al felt at least one iota of anxiety drain away.

159

At last they had something to go on.

"I'm going to find you," he said to his unseen foe.

He clutched the small rock of spharelite around his neck. He scratched it with his nail. It glowed.

"I'm going to find you," he promised Finn.

DAY TWO 15:39 (BST). Siberia

Down in his lair Kaparis listened to the Brodsky play Beethoven's String Quartet in C sharp minor and awaited events.

He raised an eyebrow at Heywood.

Instinctively the butler moved forward and dripped Château Valandraud St-Émilion '95 by pipette on to his fat silver-grey tongue.

Kaparis liked the finer things in life, very much. Indeed, he considered himself one of the finer things in life, so much so he had constructed a general theory round the very notion.

A theory he now felt absolutely certain would be demonstrated.

Not wishing to take their chances on the forest floor, they landed the Apache carefully on the horizontal branch of a common oak that was a good 200 years old, Delta putting down close to the trunk where there was no chance of movement in the breeze. The insect flying circus still buzzed round them, but at least it felt like they had a private box and wouldn't get dragged into the show.

As Finn jumped from the cab, he felt a professional sense of excitement taking hold of the crew.

Delta turned off the Apache engines to preserve their remaining fuel and they set about finalising the assault plan.

They got out maps and nailed their position in the southeast quadrant of Willard's Copse, 1,000 macro-metres outside the village of Willingham, 100 macro-metres downwind of the nest site.

Stubbs did some calculations. They had enough fuel to complete three attack runs and comfortably reach the village, "But if we get stuck in a lengthy dogfight that would be seriously reduced."

"The miracle is," Kelly said, and they all agreed, "that despite everything we've got a shot at this, and there's no way we're going to screw it up."

The attack on the nest would be pretty much as they'd prepared for back at the CFAC. The primary aim was to kill the two mature Scarlattis, then to destroy the nest, along with any nymphs or eggs. Their secondary objective was to report the position of the nest site.

It was agreed that Delta and Stubbs in the Apache would make multiple attack runs at maximum speed, firing off everything they had: twelve Hellfire missiles, a full load of Hydra rockets, a 30mm chain gun with 1,200 rounds and even, if necessary, four air-to-air Stinger missiles. A lot of bang.

"That should put their asses on ice," said Delta.

Kelly, it was decided, would be landed ahead of the first attack run to establish a ground fire position: to provide 'mopping up' fire (finishing off any eggs or nymphs that escaped the bombardment) and to prevent the Scarlattis escaping the nest. This was now even more important as the greatest threat to the mission was that one or both of the Scarlattis would pursue and attack the Apache in the air.

"As long as I go in at max speed, I'll have time to turn and waste it with the chain gun. And we can always load Stubbs up with an M27," said Delta.

Kelly shook his head.

Stubbs stated, matter of fact, "Been refused small arms access since 1994. Lost a thumb on the range. Not mine. Fellow next to me."

"Never mind. Are we good to go?" said Kelly.

"Spot of supper first?" suggested Stubbs.

"Eat? There's only an hour of good daylight left!" said Delta.

"What about me?" asked Finn.

They all turned to look at him. And then –

WHACK!

A chaffinch hopped out of nowhere to land on a branch directly alongside. Less than a macro-metre away. A tower of colour. A blur of speed. The size and build of a T-Rex.

"Kelly!" snapped Delta.

()()()()()()()()()()()()()()()()()! sang the curious bird, a crystal-clear scream in B minor, snapping its head round to get another look at them.

As one, the crew ducked to cover their ears, Kelly failing to fire. There was a sudden, violent wingbeat, and in a microsecond's blur the bird was upon them.

It screamed again and Kelly finally got his finger on the trigger.

DRRRRRRRRRRRRT!

The bullets missed, but the harsh, alien sound threw the massive bird into a blind panic. It burst into a furious flap in its desperation to escape, wings clattering the branch and almost taking out the entire crew.

Within an instant, it was gone – but the Apache was rocking dangerously on the branch. Kelly and Stubbs leapt up to steady it before it tipped over on to its rotors, just managing to bring it to rest. Kelly killed any further debate.

"We go now and we get the hell out."

Stubbs and Delta immediately began to prep the Apache weaponry, Kelly the small arms.

Finn blew up.

"WHAT ABOUT ME?"

The three soldiers took him in.

"You wait in the Apache," said Kelly.

"No way! I could go down with you! You could show me how to fire!"

Kelly raised a hand. "No combat role."

"You'd be dead already if it wasn't for me!" said Finn.

"He's right," said Stubbs.

"True…" said Delta.

163

"Those guns are bigger than he is," said Kelly and, as so often happens with grown-ups and kids, an argument briefly raged *about* Finn without them apparently noticing that he was *standing right there – HELLO??*

Kelly admitted he provided excellent intelligence on environmental threat ("Thank you," said Finn), and that, while he *could* be taught to fire an M27, it was a world away from combat ("I've done it on Xbox like a million times!"), but mainly they mustn't forget he was Al's nephew and *just a kid.*

"Forget Al! This is about me!"

"Hold up," Delta suddenly held up her hand like she was stopping traffic. She had decided something. "Kelly's right, you can't just throw in a noob," she said.

"Let alone expect one to perform under pressure," agreed Kelly.

"I'm *virtually* a teenager!" insisted Finn. "And I am *me* and I'm good at some stuff – and you're NOT cutting me out! And, by the way, my name is not Noob!" he added to Delta, who chewed on, unmoved.

Kelly held fast. A deep paternal instinct he didn't understand was in play. He couldn't help but like this kid. He squatted down until his massive head was level with Finn's.

"We all have a role. You do too. You're the one that has to stay alive."

There was silence for a beat. *Alive?* thought Finn. *Who said anything about the possibility of dying? Did they really think they were going to lose this thing?*

"Life is wasted on old people," agreed Stubbs. "Hang on to it."

"Your parents wouldn't want us to risk this," added Kelly.

"How do you know? They would have *loved* this," said Finn, feeling more certain than he'd ever felt about anything. Kelly fell back on a military protocol.

"I'm your Commanding Officer. And that's my decision," he said, and signalled an end to the discussion by going off to check the guns.

"That's no reason!" Finn shouted after him.

"He's right, Noob," Delta tried to mollify him. "I'm… a big sister," she revealed as if it was some kind of hidden gift (which to her it was), "and no way would I let Carla go. I didn't even want her to get *a pony*."

"Who the heck's Carla, and what's she got to do with anything?" said Finn.

The argument would have continued at even greater pitch, but for Kelly's scream.

"AHHHHHRRGGH!"

Finn turned. Kelly was screaming and scrambling backwards, a crab spider[19] locked on to his thigh.

---

[19] The crab spider does not spin a web, although it will produce silk to wrap up its prey or to act as a safety line. It is a hunter. It relies on stealth, camouflage and, above all, ambush. The two front legs are overdeveloped and are held aloft, either side of the head, ready to spring together and seize prey. Poisonous fangs then deliver a bite before mouthparts suck the victim dry. There are almost as many subspecies and variants of the crab spider as there are colours in nature. The Philodromidae is an active variant able to change colour to blend in with its background: in this case, common oak bark.

"Stay still!" Finn shouted at the skittering, scrabbling, shrieking SAS man.

Delta froze like there was a gap in the game code all over again and Stubbs threw his mug at the dog-sized beast. This knocked off one of its legs, but it was still attached by its fangs and Kelly was fast disappearing off the branch.

In the open stow hold of the Apache was Delta's service pistol.[20] Finn snatched it up and took aim down the barrel.

"Hold still!"

"YAAAAAARRHH!" Kelly yelled back.

"Depress safety catch with right thumb and squeeze," advised Stubbs.

"Don't you d—" started Delta, snapping out of her trance but then...

BANG! Finn felt the pistol buck in his hands and, to his astonishment, the spider blew clean off Kelly's leg.

Kelly was left clinging by his fingertips to the bark on the far side of the branch. Delta and Stubbs pulled him up. He was grey and shaking.

"My leg... Can't feel my leg..." he managed.

"You're lucky you've got one," said Delta, snatching the Beretta back off Finn, whose ears were still ringing.

"He's going into shock. I'll give him thirty mil of steroid and twenty of morphine," said Stubbs.

[20] Beretta 9mm.

"Crab spider, not fatal," Finn reassured them. "It just paralyses."

Delta turned to Finn. "For how long?"

Finn shrugged.

Delta looked west into the afternoon sun.

NINETEEN

Knit one purl one knit one purl one knit one knit one purl one...

"*Empty the fjörds, blow the seå mist
love is sö cold like a småll pickled fish...*"

Violet Allenby was not happy. Although it would be wrong to say she was the unhappiest person onboard the *Princess Hüttigeun* – chosen vessel of the 2014 Northern Delights Knitting Cruise. That distinction fell to Eskild, the ship's young Entertainments Officer, who had just broken up with his girlfriend. He had been listless while calling the bingo, had wept openly on an excursion to the Yärn Bärn in Haugesund, and had treated them so far this afternoon to three hours of improvised love songs played on an out-of-tune guitar and delivered in an affecting Norse monotone. The elderly ladies onboard were very sympathetic, though it hardly made for the advertised 'party atmosphere'.

> "*Inge-love linger, plunge ice through må soul*
> *for the forest häaf wolves unt Edvart Bergasol*"

Knit one purl one knit one purl one knit one purl one...

But what really got Violet Allenby's goat as they made their way up the Norwegian coastline, hopping from one picturesque port to the next, was the fact that Al and Finn had not returned a call in the last twenty hours.

All they'd managed was a text from Finn saying he was going to the cinema. A text she'd just followed up with a call, thinking the film must be over by now. But instead of reaching him, she'd heard a snatch of frantic technical discussion interrupted by a well-to-do voice saying, "What the devil?" before being cut off.

Knit one purl one knit one purl one knit one purl one...

Of course there might be a perfectly reasonable explanation. She had obviously phoned up during the film and the voices were on the soundtrack. And yet... She could have sworn it was the same voice. That of the tall, severe gentleman who'd turned up at home the Easter before last wearing a lovely coat. Al disappeared for a fortnight with him, returning exhausted. "Don't ask," he'd said, and had slept for two days straight.

She had to respect this; she knew he sometimes did secret work. The following weekend at the last minute he had somehow managed to get the Crown Prince of Japan to open the village fête (a local author had pulled out, 'feeling fluey').

"He owes me a favour," was Al's only explanation.

The Crown Prince had listened attentively to the plans for the hospice, but was clearly in awe of Al.

"Your son. Very brave man," he had told Violet.

Brave – the last thing a mother wants to know.

> *"She is free – she is winter!*
> *a sáuna, a splinter..."*

Knit one purl one knit one purl one knit one purl one...

If she didn't know better, she might think Al was somehow involved with this frightening gentleman again and that he'd dragged Finn along and they were now flirting with death in some calamitous situation that would mean misery for everybody who had ever loved them, and nobody loved them like...

She stopped herself before tears of distress sprang into her eyes.

For goodness' sake, Violet. Pull yourself together. Ridiculous.

Then the Captain had appeared. Again. He'd been in mild terror of her the entire trip, anxious to make her stay as comfortable as possible, hanging on her every word – what was happening to the men on this ship?

He gulped and announced, "Ah... as we *kommer* into port, please refrain from using mobile phone. For the interference with communications... Apologies." He did a little bow and hurried out.

It had been less than three minutes since she had called Finn. If Violet didn't know any better, she might smell a rat.

Knit one purl one knit one purl one knit one purl one...

A very big rat called Al, followed by a rat in a lovely coat and the Crown Prince of Japan.

"RIGHT," she snapped, throwing down her three-colour sweater panel. "Call me a taxi! Someone's got to get to the bottom of this. And Eskild, please stop that ridiculous racket!"

"Dear lady...?" started the Captain, popping up as she stomped back to her cabin to pack.

"Out of my way! I'm leaving on a jet plane and I don't know when I'll be back again."

TWENTY

"**G**O!"

Delta dropped the Apache out of the woodland evening air and hovered a few centimetres above the ivy-clad undergrowth.

"Touchdown!" called Kelly as he hit the ground. Finn was already leaping out of the port door, the weight of the M27 strap biting into his shoulder on impact.

They kept their heads down as Delta took off again and a fierce rotor wash tore at them. The moment it eased they were up again, Finn propping up the hopping Kelly, who was still getting used to his semi-paralysed leg.

They were three macro-metres downwind of the target, just outside the ring of dead animals, which were like a row of buildings at their scale. Their immediate task: to run 1,500 nano-metres in under five minutes, so they could reach the nest and establish a fire position, before Delta's first attack run. Then open fire.

Not easy even under normal circumstances, but helping a man laden with an M27 and multiple magazines of ammo and a limp while watching out for both deadly aerial attack and nuisance ground attack was another thing altogether.

But Kelly soon got the hang of his injury, his dead leg thumping out the rhythm.

Thud thud thud thud...

Finn struggled to take the weight, but didn't want to show weakness. He craned his head up when he could to scan the sky. Nothing. The ivy gave good cover. Grubs and ants, alarmed by their movement, were scattering out of the way as they progressed.

"Four minutes to go!" called Kelly. *Thud thud thud thud...*

Finn was panting and sweating. This was combat and Kelly was in another zone, all steel and determination. Finn tried to match him, but his lungs were bursting. He tried to focus on Scarlatti. He tried to find the steel.

For a moment Finn's legs gave way and he collapsed. Kelly hauled him to his feet again, let him recover for exactly three breaths, before dragging him on again.

"Go! Go! Three minutes!"

Thud thud thud thud...

They ran past the stiff, extended foot of the dead cat. The smell of the putrefying badger was beginning to hit them.

As they rounded the giant head of the cat, they got their first sight

173

of the nest. The dead badger's pockmarked body was covered in writhing, burrowing nymphs – each a vile maggot nearly twice their size.

"Visual!" Kelly yelled and they hit the ground, desperate not to attract an attack before Delta's first bomb run.

They had left the cover of the ivy and now lay panting in flattened mud and grasses. Finn thought he would throw up and his shoulder ached where he had been supporting Kelly.

"There! You see it?" Kelly pointed through the grasses.

There among the nymphs, darker than the Beta they had been tracking and lacking the distinctive white stripe of the nano-transmitter, among the putrefying guts, tending, feeding and bullying its young, was the Alpha Scarlatti... the size of an army truck to them, brutally assembled, and evil in intent.

Finn checked his watch. "Forty-five seconds."

Kelly propped himself up and aimed his M27 through a gap in the grasses. "Now where the hell is your twin brother?" he asked. The Beta Scarlatti was nowhere to be seen. "Fifteen seconds. You ready?"

"Ready," said Finn, bracing the M27 against his shoulder and looking through the sight.

"Short bursts."

"Uh-huh."

They waited, watching the Alpha tending its nymphs and then... something made it stop... some hint of something on the air... the faintest quantum vibration.

It raised its head and tasted the air with its whip-long, wriggling antennae. It tasted... **danger.**

Wwkzzkzkwkwkwkzzzwkzzkzkwkwkwkzzzwkzzkzkwkwkwkzzz

The Alpha shook itself free of the badger's guts, and its young, and took off, heading straight for Kelly and Finn.

At that very moment the Apache shot past, low overhead, and let loose every one of its rockets at the badger, describing a line of fire and hell along the bottom edge of its belly. The guts lit up and the whole mass jolted, the body almost lifting off the ground.

BOOOOOOM!

DAY TWO 17:33 (BST). Siberia

An alarm sounded in the communications wing of the Siberian bunker. Motion-detector software registering sudden movement in Willard's Copse.

Kaparis's eyes swivelled towards a monitoring screen.

The blastwave snapped through the Beta Scarlatti's body.

The urge to reproduce had been quick to kick in, the taste of the Alpha starting the flow of hormones that would transform it into a reproductive machine, and it had crawled to the opposite side of the sow badger to start laying, to ensure the developing older nymphs would not consume its eggs.

Now the blast, still ringing through its nervous system, halted everything.

And something else.

A scent.

Attack...* commanded its instincts. *Kill.

Finn's gun was blown out of his hands as the shockwave hit him. He gasped for air.

Kelly simply withstood the blast and fired and fired and fired.

DRRRRRRT! DRRRRRRT! DRRRRRT! DRRRRRRT! DRRRRRT!

The Alpha Scarlatti wheeled out of its trajectory and roared back towards the conflagration, where its writhing nymphs were fleeing or being consumed by flames.

DRRRRRRRRT! DRRRRRRRRRT! DRRRRRRRRRT!

Kelly's bullets ripped up at the Alpha, their trace red-gold in the early evening light, most of them bouncing off its extraordinary armoured exoskeleton. Only its wings were vulnerable, taking multiple hits and losing traction against the air.

But nothing could dent its rage as it turned back towards them.

"Finn!"

Finn snapped out of his shock and braced the M27 against his shoulder and began to fire as the Scarlatti flew at them.

DRRRRRRRT! DRRRRRRT! DRRRRRRRT!

The force of recoil was incredible, but Finn leant into it as he'd been briefly instructed up in the tree. The bullets hurtled out of the barrel and arced up to the Scarlatti – giving Finn an incredible feeling of a mad, uncontainable power – but apparently doing nothing to slow the beast's progress.

The Alpha Scarlatti turned into a dive, powering towards the earth, stings first, massive tail whipping. Kelly and Finn abandoned the short controlled bursts mantra and let rip with everything they had –

DRRRRRRRRRRRRRRRRRRRRRRRRRRRRRRRRRRRRRRRRRRR-RRRRRTT!

At the same time the second Apache attack run swung in and Delta let loose the full batch of Hellfire missiles.

BAAA-BOOOOOOOOOOOOOOMM!

The blast ripped through the riddled corpse, obliterating more of the vile nymphs within, the shockwave knocking the Alpha Scarlatti out of its dive and sending it slamming into the dirt, centimetres away from Kelly and Finn – who were also sent reeling.

From its new position, the Scarlatti's thousand-celled eye was able to zero in on Kelly and Finn. Again, Finn felt the massive evil eyes boring into his brain.

They fired again as the beast roused itself –

DRRRRRRRRRRRRRRRRRRRRRRRRTT!

And again the bullets bounced off the armoured core – but the wings at least were suffering, shredding. The beast tried desperately to fly the short distance to them, but its wings were reduced to furious, impotent, buzzing stubs.

Finn and Kelly carried on firing as the monster found its feet and began to crawl, massive and still deadly, across the dirt towards them in writhing, angry agony.

"Run!" Kelly screamed, blasting away at its remaining legs.

Finn grabbed him and they started to scramble away as fast as they could.

But the Alpha was buzzing and writhing and whipping itself ever nearer, a wounded, lethal foe, its nymphs aflame or in flight around it. It flicked a last stub of wing against the ground and was almost upon them.

Kelly dropped free of Finn, lay prone and fired.

DRRRRRTRRRRRRRRRTTRRRRRRRTTT!

Finn backed away and fired too.

DRRRRRT! DRRRRRT! – into the stubs of its wings, into what he thought might be the soft parts of its abdomen, into the remaining creeping, crawling legs.

They were destroying it...

Until suddenly, with an absurd and desperate flick of its tail, it fell upon them – slamming into Finn like a giant mattress, the bulging surface covered in barbed and beaded hairs, sending Finn sprawling backwards... knocking his gun well clear.

For a moment, as Finn lay on his back in the dirt, blinking back to consciousness, he thought it was all over, that the beast had died... but, as his senses returned, he could tell there was life in it yet. He heard Kelly's muffled screams from beneath the crippled beast. It tried to buzz its useless wing stubs, it tried to curl and whip its tail, but life was draining from it, the bullets were finally taking effect.

Finn dragged himself up.

He took in the massive, writhing Scarlatti as Delta dumped the last of her explosives into the nest beyond, illuminating the twitching devil's dark profile. Kelly's head and shoulders were clear, but the rest of him was trapped beneath it.

There was a grenade in the dirt just beyond Kelly's reach. Finn could run in. He could reach it. But he'd be in range of the tail.

He had to decide what to do. But, before he got the chance, the Alpha Scarlatti flicked its evil tri-stinged tail one last time, whipping it past his face, missing it by centimetres.

The Scarlatti's movement suddenly set Kelly free. He twisted. Snapped up the grenade. Pulled the pin and punched it – right up to his elbow – into an open wound in the beast's abdomen. It writhed and shot out its stings.

Kelly hopped clear and jumped on top of Finn, flattening him completely. A tonne weight forcing Finn down into the dirt, and then –

BOOM!

Finn felt it like a thump in his chest. Kelly rolled off him. They both looked over.

The Alpha Scarlatti was blown clear of them. In three distinct gooey parts.

And it was gone.

The ordeal was over.

The badger was a burning pyre.

And then, from above the flames…

WwkzzkzkwkwkwkzzzWWKWZZZWZWZWWKZWZWKZWZWKKZ

TWENTY-ONE

Kaparis's eyes flashed and skittered over the optics around his head as he tried to make sense of the destruction and action playing out on the screens. The limited resolution on the Willard's Copse camera meant it was difficult in real time, but there seemed to be little doubt that the nano-team were causing considerable destruction.

Heywood and the two other staff members stood frozen in fear. Kaparis rarely lost control, but when he did...

His heart rate rose further. Heywood adjusted the iron lung to take deeper, faster breaths, as Kaparis fought to remain calm and reason through events.

1. The nano-team had clearly escaped the crash and pursued their objective, unbeknown to the authorities.

2. To maintain the credibility of the threat the remaining Scarlatti or nymphs must be preserved.

3. If the nano-team completed their mission then they must be caught and destroyed before they could communicate as much.

"How many Tyros do we still have in the UK?" he asked.

"Only Kane, sir."

"Get him. Now."

"Bombs away, run good," shouted Stubbs.

Delta banked sharply at the end of her third run, the Apache hugely more manoeuvrable after shedding so much weight. Her heart was pounding. No matter how many times you did it, firing ordnance was incurably exciting – and now the craft was so light it felt part of her, like a running girl.

"Final pick-up," said Stubbs.

"Check."

She tipped the stick forward and hammered the thrust to rush back through the wood to the smouldering target.

Then beneath them they saw it.

The Beta.

Kill kill kill kill kill kill kill kill kill kill…

An attack on the swarm.

Every fight receptor in the Beta's brain was on fire. Every cell in its body was hyper-sensed. Every muscle, every sinew, every nerve was geared to kill to protect the few young now wriggling and scattering across the earth and undergrowth.

The smoke confused it. A bullet punched and confused and angered it. Another.

Then it saw the Queen. Dead. Dead… And it saw and smelt them.

Kill kill kill kill kill kill kill kill kill…

Finn and Kelly lay in the dirt with a single Magnum 9mm handgun, surrounded by abandoned guns and spent shell cases.

The Beta curled into a death-dive, poised to strike. Delta gave everything she had to the 30mm chain gun slung beneath her nose cone.

DRTDRTDRTDRTDRTDRTDRTDRTDRTDRTDRTDRTDRTDRTD-RTDRTDRTDRTDRTDRTDRTDRTDRTDRTDRTDRTDRTDRTDRT-DRTDRTDDRTDRTDRTDRTDRTDRTDRT!

The shells split the air, ripped off two of the diving Beta's legs and tore a flesh wound in its abdomen. The pain and impact forced it into a reflexive wheel for cover, for safety, and to get an angle on whatever was attacking it.

"We don't have enough fuel for this," concluded Stubbs as Delta threw the chopper back round the target area in a tight arc to max the distance between them and the wheeling Scarlatti.

"You want to leave them to that thing?"

"I'm simply providing 'real-time updates'," Stubbs replied, using bunny fingers to illustrate his quote marks. "Don't shoot the messenger."

Finn and Kelly ran for the cover of the ivy, unsure if Delta had seen them or if she was simply trying to take the Beta out.

They were joining a nano-scale exodus of ants, earwigs, woodlice, assorted forest-litter bugs and even earthworms, all fleeing the smoke and fire.

BANG! BANG! Kelly blasted escaping Scarlatti nymphs with his sidearm as they went.

The nymphs were heading for the ring of slain birds and mammals around the burning badger. One was crawling over the head of a dead crow trying to burrow frantically under the feathers. One nest was becoming five.

There were never going to be enough bullets. But if they could slay the Beta Scarlatti, the grubs would be starved of growth hormone and that would kill them all.

The Beta fizzed with anger, unable to locate its airborne foe, but fixing again on the scent of its tormentors.

Kill...

Wwkzzkzkwkwkwkzzzwkzzkzkwkwkwkzzzwkwkkkwkkwkwkwkw!

"It's coming back!" said Finn.

Kelly grabbed him, looked him square in the eye, intense, like the son he never had.

"Listen to me now, Finn. Don't look back, whatever you do, don't look back. Now – RUN! RUN!"

Finn ran... Finn looked back.

Kelly took out two grenades. Three.

Kelly *stood and waved like crazy at the Scarlatti.*

"BRING IT ON!" he roared at the beast.

Finn realised Kelly was going to sacrifice himself... that he was inviting death.

Kelly looked back. "RUN, I SAID!" he yelled, levelling the Magnum at Finn. "I fire at him or at you!"

Wwkzzkzkwkwkwkzzzwkzzkzkwkwkwkzzzwkzzkzkwkwkwkzzz

Finn turned on his heel and started to run again as the Beta again went into a death-dive.

Aiming directly at Kelly.

"Come on then!" shouted Kelly at the diving beast above, offering himself as a sitting target and blasting away with the Magnum. Pulling the pins on the grenades. One. Two. Three...

But Finn could not run and let Kelly die. This was the only thing he knew. Nothing else.

The Scarlatti twisted in its dive, veering away from Kelly and heading towards...

"FINN!" Kelly shouted.

Oh crap. It's me, thought Finn as the Scarlatti sped towards him. He was caught. Stuck. Helpless before death again. The awfulness and the inevitability. The weakness. Time seemed to slow. Would he get some kind of answer when it hit him? Would he get it in the moment of death? Answer to what? He was as confused as he was weak as he was helpless. It was exactly how it was the morning his mum died.

BOOM! BOOM! BOOM! Three grenades burst in the air just before the Scarlatti struck home.

The beast and Finn were both knocked sideways. The beast ploughed into the dirt, grenade shrapnel burning, stuck fast in its armoured thorax. Stunned.

Finn opened his eyes. The face of death was over him. Upon him. It twitched as it came to… opened its great mouthparts and dropped its fat tongue down to taste him. Then buzzed furiously to life – *WKWKWKWWKZZZWZKWZKZKKZKZ!* Rising and flicking its tail round at once to…

DRTDRTDRTDRTDRTDRTDRTDRTDRTDRTDRTDRTDRTDRT-DRTDRTDRTDRTDRTDRTDRTDRTDRTDRTDRTDRTDRTDRTDRT-DRTDRTDRTDRTDRTDRTDRTDRTDRTDR!

The Apache's chain gun spun, spitting fire, centimetres above Finn's head, blasting away the Beta, paying out spent cartridges like a slot-machine jackpot, the downdraught beating Finn against the earth.

The Beta Scarlatti took the full force of the 30mm rounds against its thorax, and again, while they did not penetrate its exoskeleton, they blew it into an instant retreat.

The Apache door opened. Stubbs reached down. Finn reached up.

He was back.

"Kelly!"

Delta hopped the aircraft the few nano-metres over to Kelly who was scrambling up, just as the Beta screamed towards them from the chain gun's blind side. Skimming the undergrowth on a collision course.

WWKWZZZWZWZWWKZWZWKZWWZZZWZWZWWKZWZWK-ZWZWKKZ!

Kelly grabbed hold of the hardpoint weapons mount braced to the fuselage and screamed, "GO!"

Delta hauled on the stick, spinning and rising and firing all at the same time, corkscrewing the hell out of the nest area, heading for the tree canopy.

Kelly held on for dear life, gravity and centrifugal force trying to tear him away.

Bip bip bip bip bip bip bip bip bip... sounded the fuel alarm as Delta ascended.

"Fuel alarm," Stubbs deadpanned.

Delta levelled out. From right beneath her the Beta came.

She put the aircraft into a dead drop, trying to lose the beast – but not shake off Kelly – and at the same time get a fatal shot off at the Scarlatti with either the Stingers or the chain gun.

She had to get behind it. The Scarlatti jackknifed and dived down with her, down through the wood, banking past the smouldering nest site, skimming the ivy and underbrush, centimetres behind.

Bip bip bip bip bip bip bip bip bip. The fuel alarm echoed the stress within – and without: Kelly was slipping.

"We're losing Kelly..." said Finn.

"We're losing power..." said Stubbs.

187

"Shut up," said Delta and banked hard left and along the course of the stream, inky black in the growing dusk. "Tell him to drop when I hit the brakes!" she said and slammed the aircraft into almost a dead halt. They watched the Scarlatti slingshot by and try to turn.

Finn leant out of the chopper as far as he dared. "Drop, Kelly! Drop!" he yelled.

Kelly let go of the hardpoint. He seemed to Finn to hang in mid-air an age… then *SPLASH!* hit the water from twelve nano-metres.

Delta was at last behind the Scarlatti.

DRTDRTDRTDRTDRTDRTDRTDRTDRTDRTDRTDRTDRT-DRTDRTDRT!

Bip bip bip bip bip bip bip bip bip bip bip bip bip bip bip bip bip

DRTDRTDRTDRTDRTDRTDRTDRTDRTDRTDRTDRTDRT-DRTDRTDRT!

Bip bip bip bip bip bip bip bip bip bip bip bip bip bip bip bip bip

"Low on ammo. Low on fuel," said Stubbs as Delta again hauled the Apache round in a tight circle to take the dogfight downstream.

"Grab that M27!" she yelled. "Get off some lateral shots!"

Before Stubbs could move, Finn grabbed it.

The flank of the Scarlatti briefly appeared through the open door and Finn let rip –

DRRRRRRT! DRRRRRT!

"Hold on!" said Delta and threw a corkscrew, turning them upside down at the equivalent of 120mph along the course of the stream, then pulling hard on the stick to end up directly behind the confused Scarlatti, like a World War Two ace.

Bip bip bip bip bip bip bip bip bip bip bip bip bip

There it was, the softest part of its abdomen, right in the crosshairs of the chain gun...

They had followed the course of the stream out of the woods now.

Delta hit the button.

DRRRR— The Beta veered away at the sound alone. *Clickclickclickclickclickclickbeeeeeeeeeeeeeeeeeep...*

"Out of ammo. Out of fuel."

"I know!" shouted Delta as the engine died. The rotors were still whizzing, they could glide to the bank... but where was the Beta?

In the sudden silence they heard the roar of a patrolling macro-aircraft overhead and their radio finally crackled to life.

"*Come in, Messi, come in, Messi? This is Ronaldo, repeat, this is Ronaldo. Over,*" said an RAF voice.

Stubbs grabbed the mike. Too late.

The Beta Scarlatti sensed their weakness. With a burst of energy, it thrust down at them, stings first – *SMACK!* – into the rotors of the gliding Apache. The rotor blades sheared from the aircraft and the Scarlatti was flung against the bank.

SPLASHSHSHHSHHHWCKDHDSHSHH! The Apache spluttered into the water upside down, the rotor scything off alone downstream while the rest of the craft tumbled head over heels into a floating bed of weeds, the force of which caused them to detach from the bank and drift into the fast water.

Finn – thrown clear of the cabin – found himself losing

189

consciousness as he was assaulted by water on all sides, water trying to crush him and wrench him and spin him all at once. A memory of being in the flume ride with Grandma and Al flashed to mind, before more water tried to force its way into his lungs as the current sucked him under and kept him there, his every instinct and nerve ending screaming FIGHT as he struck out at the water, trying to reach the light...

...as a shadow arrived... and hovered over him... waiting...

...*Kill*...

PART THREE

PART
THREE

TWENTY-TWO

The tiny, blurred movement of a white line on a screen.

First it moved this way, then it moved that.

Keep going, thought Al. It had been his internal mantra since the Cooper-Hastings video had come through and, whenever he slowed down, whenever he doubted, whenever things seemed hopeless... *Just keep going* (and stay one step ahead of your worst fears).

For nearly two hours they'd been clutching at straws. The white line was just the latest. Al had split the scientists and technicians into small groups and told them to think "outside the box".

Could there be any clues in the reflections in Cooper-Hastings'

eyes? (No, the resolution was too poor.) Could there be a coded message in Cooper-Hastings' mannerisms and speech patterns? (None could be detected.)

The only hint of a lead they had was that analysis of the brief 'nest site' clip had suggested a background plant distribution more likely associated with the loamy soil found to the southwest of the search area, thus search aircraft were patrolling the quadrant more heavily.

It was barely scientific, but it was a straw, and Al made damn sure they clutched at it.

Other teams sought to track the source of the video, examining any trace of the digital pathway. And one group had been studying blow-ups of various background details in the main part of the video.

And it was this group who had spotted the blurred white line. Who had spotted – movement.

"...*pack the Cambridge Fat Doughnut Accelerator into two shipping containers and have them placed freestanding on the deck of the container ship* Oceania Express... *steam along the Great Eastern sea lane, there to await further instruction...*"

First the white line moved this way, then it moved that.

"Run it again," said Al.

At the opposite end of the gallery, Commander King was attempting to keep order among a collection of seriously rattled global heavyweights.

The 18:00 deadline was about to pass, and everyone wanted

answers. He felt like a holiday rep trying to explain to a group of disappointed tourists why their flight had been delayed. He did not know how or why. They knew he did not know how or why. They just needed to let off steam. And in the meantime he must maintain perfect calm and remain courteous in order to preserve the only sensible strategy: "To keep as many options open as we can, for as long as we can."

"But we're going to have to meet their demands, surely?" said the British Prime Minister.

"It's got to be preferable to a nuclear strike," said the US President.

"No Scarlatti, then no more threat," agreed the German Chancellor.

"Hand it all over," ordered the US General Jackman. "Then you can just worry about how you chase the bastards down."

"I must say I have to agree," said the UK's own General Mount. "Even the Royal Navy can't lose 110,000 tonnes of cargo ship in the North Sea."

"Just give *everything* away?" asked King. "Just allow ourselves to be blackmailed?"

"Sometimes you have to trade with the horse," said the French President.

"I see, is there anything else you would like to give away while we're at it, Monsieur? Your independent nuclear deterrent the Force de Frappe? The American Pacific Fleet? Deutsche Bank? Or perhaps, Prime Minister, a minor member of the royal family? I'm sure they'd be delighted to oblige. Any takers? No...? Because it would be as absurd as it would be cowardly," said King. "We have no real idea who we're dealing with, let alone whether we can trust them."

"True," said the American President, "though we are talking about Armageddon, not buying a used car – and *we* had a deal *and* a deadline. It is 18:00 hours, and there are no other alternatives on the table, so surely it's now time to coordinate evacuation and plan for the nuclear option."

"Well? Are you going to evacuate?" asked the French Conseiller Scientifique.

King called up a map and some faked aerial footage of fire crews and emergency services in heavy protective suits dealing with an overturned chemical tanker on a section of motorway.

"These pictures are being released to the media now. We're going to announce that a chemical tanker has overturned causing a spill that requires the evacuation of a small area. This will, by degrees, be expanded in order to achieve a phased evacuation, thus avoiding mass panic. When there are no other options on the table, we will begin to break up the Large Accelerator and prepare the nuclear warheads."

"And when do you judge that to be?" asked the Prime Minister.

"We'll have to begin the process at midnight tonight. In six hours."

"And the nuclear strike time? Should the deadline pass at noon tomorrow?"

"We can't at this stage give a precise—"

"*Non!* This is not an acceptable answer. France will be next. Then the world. Are you prepared to destroy this thing or are you not?"

King said the last thing he wanted to say, the last thing he wanted to think about.

"If by noon tomorrow we have acceded to our enemies' demands and they have not honoured the deal and given us the location of the nest site, and if we have not discovered it ourselves, then, given the increasing likelihood of a swarm, we will be forced to detonate."

"Hold your fire!" said Al, bursting in on the conversation with a laptop. He hooked it into an available terminal. "Nobody's doing any deal without my say-so! Remember, I have the sequencing codes. In the meantime, we may yet be able to find these bad guys – and our little people too."

"Oh, come on! You don't *still* think for one moment they survived?" said General Jackman in Washington.

"General Jackass!" Al shouted. "May I remind you you've had to kiss my butt before and if I find my nephew you will be kissing it again!"

The American General harrumphed. Al had driven him to fury over the Fukushima business, and had been absolutely right.

King half closed his eyes. He hated discourtesy and name-calling, but he also loved to see Al in full flight and with fire in his belly.

"Well, what the hell is it then!" roared Jackman. "What have you got?"

"Calm down, Linden," said the US President.

"Yes, sir, Mr President."

Kill...

The Beta Scarlatti hovered over the water.

Its compound eye was confused by the foaming, turbulent surface and not sensitive enough to penetrate beneath. Its senses clung to the multiple scents... although the chaotic air was confusing and dispersing these too, and it was even in danger of losing the scent of its nest... yet still it hung there...

Wkwkzkzkwkdkdkwkxzxhxkxkwwkwkwkxxzzzzz

...wanting to kill with every fibre of its exhausted being, but its purpose was the swarm.

It latched on to the last of the swarm pheromone and, slowly, rose and turned back.

Finn kicked towards the sunlight, needling through the crazed, rushing water, lack of oxygen crippling mind and limb alike. As his lungs reached bursting point, the very zenith of pain, he felt himself break the surface of the water, out of death and back to life – GASP...

Cool, life-giving oxygen flowed through him.

GASP...

Live...

GASP...

He choked and his limbs began to thrash and he realised he was being dragged down the course of the stream at tremendous speed. The banks rushed past. He could just see, further down the rapids, the stricken Apache sticking out of the clump of green weeds where it had crashed.

He could hear something too. A voice.

"Noob! Noob!"

Delta!

He caught a glimpse of her as the water spun him around again. She was scrambling across the floating weed bed outside the aircraft, trying to get to him. Stubbs was there too, attempting to pull himself up the fuselage.

Finn raised his hand to signal and – *SWOOOSH* – the current sucked him under again.

He was tossed around 360 and emerged in slower water that deepened and darkened.

The playground-sized clump of weeds was still a good distance away, but Delta was now at its edge.

"FINN!" he heard her call, using his name at last.

"Here!" he yelled back.

He kicked towards her, but the current and his soaking clothes made progress slow.

As he thrashed away, the stream ran clear of the woods. He got snatched views of fields above the banks.

Ahead Delta was trying to manoeuvre a twig off the weeds to use as a boathook.

Encouraged, Finn kicked on. Then he realised he was gathering speed.

"Get out of the current! Get out of the current!" Delta called.

The weeds had drifted into slower water on the right bank while he was now in the fast water, about to shoot past.

Finn kicked with all his might. Delta stretched out with the improvised boathook.

"That's it! Go on!"

He thrashed and flapped. Delta was right at the edge of the weed bed, half immersed herself.

Finn's fingertips brushed the end of the twig and he threw everything into a snatch… and just managed to get hold of the end of it.

Yes.

Then Delta looked over his shoulder and roared, "AHHHHHHHH!"

Finn turned to see a gigantic duck launch itself like a ship from the opposite bank – vivid green and blue in plumage, and bearing down, fast and curious. Finn kicked wildly, desperate to make it to the weeds.

Stubbs, back at the Apache now, yanked open one of the stow holds.

The bird loomed over Finn, jolting its beak from side to side, bemused.

A red distress flare, fired by Stubbs, arced out of the remains of the Apache and hit the duck, glancing off its chest and causing feathered pandemonium.

QUUUUUUUUUAAAAAAAAAAACKCKCCKCK!

Finn dived under to avoid being decapitated by a wild wing. When he emerged, the duck was hitting the opposite bank in comic flight. And Delta was still on the other end of the stick.

She hauled on it and, with a last scramble, she managed to help Finn up on to the weeds.

With a double *ker-splash*, they both fell back on to the jelly-like surface. They lay there a beat, panting.

"Not a textbook landing," said Delta to break the ice.

"Kelly…" said Finn. "Where's Kelly?"

He raised his head. The stream slid by. Acres of black water. No sign, no hint of anyone.

TWENTY-THREE

BBC NEWS 24 FLASH 18:23 HRS BST

"A chemical tanker has overturned on the M25 slip road at Junction 14 in Surrey and a cloud of gas is escaping from the vehicle. Police say the cloud is 'potentially hazardous' and have started evacuating the immediate area. They stress the move is 'purely precautionary', although the villages nearby will be put on standby. In fact, yes, we have pictures from the scene now..."

SKY NEWS – BREAKING NEWS! 18:24

"...utter devastation! A cloud of lethal toxic gas, possibly cyanide, is already spreading through local villages, filling the lungs and the lanes

of leafy Surrey with death and devastation. The emergency service
advice is clear and unambiguous..."

THE SUN WEBSITE NEWS FLASH 18:24

'RUN FOR YOUR LIVES! Celebrities caught in poison gas
dash...'

GOOGLE ANALYTICS 18:25

String = 'SURREY GAS CLOUD': NEWS – 3,765 new articles.
WEB – 127,823 hits in 0.38 seconds. TWITTER – 134,877
related tweets.

They watched the water intently for five minutes or so.

"He'll make it," said Delta. "He'll figure it out and he'll make it
downstream. We just have to wait." She set her jaw and allowed no
doubt whatsoever.

Soaked through, Finn felt the cold grip him. The stream alone
was like the Amazon at their scale – and fast – the woods like its
great forests with multiples of its lethal threat. And Kelly was
already injured. The Scarlatti? It would sting him – surely – if it
picked up his scent on the way back. Finn felt sick. He should
have let Kelly blow it up when he had the chance. Stupid. Now
they were all in danger, much worse danger. He should have

obeyed... To save one life he risked six billion. What kind of maths was that?

He reached instinctively for the spharelite stone at his chest, but it wasn't there.

"This is the movement of a pull-cord light switch, 120 millimetres long. It's from the background of quadrant four." Al slapped a display playing the Cooper-Hastings video on a loop, pointing out the dangling light cord in the background to show the world where the white line on the blow-up on the main screen came from.

"This is a breakthrough?" asked General Mount.

"This cord moves very slightly back and forth during the course of the video, but not like a pendulum as you'd expect. In irregular oscillation. Mysterious, unless you've never thrown up on a cross-channel ferry."

"He's at sea?" said King, getting there first.

"Correct," said Al. "This movement is consistent with that of a twenty-metre craft in a moderate swell. If we can find the right weather, in the right sea area, at the right time... we might be able to find the right-sized craft, and then we're on to something!"

The watching world chewed it over. All the resources and technology at their disposal had been trumped by a piece of string? If anyone else had come up with this, it would have been called crazy. But when Allenby got hold of an idea...

"Alert the coastal commands of every European nation," King ordered.

"Satellite feeds! Naval intel! Now!" General Jackman barked in Washington.

"*Préfet Maritime! Vite!*" ordered the French President.

"Let's go, people!" called Al. "I want the Royal Navy, the coastguard and every pirate in the land scouring their screens to find this thing!"

Just keep going.

Finn, Stubbs and Delta secured the weeds as best they could to the bank and waded ashore.

With a line and pulley, they managed to haul the Apache carcass off the weeds and on to the muddy bank.

Stubbs worked away, soaked and largely silent. The old man was in survival mode, moving steadily from task to task, occasionally stopping to cough up some of the stream.

The blink of a strobe light began to flash across the scene. Stubbs had turned on the Apache's landing light to act as a beacon.

"Kelly," he said, and Finn and Delta nodded.

Now securely on dry land, they took in their landing place properly for the first time. The mud had been pressed flat and there were huge rubber bootprints and flowers. Further up the sloping bank was short mown grass, a path and, looming large above it all, a wooden structure twenty storeys high.

"Shed," said Stubbs.

Leaving the Apache landing light on, Finn, Delta and Stubbs climbed the bank.

When they reached the top, they came upon an Eden – a sunset garden of breathtaking beauty, colourful and carefully planted, designed to ramble and enchant, with beds of flowers backed by shrubs and trees and dry-stone walls. Jasmine scented the warm air and the 'magic hour' light seemed to lift and define everything it touched.

Looking like they'd been dragged backwards through hell, Finn, Delta and Stubbs regarded it in wonder.

Climbing up a rock and using Delta's field glasses for a better view, they could see the path led up a perfect lawn to an ancient house that spread itself out across the loveliest spot in the valley.

And they could see open windows. And the distant flicker of movement inside.

Finn's heart – which had felt frozen at the stream – jump-started and began beating hope all over again.

Somebody was home.

Contact.

"How far d'you think it is?" asked Finn.

"At nano-level? Fifteen to twenty K," Delta said.

That might take two hours running flat out in perfect conditions.

Their orders were clear: if they couldn't destroy the nest site – and without transport and ammo there was no going back – they were to make contact with a patrol and report its location.

All that mattered now was contact. The macro-radio on the chopper's

206

underside had been shattered in the crash, but the house gave them hope. Finn took it in again as the sun set. It looked perfect and homely. He wanted to eat cake in front of the TV with Grandma and Yo-yo on a Sunday evening while Al ranted and drank in the background.

The door to the shed had been left open a crack and inside they found a mass of old mowers, gardening equipment, bits of string and a spoil heap of plastic toys. To Stubbs – Disneyland. Invention glittered in his eyes and bizarre potential vehicles formed in his imagination.

They had taken what they could salvage of their supplies out of the stricken Apache. They badly need rest, but the original mission time ran to 06:00 hours, after which a mass-evacuation plan came into effect. The survival of the Beta Scarlatti and the nymphs left them with only one possible objective – they had to report the location of the nest site before it was too late.

"We just have to get to that house, find a phone and hit 911," said Delta. "We don't need a reception committee. We just need a landline."

They had been through it in one of the 'emergency fallback' briefings back at base. Any mention of the word Boldklub or Scarlatti to the operator would get them put straight through to Hook Hall.

"It's 999," corrected Finn. "If they have a grandma, they'll have a landline. Grandmas think mobiles fry their brains."

Thinking of Grandma made his heart jump again. Made him impatient. "Let's go," he said.

"I'll stay. Wait for Kelly. I'll only hold you up, and I'll see what I can find in the shed," said Stubbs. Finn and Delta nodded.

"We can take an M27 and your Beretta and Stubbs can take the Minimi," said Finn.

Delta pointed up at a cloud of midges hovering above them.

"If we wait, we can avoid those dive-bombing our butts and help Stubbs set up. Kelly may even show up meantime."

"Very unlikely. With that leg…" said Stubbs, adding to Finn's guilt.

"He was a warrior, he was boss. Could have survived anything," said Delta.

"I note you use the past tense…" said Stubbs.

Delta was about to reply when Finn interjected.

"Hey, I think something's happening at the house," he said, pointing up the garden.

Delta and Stubbs looked up. Finn grabbed the field glasses.

Lights were on in every window all of a sudden, and figures were running from room to room. As they watched, a large 4 x 4 backed up to what must have been the back door and its tailgate swung open.

They all took a turn with the field glasses.

"What are they doing?" asked Finn.

A loud voice rang out through the silent garden.

"*Attention! This is a police announcement…*" came a voice through a loudhailer, distorted as it travelled past on a road beyond.

"*Prepare for evacuation overnight in an orderly fashion. You are in no immediate danger. Help elderly or vulnerable neighbours to prepare and* contact the authorities if you need further assistance. Keep tuned in to local radio and television for..."

"They're getting the hell out," said Delta. "Already."

"What does that mean?" asked Finn, looking at Stubbs.

"They think we're dead."

DAY TWO 21:03 (BST). Siberia

In Siberia it had been 'night' for over six hours. The sun, that barely dips below the horizon in summer, was at its lowest point, the temperature well below zero.

Kaparis and his team had spent the last three of those hours monitoring communications around the declared exclusion zone and, naturally, around the nest site at Willard's Copse.

Despite Li Jun's best efforts, they were still locked out of Hook Hall, but progress was being made on local telecoms systems.

Kaparis had not allowed himself to relax, but at the same time his stress levels were subsiding.

Footage from the nest site had been exhaustively studied. The crew had made it to the site and destroyed the Alpha. But the Beta lived, and had pursued them, so based on this and on rational assumptions (of logistics, morale, supplies, etc.), Kaparis's military analysts predicted only a 13 per cent chance the crew had made it further than 200 metres beyond the nest site.

There was nothing to suggest otherwise. No communication intercept.
No pause in the evacuation.

Thus far the threat held.

The Beta had bucked its instinct and willed itself forward. Into the smoke. Into the pyre. Fury and swarm preservation inflamed its forebrain.

It had dropped on to fleeing nymphs, seizing them and depositing them on to one of the new hosts.

To those nymphs already burying themselves in the new corpses that lay scattered around the nest it fed deposits of hormone.

As the minutes passed and the smoke subsided, it began to collect and farm the dead nymphs. It landed on them, razored through their outer membrane with its mouthparts and sucked them dry.

It then flew to the living nymphs and regurgitated the vile remains into their gaping maws.

After an hour, it moved on to the Alpha corpse and devoured that too. It carried on past exhaustion, supping its dead twin, vomiting its remains over its young, passing on its rich hormone load. The nymphs must mature and fulfil their destiny...

Swarm.

By the time the sow badger had stopped smoking altogether, the temperature was dropping fast.

Rest... rest... its every cell needed rest... protein to repair.

It burrowed into the swollen gut of the cat, already half consumed by the nymphs, and fed, sunk its jaws into the warm, rich, fizzing innards, drinking it, draining it of life-giving, cell-repairing, replenishing gall.

Live...

Kill...

"Diddly dee diddly dah, diddly dee diddly dah..."

The little kid kept repeating his impersonation of a train. He was a small boy in a pirate T-shirt with a mop of red hair. Young enough and dumb enough to stare at the stranger sitting opposite him in the carriage, trying with childlike curiosity to see the face beneath the shadow of the hood.

The kid made Kane sick. Crazed. The hyper-sweet aroma of artificial strawberry and vanilla from the bag of sweets he kept digging into. The stains around the kid's mouth, from drying sweet saliva that couldn't help but leak out. The constant—

"Diddly dee diddly dah, diddly dee diddly dah..."

The train had been largely empty since it left East Croydon. At Waterloo it had been packed with commuters returning home, and full of a most unusual thing for a London commuter train – talk.

The evening newspapers, snatched for once from the hands of their vendors, had screamed 'Toxic Gas Alert'. In calls to loved ones, to friends, and in person to each other, the Surrey commuters discussed one thing – how fast they were going to get out. Trains travelling in the opposite direction were already packed. Rumours of looting and imminent disaster were traded, and overexcitement led to small acts of recklessness (one woman ate six chocolate muffins).

Everyone avoided Kane. The way he carried himself was warning enough. Face deep in his hood, gaze fixed on his phone, bad music distorting from filthy earphones, repelling those around him like a force field.

Fear.

Everyone understood fear. Everyone apart from this one irritating, sweet-munching, stupid little kid.

"Diddly dee diddly dah, diddly dee diddly dah..."

Kane had an IQ of 196 and, like every Tyro, an ingrained sense of absolute superiority.

They had passed the first of the stations in the 'affected area' and entered the newly established Exclusion Zone. The kid's mother was tearful as she made arrangements with her husband over the phone.

Willingham was coming up. Kane's stop.

"Diddly dee diddly dah, diddly dee diddly dah..."

Those sweets... That smell...

Kane pushed back his hood a fraction and stared.

The boy saw a face. Not black, not white, not Eastern, not Western... Alien. A face set to kill, with speckled eyes that bore into him. The boy froze. Fear gripped him. He could not break the stare. His eyes filled with tears.

As the train came to a halt at Willingham, Kane's arm shot forward, snatched the boy's sickly sweets and pinched the skin on his arm as hard as he could. Drawing blood. And screams.

By the time the boy's mother could react, the train doors were closed and Kane was gone.

The boy was six years old.

TWENTY-FOUR

Finn glanced back as he and Delta took off up the path to the house, but Stubbs had already merged into the dark. He wanted to say good luck, or at least goodbye, but that wasn't Stubbs's way.

Finn jogged on, keeping up with Delta.

"Sure you're up to being my wingman, Noob?" she'd asked before they set off.

"Sure you're up to being mine?" said Finn.

"Good job."

They were running right up the middle of the garden path. It was made of smooth sandstone and they wore LED headlamps to scan ahead, so they could travel relatively fast.

The path gave them clear sight of any threat. Only black ants and disinterested small beetles had crossed ahead of them so far. Nocturnal predators would more likely be lurking in the lawn – spiders, rodents out looking for grubs, grass snakes, adders...

Just keep going, thought Finn. Concentrate on the run. One step at a time.

Easy enough to say. He was already starting to struggle. As well as the M27, he carried a backpack containing, among other things, a spare ammo clip, two litres of nano-water and three of the remaining flares – red, white and blue.

After ten minutes of steady, lung-bursting running, Finn was extremely pleased to hear Delta call, "OK, let's take a minute."

They stopped and panted, leaning against each other for support, the beams from their headlamps cutting through the total darkness like lightsabers.

Then from somewhere above they heard – *SCHHHHHRRRERE-CCHH!*

"What was that?"

Their headlamp beams wheeled and searched. Delta drew her pistol.

"I think it was just an owl..." said Finn. "We're too small for an owl. It's probably just calling its young anyway."

Up at the house, they could see the family still packing up and a row was breaking out about what was going to make it into the back of the 4 x 4.

SCRATCH.

Another sound on the path ahead.

They swung round and their beams bounced back at them off

the shining exoskeleton of a stag beetle the size of a camper van, its terrifying, extraordinary gloss-black antlers raised as if to strike.

"Wait!" said Finn, again holding back Delta's gun arm. He was bowled over, not just by its size but by the shiny detail and textures on the stag's hammer head. "He's just a big vegetarian!"

The stag's mouthparts twitched and sampled their scent.

"With that rack on his head?"

"Just for show."

"Men…" sighed Delta with a shake of her head. The stag turned his mighty frame and scurried back across the path, back to black.

"Let's get out of here. You good?" said Delta.

"I'm good," said Finn.

SMACK – something hit the ground ahead of them.

"What was that?" said Delta.

SMACK – behind them now. They spun.

SMACK SMACK SMACK

"Uh-oh…" said Finn as – *SMACK* – what felt like a bucketful of water exploded on the ground at their feet. "Rain!"

"Go!" yelled Delta.

SMACK SMACK SMACK SMACK SMACK – merciless fat raindrops the size of basketballs started hammering down as the skies opened and a heavy summer shower broke.

BOOSH! Finn copped a direct hit and fell to his knees, punched from on high and drenched. He struggled up, trying to get his breath.

BOOSH! Delta copped one beside him. She tried to shout

something, but all he could hear was *SMACK-A-SMACK-A-SMACK-A-SMACK-A-SMACK-A-BOOSH!-SMACK-A-SMACK-A-SMACK-A-SMACK-A-SMACK-A-BOOSH!-SMACK-A-SMACK-A-SMACK-A.*

Water exploded all around them. They clung to each other and tried to keep their feet, but the path was turning from yellow brick road to raging torrent as water cascaded down the impervious slope bringing with it a speeding shrapnel of vegetation, grit and insects curled into rock-hard balls for their own protection, some heavy enough to – *BASH!* – knock Finn clean off his feet.

Down Finn went, torn along the path, tumbling over and over in the flash flood, fighting to stop himself, fighting for breath.

With some relief, the stone path gave way to thick, soft mud which gave way in turn to firm lawn grasses which at last slowed his progress, if not the flow. Up to his chest in rushing water, he fought to cling on and find his feet. Around him was a violent blur.

He tried to call out, "Delta!" but it was hopeless.

SMACK-A-SMACK-A-SMACK-A-SMACK-A-SMACK-A-SMACK-A-SMACK-A

There was no point in trying to move in the downpour. He anchored himself as best he could and held firm. He had no real idea of how far he'd been driven from the path or where Delta was.

After a further five minutes of relentless noise, the deluge – almost as suddenly as it started – began to fade out.

Finn's ears rang. The water sank around him, diminishing into a quagmire. Mud and trickle.

"Arrrrrghghhhhhhhhhhhhhhhhhhhh!"

He called out – "Delta!"

"Arrrrrhggghhhhhhhhhhhhhhhhh!"

"Delta?"

Slosh slosh slosh – Finn slogged through the dense, uniform lawn grasses, trying to cleave a way through the tall stems as if through a field of sweetcorn, headlamp picking out a pinprick path ahead.

"Keep screaming!"

"Arrrrrrrrrrrgghhhhhhhhhhhhhhhhhhhhhh!"

She sounded like she was being eaten alive. Why wasn't she shooting?

Slosh slosh slosh

When he saw her, his stomach turned.

There were thousands of them. They were crawling over every bit of her.

"Arrrrrrrrrgghhhhhhhhhhhhhhhhhhhhh!"

Translucent baby spiders, trapped in the fishing net of a web, covered her; each the size of a rat, each in a frenzy; a colony reacting as one to attack. A garden spider's nursery web[21] must have been beaten from the shrub above them and she'd somehow run into it.

"Aaarrghh!" she screamed, convulsing.

Finn tried to scrape and slap the beasts from her, but there were too many.

---

[21] A cone-like structure rarely more than twenty-five millimetres in diameter that acts as both incubator and playpen to 200 or so newborn young.

He grabbed the top of her pack and dragged her backwards through the grass and mud, trying to shake off the glutinous web. She kicked and pawed and, bit by bit, like she was wriggling out of sleeping bag, it came away – taking most of the vile creatures off with it.

"They're biting!"

"It's OK, it'll wash off!" Finn said, splashing and soaking her and slapping off the last glassy, skeletal young, scraping the slime off her. "It's only acid."

She scrambled up and grabbed him. Gripped him round the throat in pure aggressive terror as if she was about to kill him.

"Acid! Only acid!" she barked, shaking in shock and struggling to control herself. "When I get out of here, I am going to kill your goddamn uncle!"

"It's OK," he said to her. "It's all right to be afraid every now and then, y'know..."

"Who said I was afraid? I am not afraid of goddamn spiders! I hate them. But I am not afraid. You get me?"

"OK, I hear you. Not so hard, I've got to breathe," Finn gasped.

"OK. I'm going to let you go now... I'm going to let go... Three... two... one..."

She unclasped and he fell back. She was still shaking. Rebooting. She'd briefly regressed to a traumatised child, now the adult was fighting back.

"Don't ever tell anyone about this... or I'll have to kill you too."

"OK!"

"Joking. I joke, you know…" said Delta, regaining control.

"You're never going to make it as a clown," said Finn.

"Don't be such a smartass! You're worse than Carla."

"Your sister?"

"Uh-huh. She's like you. Louder maybe."

And for a moment, as her anger faded and she thought of her sister, she looked vulnerable. Not so superhuman. Normal. And Finn suddenly thought of his mum, and wanted to say what he couldn't say. About how he missed her, yet how she was always never very far away. Which made it worse yet better all at the same time. Stupid stuff like that which you can never say so he shut up. Then, for a fraction of a moment, he thought she must have sensed it because Delta drew breath and said: "Oh Momma…"

Finn's heart skipped – right up until she grabbed him and threw him down – *SPLASH!* – on to his back and out of the way of the jaws of a vast, seriously ticked-off mummy spider, a climbing frame of implacable rage.

Delta growled and snatched at her Beretta – but it had fallen from its holster.

As the mother monster rose to strike her down – fangs scythe-sharp, extended, about to pound through her – Finn *just* managed to get his finger on the trigger of his M27.

DRTRTRRTRTRTRTRTRTRTRRT!

The bullets whizzed and cracked through the spider's skull, taking its head clean off and leaving the rest of its body to collapse on top of him, oozing yellow goo.

Delta dragged him out.

They were soaked, exhausted, they'd lost one of the weapons already, but at least...

Finn felt something wriggle beneath his foot. He jumped.

"Ahhh!"

What the...? He aimed the gun at the mud. A shiny-wet copper head appeared – an earthworm the size of a crocodile that writhed out of the ground.

"Let's get out of here!" Delta shouted, then spun and stamped as behind her a much larger one poked its head out.

"Heavy rain brings them to the surface," said Finn. "We need to find the path. Fast."

"Aren't they harmless?"

"They are – but the things that feed on them aren't."

Right on cue – THUD-SPLASH – an elephantine spiked dinosaur charged and bit into the wriggling earthworm with evident, beastly delight. A hedgehog, but definitely not the cute creature of children's stories.

"This way!" Finn cried, and they pushed on...

Slosh slosh slosh slosh slosh

...until they found themselves in a bald patch of lawn, right now a mudslide.

They skidded into what seemed like another worm – until it twitched.

A tail.

CHITERTERTERTEER!

Finn slid right to see a wood mouse – a bus-sized, black-eyed beanbag of a thing – also clearly slaking its bloodlust, tearing the worms to pieces and making the most of the unexpected bounty.

"Get back!" barked Delta. But before they could scramble away to the grass, the mouse caught their lamps in its peripheral vision and, in a heartbeat, twitched round to face them.

"Run!"

Slosh slosh slosh slosh slosh slosh slosh…

They made it to the grass but then – *THUD* – the mouse pounced, landing alongside, intrigued by the dancing headlamps, trying to make sense of them, trying to keep up – *THUD.*

Finn reached for the M27, but as he swung round to fire he tripped, the dense grass suddenly giving way to the path again, and he landed heavily at its edge, the butt of the gun taking his impact, the ammo clip cracking out and skittering across the surface.

THUD. The mouse was on him.

Delta roared and ran for him, slipping and falling as the mouse opened its mouth and bore down…

Then froze – its black eyes literally popping out.

Over it, above it, the jaws of a giant fox cub had snapped shut – blood-slick fangs the size of tusks emerging from the furry red cliff of its face.

The cub bit down hard and shook the mouse back and forth for the sheer primal killing hell of it.

Blood sprayed everywhere, the cub's massive head whipping to and fro, before it tossed the corpse aside to run and snap up the next rodent.

Finn and Delta just lay there for a few moments on the wet path, covered in blood, waiting until their hearts stopped pounding against their ribcages.

"And that's what they call the circle of life," said Finn.

TWENTY-FIVE

*R*adar-cloaked and powered by whisper jets, the drone cut through the night sky, maintaining a cloud-cover trajectory and dropping to 2,000 feet as it prepared to release its cargo.

Advanced aerodynamic and navigation technology meant the payload could be floated within two metres of the target. Cold gas vernier thrusters had been fitted to control the descent as required.

At 21:34:23 BST the drone released its payload at a speed of 163mph. Parachutes deployed after 5.8 seconds and, after a descent lasting 111 seconds, the thrusters kicked in, guiding it, hissing, to its final destination.

Kane waited. He had finished the sweets. A sugar-slick coating covered his tongue and mouth.

To come across Kane in a dark wood was the stuff of nightmares. But he was quite alone.

He checked his phone again and looked up into the wet night sky, plucking the canister out of the air as it fell to the earth.

Inside the package, among other high-tech gizmos, Kane found an ultra-sensitive thermal-imaging device.

He tested it, pointing it into the woods. The display showed the wood alive with glowing orange pinpricks of life. Half a dozen small rodents nosed through the leaf litter while the trees contained nesting birds and sleeping squirrels.

Satisfied, he slogged on into the woods.

"We need to regroup. We need a vehicle, and firepower," said Delta. "It's a jungle out here."

They were still lying flat out on the path, recovering.

"Just keep going," muttered Finn.

"What?" said Delta.

"Got to keep going," said Finn. "It's a family tradition. Don't you have family traditions?"

"Just court appearances in the Pennsylvania Family Division," said Delta.

"Kelly would keep going," said Finn.

"Kelly would chew off his own arm."

"You think he's dead?" Finn asked.

She looked at him. Finn tried to stop it all spilling out, but lying there on the path in the darkness he couldn't help it, after being in the Grip of the Spider Woman, he felt he'd been let in on a secret and now he owed one.

"Kelly... he could have killed the other Scarlatti too, but I messed up and he had to save me instead. I should have just done what he said and now he's probably dead. But I thought he was going to blow himself up and I couldn't help it..."

Finn looked back up at the night sky.

Delta didn't usually get close to people like this. She generally kept them as far away as she could. But he looked so young suddenly. She tried to think what she'd say to Carla.

"You can't care about Kelly. It's what they train us for. All that matters is the mission. We are what we do. You don't want to be like us, Noob. We walk with death. If you lose someone, the training kicks in: you shut down, collect the XP and move on."

"Collect the XP... Do you treat everything like a game?"

"Only thing I know. Apart from Carla."

"You play online?"

"Sure."

"Tag?"

"West Pole, like North Pole or South Pole, y'know," she said, reaching into her jacket and flicking out a gum, as Finn lifted his head off the path, open-mouthed, to lay eyes on a legend.

"*The* West Pole? *Black Ops* number one ranking of all time West Pole? Shot me twenty-two times in one deathmatch West P—"

"Yep," she said, expecting him to reel off her stats.

But he'd stopped mid-sentence. Because beyond her he could see something else.

"The lights... They're going out!" he said.

"What?"

They jumped up.

First upstairs and now down the lights in the house were going out in sequence as the last family member tracked back through the building. Soon there would just be a silhouette against the night sky.

"We've got to get there and stop them! HALT! HALT!" Delta called.

"The signal flares!" said Finn, and Delta ripped one out of his backpack.

She pulled the ripcord on it and – *SWOOOOOSH!* – red fire arced up from her hand into the night.

Then she pulled out two hand flares from her own pack – the kind used to guide planes on to aircraft carriers – and waved them madly as if guiding in a hyperactive albatross.

Finn snapped the ammo clip back into the M27 and fired into the air.

DRTTRTRTRTRTRTRTRTRTRTRTRTRTRTRTRTRT!

"OVER HERE!"

But it was ridiculous, and they knew it – the flares would be barely a glimmer at this range and scale.

227

The last light went out. The 4 x 4 coughed to life.

In the weird red light of the glow flares they were the picture of despair. Finn was just about to break into a string of his worst playground expletives when...

WHKWHKWHKWHKWHKWHKWHK

...from nowhere, over their heads, they felt a powerful downdraught followed by the flicking, whipping brush of stiffened silk.

"Oh, what *now*?" Delta snapped, ducking.

But Finn was in awe, looking up at the most brilliant orange and black moth he had ever seen.

"Woah..." said Delta, held by the strangeness of the rapidly beating wings, the moth held in turn by—

"The flares!" said Finn. "Don't move your hand. It's caught in the light..."

They held still. The moth continued to hover, a fantastic thing, a horse of a thing.

"It's a tiger," said Finn. "A tiger moth." He looked over to the house. The 4 x 4 was still there. Barely daring to do so, he reached out and grabbed one of the moth's dangling feet. They were rough, alien almost, covered in brittle hair – but strong.

"What the hell are you doing?" asked Delta.

"Keep the flares right where they are!" Finn insisted.

He reached up and grabbed a second foot, then pulled on both, testing, seeing if the hovering beast would take his weight.

WHKWHKWHKWHKWHKWHKWHK

It did. He hung there easily. He couldn't believe it. He looked at Delta.

"Come on! Put them both in one hand a sec, then hang off this foot. Do it fast!"

"You're crazy..."

"They're going! They're leaving!"

"I like the way you roll, Noob. You know that?" Delta said, and took her heart in her mouth as she stepped forward to grab hold of a foot herself. The fluttering beast seemed so strong and so strange.

"Now pass me one of those..." urged Finn, excited, feeling the moth reel, confused.

Delta leant towards him and Finn grabbed one of the flares from her. Quickly he held it directly under the creature's head. The moth moved instinctively towards it. Mesmerised. When Delta held her flare out as well, the moth sped up.

WHKWHKWHKWHKWHKWHKWHK

"It's working!" said Finn as they picked up speed and the ground began to rush beneath them.

Their arms ached as they dangled, the ride as painful as it was precarious, but by holding the flares to the left or right they could, very roughly, steer the thing.

"Back to the path! Keep on the path!" yelled Delta.

WHKWHKWHKWHKWHKWHKWHK

Suspended in the machine-gun beat, they shot along a few nano-metres off the ground, hours of effort blitzed in a few terrifying moments of flight.

They held their breath and Finn prayed – to Mum and Dad or

Richard Dawkins or the Queen or God or David Attenborough –
"Please don't let me let go."

He was just starting to fear the moth would never slow down
(the house was suddenly looming large) when, for a fraction of a
fraction of a moment, he glimpsed a face. A terrible, snarling mask,
wide red mouth, razor teeth, travelling at incredible speed.

SMACK!

Finn felt himself spin through the air.

TWENTY-SIX

Swarm...

The Beta woke. Stirred. Something was coming. Swarm. It was still just warm enough to flick its, wings and take flight...

Kane reached the nest site. The badger had long ceased smouldering, but the smell of charred and burnt flesh hung in the damp air, a foul miasma.

Swarm...

The Beta Scarlatti flew to him. Straight at his face. To touch him. To taste him. To crawl across his warmth and taste the toxic sweet traces around his lips.

Swarm...

Kane opened his mouth and let the Scarlatti dip its tongue into any remaining sweetness in his saliva. It buzzed happily –

Wzkxzkxzkxzzxzzzz! – and Kane felt an urge, an instinct to protect. To nurture. To swarm.

He had been sick at first when the injections started.

Spiro had created a zombie bacteriophage from the DNA of the Vespula cruoris strain (source species of the Scarlatti) and repeatedly infected Kane with it until his body no longer resisted. The infection would turn him slowly, cell by cell, into a wasp-human hybrid. It was an impossible cross, and the process could kill him within weeks. But it would also afford him immunity from attack by the Scarlatti, allowing him to release and work with it directly. Much of his cell DNA was already mutating. There was a counter-virus waiting to reverse the process back in the Carpathian Mountains. If he made it.

It mattered not. It was for the Master.

The Scarlatti finished tasting Kane's saliva and flew back down to tend the swarm.

The badger corpse was nearly obliterated, but five of the corpses around it – three crows, the cat and a fox – were just enough to sustain the dozen or so nymphs that remained. They were fat and healthy, and from the empty carcass of the Alpha and scattered dead nymphs, Kane could see the Beta was feeding them a rich supplement. Indeed, one or two nymphs were beginning to discolour and look more like adults with viable wings.

He flipped open a small cryogenic container from his pocket, picked up a nymph and placed it carefully inside. He pressed a button to open a small liquid nitrogen vessel and instantly froze it.

He glanced at the electronic eye in the tree and held up the container for the Master to see. Then he pocketed it and headed back through the woods. Towards the village.

The Scarlatti, refreshed by the contact, writhed among the growing nymphs. Renewed. Feeding. Healing. Tending.

Swarm…

For a brief moment Finn didn't know who he was or where he was or when…

…all he could see was the frozen momentary image of the face, and from deep in his hindbrain it formed into something that made sense… a building block of sense and civilisation… a Latin classification… *Pipistrellus pipistrellus.*

He laughed to himself through a mouthful of mud as everything rushed back to mind.

"A bat ate our ride!" He lifted up his head, looking for Delta, and realising he'd dropped face down into the soft mud of a flower bed.

Right by the 4 x 4.

Finn scrambled to his feet. He couldn't find his gun or his backpack and he couldn't see Delta, but he knew what he had to do. Standing before him, barely 100 nano-metres away, was a gargantuan child, 100 times his size.

"HEY! *HEEEEEYY!* DOWN HERE!" He started to wave and holler.

"Get in the back of the car, darling! NOW!" shouted Mummy.

She was one of those perfect mummies you see perched high up in shiny 4 x 4s, only less so right now – panic having aged her ten years in two hours.

"I'm not going without Zizou!" said the little girl.

She had long hair, a rag doll and angry tears stained her cheeks.

Mummy took a deep breath. "But we can't find Zizou, darling, and we have to go…"

"I'm NOT going without Zizou!" She stamped her foot and stood firm.

"Fine! I'm getting Daddy!" said Mummy, storming back to the car.

Finn saw his chance. "DOWN HERE!" he yelled, leaping about in the dark.

Then, a few nano-metres away, he heard, "YO! OVER HERE!" and saw Delta staggering to her feet, still holding one of the red flares and waving it like mad.

They were within a macro-metre of the child now, and would be easily crushed if she took a step forward. But still they waved and roared.

The little girl thought she noticed something sparkle on the path; thought she could hear something squeaking. She stepped forward.

Yes! It was a sparkle. Or more a glow. A red glow… and two tiny pinpricks of light… She put her head right down.

Kane entered a housing estate on the edge of the village.

It was already empty, the young families who lived there having evacuated quickly. Further into Willingham he might have to deal with the lingering old and lonely, but here no one heard the smash of glass and splinter of wood as he began to break in and search the houses one by one.

The thermal sight revealed the odd mouse, nothing more. It was worse than trying to find a needle in a haystack – more like a miniaturised needle in a giant's haystack.

But the Master had ordered it, and the more difficult the task – the more resilience and concentration it demanded – the more Kane and all the Tyros loved it.

The giant girl bent down, and Finn saw above him a looming, terrified face, with two expanding, pond-like eyes, fighting to comprehend what was in front of her.

"IT'S OK. DON'T BE FRIGHTENED!" said Finn, with an exaggerated smile, trying not to scare her.

"LISTEN UP, LITTLE LADY! DIAL 911!" Delta jumped in. "YOU WILL BE REWARDED WITH ALL THE CANDY YOU CAN EAT!"

Finn literally had to shove Delta aside.

"DON'T BE FRIGHTENED! IT'S ALL GOING TO BE OK… WE'RE YOUR FRIENDS! DON'T GET TOO CLOSE!" he added, getting caught up in the end of her hair.

She reflexively pushed it over her ear as her daddy appeared. "Listen, poppet, do be reasonable," he began, exhausted and peeved. "We'll get you a new Zizou – we'll get *two*, how about that?"

He positioned himself to scoop her up and sling her over his rugby-playing shoulders. But he didn't stand a chance. The little girl shot straight past him and dived into her mother's lap in the front of the car.

"Mummy! Mummy! There are these... people! There are these little people!"

"At last! Sit round properly, dear," said the mummy. "Duncan! Get in the car!"

And Daddy, feeling quite pleased with himself for somehow finding the magic words, sauntered back to the 4 x 4.

"NO! DUNCAN! NO!! COME BACK!!" Finn ran after the man.

"HEY! DIPSTICK!" shouted Delta, throwing the hand flare at him and extracting her last distress flare.

SLAM went the door of the 4 x 4.

"NOOOO!!" called Finn.

VRRRRRROOM! went the engine as it started to pull down the drive.

Delta pulled the ripcord – *SWOOOOOSH!* – fire arcing up from her hand and speeding after the receding car.

But even if Daddy did catch a flicker of it in the rear-view mirror, he must have dismissed it as a trick of the light, because he drove straight on.

They watched as the tail lights disappeared.

Then a second later – BLINK – the security light cut out and they were left staring at darkness.

"Way to go, *big sister.*"

TWENTY-SEVEN

It had started with a speck of light. That was all he saw.

Something glinting through the trees on the surface of the water. He'd ignored it at first, thinking it was just reflected starlight or something, but the further south he travelled, the more insistent it became.

Kelly had spent almost six hours in continuous combat of one kind or another.

First, just after he'd been dropped by the Apache, he was taken by a small pike in the stream (although 'small' in this case meant ten times his size – bigger than a great white shark at macro level).

It had almost bitten off his leg, but Kelly had managed to sink his knife into its forebrain before it could take a second helping.

Then he'd drifted ashore to escape the rapids and had made his way slowly through the woods, his recovering leg still slowing him down. Robbed of Finn's specialist knowledge – and on so many occasions he'd willed him to be there – Kelly had reverted to his 'attack first, ask questions later' tactic. He had lost the Magnum, so only had his bowie knife for protection, which some time ago he'd lashed to the end of a stick to make a spear.

He'd roughly followed the course of the stream and on the way been attacked by, among other creatures, newts, frogs, a scorpion (or some kind of weird red earwig thing), dragonfly larvae and dive-bombing, kamikaze mosquitoes (may have been gnats).

And then… he'd seen the speck of light.

The nearer he got to the shoreline, the more he became convinced he was dealing with artificial light reflecting off the water, and it soon became clear that it was flashing; some sort of strobe anchored somehow to the opposite bank.

Yes! Stubbs. The Stubbster. The Stubbsulator.

He'd gone back upstream, constructed a raft and set about crossing the rapids (in the middle of an almighty downpour).

Finally, he'd reached the other side. There he'd found the Apache's landing light blinking on the APU[22], together with a short note in Stubbs's handwriting that said simply – '*Gone to shed.*'

[22] Auxilliary Power Unit

239

Kelly climbed the bank with some difficulty, saw light coming from under the shed door and burst in to find... an improvised workshop that was something to behold.

Stubbs had laid out the dismembered components of the T700 jet engine he'd removed from the Apache and set up an A-frame lifting rig, ready to hoist the engine into place aboard an old radio-controlled toy jeep that was about five times their size, but what the hell.

Stubbs stood in the middle of an explosion of parts and tools, lost in his task. As Kelly approached, he looked up and said, "Ah... You. Good. I needed a volunteer."

The jet engine had to be adapted to burn macro-fuel and fitted to the basic vehicle; then steering, power and braking systems all had to be addressed. What Stubbs was undertaking was a massive task for any normal engineer, let alone one of his current size... and he loved it. Kelly respected his knowledge and skill, and had to admit he hadn't seen him so energetic or engaged since their original work on Boldklub. No doubt about it, the little old man was on fire.

And I might soon be too, thought Kelly, because he found himself a few minutes later standing before Stubbs's new creation – the 'Adapted Distillation Apparatus'.

It was an old medicine bottle half full of lawnmower fuel, tilted over a crude burner. One pipe fed fuel into the medicine bottle from the lawnmower, while another led to the bottom of a tank of water.

The idea was to boil the lawnmower fuel and feed the vapour through the water so that it condensed on the surface. This refined fuel could then be collected and used to power the "T7-S Mark 1" (Stubbs), or the "Toy Jeep" (Kelly).

"What are the odds of this thing going boom?" asked Kelly.

"About fifty-fifty."

"Great. Why don't I do your job, and you light this, because you know what, Stubbs? I've been putting it on the line rather a lot lately!"

Stubbs looked thoughtful. "Can you ream out turbo-jet feed nipples?" he asked. "Do you have advanced engineering experience? Can you calculate compression-thrust ratios? Remind me – what was it you so briefly studied at university before they chucked you out?"

"History of Art."

"Huh huh huh." Stubbs actually laughed, in a wheezy old man way.

"All right, just give me the damn lighter!" barked Kelly.

Stubbs took out the lighter, then turned and walked away. "Wait. I should be a minimum of twenty nano-metres away."

"What about me?"

"As you're injured anyway, you are technically 'mission expendable'," Stubbs explained.

He retreated the required distance then under-armed the lighter back at Kelly who snatched it from the air with a growl. Then Kelly turned to the Apparatus and reached forward to ignite the fuel.

WHOOOF! A cloud of vapour went up in a mini fireball that knocked him on to his backside.

"Control the flame by pulling over the damper," Stubbs advised from afar. "If the bottle fractures, remember to run awa—"

"I can kill people with my bare hands! That's all you need to remember!" yelled Kelly.

He was beginning to miss the pike.

"For future reference, that is not how you talk to a kid. You don't bark 'Listen up, little lady'," said Finn.

As they retrieved their bits of equipment from the flower bed, Finn and Delta bickered.

"You do in Philadelphia," Delta replied, retrieving the M27 from a clump of freesias. "Bail-out training kicked in: 'How to address a civilian in an emergency' – you fall out of the sky on a mission, they'll likely be in shock so you have to make yourself absolutely clear."

"She was about seven years old!" Finn pointed out, dusting off his backpack and realising the dust was bright orange from the wings of the tiger moth. He left it on, tribute to a fallen comrade. "Have you actually met any 'civilians'?"

"Never been shot down."

Finn looked up at the vast house. They had a grappling hook and some titanium line in one of the packs, but it was never going to scale that, he thought.

"Ever broken into a house?"

"Long time ago. Misspent childhood," said Delta.

"Well then, if we don't get in, I'm blaming you."

They had to jog for five minutes or so until they reached the back door, but when they did – and crawled along to try and find a gap underneath – they found a stiff insulating seal that created a barrier impassable to cold draughts and nano-warriors alike.

"What we need is a friendly, seven-year-old girl," said Finn. "With a key. If only—"

Delta grabbed him.

"When we get out of this, I promise to whup your ass on *Black Ops, Halo, Gears of Wa—*"

"Keyhole!" shouted Finn, spotting its shape beneath the silver door handle. "What about the keyhole?" Then he caught the trail of something in his headlamp.

Silk.

Keeping steady, he traced the line of silk down from the door handle. Sure enough, descending fast at the other end of it was a spider about the size of a dog.

Delta froze.

"It's OK," said Finn, "it's a money spider. It's good luck."

"Oh yeah. Bite me."

Just before the spider reached the ground, Finn ran forward and grabbed it. It struggled hard, trying to draw itself back up the silk, but Finn fought to keep hold of it, while at the same time avoiding being nipped by its fangs.

"Get the hook!"

Delta took out the grappling hook and line. They secured it as best they could round the struggling critter, looping the line round its thorax and leaving eight wiry, kicking legs free.

"Let's see if it'll take the weight."

Without pause, the spider shot back up the silk like a bottle rocket, dragging the titanium line after it.

"Yes!" said Finn.

The spider slowed as it reached the door handle, the weight of the dangling line telling. Then it seemed to rest and take stock. Motionless.

"Go inside... Go inside..." muttered Delta.

Finn simply raised the M27.

DRRRRT!

The money spider fled straight through the keyhole.

Finn felt the line slip away through his fingers and realised he'd now have to pull it to engage the grappling hook and in all likelihood crush their saviour. Delta happily grabbed the line and hauled on it before he could stop her – *CRUNCH.*

She tested the weight. It held. She clipped a safety tether to the line.

"You want to go first?"

Finn took hold and started to haul himself up. It was like climbing the school gym ropes, but the energy/mass ratio worked hugely in his favour. He made rapid progress and was soon standing on the aluminium edge of the keyhole. He dropped the safety line back down to Delta, then felt the line go taut at his feet as she made her way up.

When Delta was safely up, they pulled in the line, and then, being careful not to fall into the depths of the lock mechanism, they made their way through the interior of the lock to the other side, passing the remains of the money spider on the way.

"Home sweet home..." said Finn. "Told you they were lucky."

TWENTY-EIGHT

"**N**ice place," said Delta.

For the first time in – how long? – Finn felt safe. Warm. Perched inside the keyhole they could take in most of the ground floor. These people had *pots* of money. The wobbly ancient outside walls were still in place, but much of the rest of the downstairs had been knocked through to create a huge kitchen and living space, freshly painted, with lots of groovy furniture and fittings (unlike at Grandma's, where there was lots of dog hair, Post-it notes and a serving hatch to the lounge).

Exactly like Grandma's though, there was a desk tucked in a corner with a computer and a wireless hub.

Bingo.

They abseiled down – Finn under careful instruction, Delta

retrieving the line – and in the subdued glow of dishwasher LEDs and cooker read-outs made rapid progress across the kitchen floor, the sounds of the lethal night garden replaced by the hum of the fridge.

Apart from the occasional aimless silverfish[23], the place was mercifully bug free.

They reached the desk and Finn led them behind the printer to a nest of cables that ran from overloaded sockets up to a hole in the desk above. The dust was thigh deep amid the twisted cables, great drifts of it, and there were fallen birthday cards, lost paperclips and huge coins that spoke of untold riches. There was also a landline phone socket. With nothing in it.

"I knew it," said Finn. "No Grandma. Or the phone's upstairs somewhere."

"Never mind. The data line is connected to the hub and the power is still on. Let's go."

The cables that hung from the desk were like jungle vines, and again an easy climb. They soon pulled themselves up on to the desk where a desktop computer lay finally at their mercy.

Finn started to wish he could see how Al was going to freak out when they got back in touch.

Delta surveyed the massive blank screen. "Let's power up." The switch was embedded in the top left-hand corner of the keyboard. Just a narrow rectangle, a nano-metre long, with an inbuilt LED that

---

[23] Lepisma saccharina, a small wingless insect in the order Thysanura.

would come on once the button had been depressed with a satisfying click.

If they could make it click.

They stamped, they levered, they jumped, they tried loading it with all the weight they could find and jumping on it. Fed up, Delta got out a pad and pencil and began some complex mathematics.

"What are you doing?" asked Finn.

"Blasting it," Delta said.

"Blasting it?"

"But we have to get the charge just right. If it takes 7 kilopascals of macro-pressure to depress this switch…" she muttered and scribbled, taking a pack of C-4 explosive[24] out of her pack to check the data.

"…and the detonation velocity is 8,092 metres per second…"

Finn wanted to check too, but she was using equations which made his brain hurt.

Eventually she decided on a golf-ball-sized lump with a cigarette-sized detonator poking out of the top.

"That oughta do it."

They took cover behind a stapler and she offered him the detonator remote. "You want to press it?"

"Of course I want to press it, I'm twelve."

"Three, two, one…"

Finn pressed.

BANG!

[24] Plasticised cyclotrimethylenetrinitramine.

Should have checked the maths, thought Finn.

Shattered fragments of brittle plastic skittered across the desk. The switch cover had been blown to smithereens. But it was followed by one of the sweetest sounds Finn had ever heard.

Beeeeeeeep.

DAY THREE 00:24 (BST). Siberia

In Siberia, Li Jun responded to an alert line on one of her screens.

013828234827 GU26 7BX #hwbdcuHHm777/Lanyard House, Coppice Lane

"We have another coming online. Not in the immediate search area."

She had diagnostic software running on every local web server, the mobile phone system and the emergency services network, trawling for any sign of unusual activity.

Kaparis was just enjoying breakfast, a foam his chefs had prepared of Monte Cristo caviar, coddled quails' eggs and Chambord champagne cocktail.

"Put it on the watch list."

"Yes, sir."

There had been alerts throughout the night as people had finished packing and gone online to send a hurried email or two.

Li Jun would have to report these communications to Kaparis, which

he loathed. Comforting banalities like "take care", "we'll pull through",
"I love you" made his skin, what little skin he could still feel, crawl.
She prayed this one would come to nothing.

"It's working!" Finn said gleefully, as he skidded across the touch pad in his socks, sending a pointer across a screen the size of a football pitch. He skidded it over to a search-engine icon.

"Now, jump! Double click!" said Delta. Finn hopped up and down. A window snapped open and offered them the Google home page.

"Yes! Yes!" Finn jumped off the touch pad and danced a brief jig. "What are we going to do, Skype?"

They looked miles up at the webcam in the top of the screen.

"Forget it, it's not even loaded on the machine."

"Then email? Facebook?"

"Facebook! Someone's bound to be checking our Facebook, and if not we can send an alert to all our followers."

"But who's going to be online this time of night?" asked Delta.

Finn looked at the kitchen clock; she was obviously more tired than he was and had forgotten the time difference.

"America."

They reached the Facebook page and laboriously signed into Delta's account. It took much longer than they thought as they found they had to jump together on each key to get a character to register. Once they got into their stride though, they managed to type out her address and password.

Finally, Finn jumped back to the touch pad and double hopped.

Up came Delta's page. She had exactly two friends. She offered no personal profile, but her photo was from her military ID and bore her real name.

"*Delphine* Salazar?" said Finn and raised an eyebrow at her.

"That was my birth name. I had issues with my birth mother. A colonel christened me Delta."

"You have two friends: do you have issues with Facebook too?"

"Why should I tell anybody my business?" said Delta defensively.

"Well, it might help right now..."

"I'm friends with Carla and the USAF."

"So are 1.1 million others! They're not going to notice your messag—"

But right then, unbelievably, someone starting posting – live.

"Look, someone is online now..."

A live chat picture popped up of Carla, a girl with kooky black hair and big brown eyes about Finn's age.

"Nooblet..." said Delta, stunned to see her.

"'Nooblet'?" said Finn.

They watched her message spool out live.

Hey Delts are you coming next weekend? Otherwise I have to go to Wilmington for extra rehearsals with the orchestra ☹ ☹ ☹ and I haven't practiced for like months

**because of SATs. I tried to call you BUT YOU'RE
ALWAYS ON VOICEMAIL!!!! I HATE VOICEMAIL!!!! YOU
KNOW!! OK, I'm over it. Call or message soon as I
NEED an excuse here. Btw have you heard of this
really old group called White Stripe?**

"What shall we say?

"Say it's *The White Stripes* otherwise she's just going to embarrass herself... NO! I was joking! Tell her to call the Pentagon right now!" Finn almost shrieked.

Together, over the next thirty minutes, Finn and Delta scrambled over the keys and typed out their message.

**C!!! REAL EMERGENCY! CALL DR AL ALLENBY UK
NOW +44 09776 778 87363 OR 911 PENTAGON OR UK
+44 999 WE ARE AT GU26 7BX COME AND GET, SAY
"SCARLATTI LOCATED, CREW ALIVE" NOW!**

They wondered if they should add 'do not nuke' too, but decided what they had written would be alarming enough (they were particularly pleased with the postcode which they'd found on an unpaid utility bill).

All they had to do was hit Send and it would go straight to Carla. If she was still online.

"Ready?"

"Ready."

They held on to each other and got ready to jump hard on the big Return key when they heard a clatter.

"What was that?"

They turned. They could hear no footsteps.

Finn looked over to where they'd dumped the M27 and most of their gear by the stapler. It wouldn't take a second to run over and pick it up if they needed to attract attention.

"Maybe it was just something falling over?" said Finn, but then Delta saw it over his shoulder. "Uh-oh…"

Finn spun round. A beautiful black and white cat, the size of a dozen elephants, long-haired and of infinite distinction, had silently hopped up on to the stool and was regarding the screen. Around its neck was a red collar emblazoned with its name: Zizou.

Despite such beauty, its black eyes were drawn instantly to the two tiny creatures on the keyboard.

"Easy, kitty… Easy now…" said Delta.

Trip. Trap. Play, thought the cat, exposing its dentistry.

"Hit it!" cried Delta. They scrambled for the Return key.

A soft paw swatted them experimentally, to see if they stung.

For Finn it was like being hit by a wall. They were sent flying off the keyboard.

Landing at its edge, they tried to roll under it as the cat snapped out its claws.

Showtime!

"Get in here!" yelled Delta, crawling under the keyboard, and dragging Finn after her. There was just enough clearance for them to scramble around on their bellies, but SWIPE came the cat's paw again, catching Finn's trailing foot, a tusk-like claw driving clean through the ankle of his jeans.

For a moment he was dragged back out, but Delta grabbed his arm and pulled.

Riiiiipp!

The bottom of his jeans was torn free and Finn was sent spinning back under the keyboard by a clip from the cat's follow-up paw.

"Get right under!" Delta said, bellying across the desk as *CRASH!* the whole keyboard above them shook, shifting and almost exposing Finn again.

C!!! REAL EMERGENCY! CALL DR AL ALLENBY UK NOW +44 09776 778 87363 OR 911 PENTAGON OR UK +44 999 WE ARE AT GU26 7BX COME AND GET, SAY "SCARLATTI LOCATED CREW ALIVE" NOWnjwefnl;"wfedwwsxxsxssssssf dfdc sjh54 1232sssxcxx\\\\\\\\\zz\2333ljkfewiufeiy889894ijaSASwwsb

Hsssssss! The frustrated cat pressed its face to the desk, its great whiskers poking at them as it tried to seek them out, paw trying to get the keyboard to move, but it was now wedged between the wall and the angled PC stand.

WHACK WHACK SCRATCH

"We need that 27," said Delta. It was at least a twenty-nano-metre dash across the desktop to the machine gun.

The pawing stopped as the cat took stock.

Finn and Delta crawled its way a little so they could see what it was doing. It seemed to be licking a paw.

"It's losing interest," said Finn.

Sure enough, a few moments later, they heard the soft *PALLUMP* of it jumping down. They crawled to the edge of the keyboard. Finn snuck out and moved tentatively towards the backpacks.

With a hiss, the great cat leapt up from its crouched position on the stool – not so dumb after all.

Finn sprinted for the gun. The first paw hit him five nano-metres short.

"HEY!" called Delta, base-sliding out from under the keyboard. "PICK ON SOMEONE YOUR OWN SIZE!"

The cat twitched – caught momentarily between the two. It was all Finn needed.

As the cat dived for Delta, Finn lunged forward and grabbed the M27, firing at its flank.

DRRRT! It was the last of the ammo, but it was enough.

YEOOOWWFSSJKSKSK!!!

The cat reeled like it'd been hit by a whip, skittered off the computer table and shot across the kitchen floor, hair expanding in every direction at once, hitting the cat flap in a puffball of panic.

As Finn recovered on the desktop, he turned and noticed the screen.

The cat must have hit Return when harassing them and posted. Below the post was a comment.

MESSAGE INTERCEPTED HOOK HALL.
PLEASE CONFIRM.

Finn began to laugh. He scrambled up, grabbed Delta and almost in delirium they managed to mount the keyboard and hit a capital Y.

After a brief pause, the message came back:

We are on our way.

King *Li Jun added, as a sign-off.*

"Is there a webcam?" asked Kaparis.

Li Jun rattled away at the keyboard and brought a live image of the kitchen up onscreen.

"Adjusting exposure."

She remotely zoomed the webcam out as far as she could, then scanned down to a grainy detail at the very bottom of the screen: two tiny people celebrating like fools.

"You're sure the message is contained?"

"The whole communication is isolated, protected and undetectable," reported Li Jun.

"Very good," said Kaparis.

Li Jun blushed fiercely.

TWENTY-NINE

At that very moment in the darkness over the Bay of Biscay, six members of the French maritime special forces – Le Commando Hubert – waited upside down to make their drop. They had been scrambled from Bordeaux-Mérignac airbase and briefed en route. Total prep time: seventeen minutes.

They left their transports at 20,000 feet (falling upside down out of open fast jet canopies) after a flight of only nineteen minutes.

They dropped into sea area FitzRoy, sixty kilometres north of La Coruña. They reached speeds of over 120mph. They would not deploy their specialist chutes until the last possible moment.

The tall guard with the scar took a call on the satellite phone.

He passed it to Stefan who connected it to his laptop.

The message came in the form of a data burst, the regular half-hourly call and response routine between the yacht and 'North Star'.

Cooper-Hastings stared at them from his chained position, on the floor at the back of the main cabin.

"I want to speak to her again. To make sure..."

Stefan twitched in annoyance. If he heard the pathetic plea again, he would cut out Cooper-Hastings' tongue. He closed the laptop and walked across the cabin to start beating the chained man again.

The tall guard, unable to watch the boy's casual brutality, took himself out on the bridge to smoke.

He hoped they would be allowed to kill the scientist soon, to dump his body at sea and then get into port. He was just wondering how – strangle? Shoot? – when he had the extraordinary sense that the sky was about to fall on his head. He looked up. The suddenly billowing parachute made the commando seem like an angel of death.

A tranquilliser dart hit the centre of his forehead.

Within nineteen seconds, all six commandos had landed, feather soft, onboard the moving motor yacht. An infra-red assessment during the descent had already established there were three more figures onboard, two in the main cabin, one in the sleeping quarters.

Two commandos entered via the rear hatch and detained the sleeping guard.

Three more entered the cabin where Stefan was still beating Cooper-Hastings.

Stefan was shot with a tranquilliser dart in the back of the head and fell immediately to the floor.

Cooper-Hastings looked on in astonishment at the black-clad figures.

Like something from a Parfum Pour Homme *advert, a commando took off his mask, shook out his tousled hair and checked a picture of Cooper-Hastings on a wrist-mounted data screen.*

"Docteur Coopeur-Hassteang, je suppose?"

Cooper-Hastings stammered, "I... I... Yes..."

"Bon."

Sitting in the Élysée Palace watching events unfold (alongside other world leaders via the Hook Hall feed), the French President did all he could to resist a patriotic cancan, quietly repeating: "*Bon.*"

Finn and Delta greedily ate a celebration meal out of the ration packs and waited, listening out for sirens and checking for further messages onscreen.

Finn looked at the picture of Carla again. She looked interesting, inquisitive. A more open version of her big sister, although even she was beginning to relax now the mission was nearly over.

"What's she like?"

"Nooblet? So cute she got adopted by the judge in the family court. Not any more though. Now she's more like you."

"Thanks."

"Maybe you should come visit when this is over? We have – they have – this cabin in the woods where we all go. You can go fishing, hiking, white-water rafting…"

"You want *me* to come? To America?"

Delta finished her rations and thought about it.

"Think of it as a mission."

"A mission?"

"She gets bored with me and the judge. Says she's bored."

"She sounds great."

"She really is. But she doesn't like gaming or combat. She's the one person, legally speaking, that I'm allowed to tell what I do. I don't think she even believes me."

"Shall I tell you something terrible that kids don't tell grown-ups?"

"What?"

"They're *really* not that interested in them. Especially not members of their own family – at least until they lose one."

Delta considered this. Made a serious mental note.

BANG…

"They're here!"

CRACK…

They were coming through the front door on the other side of the house.

"HERE! OVER HERE!" they called out excitedly.

Glass smashed and still they called.

It was only when they saw, in a gilded mirror, a boy in a hooded top struggling through the remains of the front door that they paused.

"No cars? No sirens? And who is *he*?" Finn said.

"I don't know," said Delta. "But I know the type."

So did Finn. He'd seen them in the playground. Avoided them at night.

"I've got a bad feeling here..." said Delta.

CLICK – suddenly light blinded them as the boy hit a switch. Finn and Delta fell back.

"RUN!" she shouted.

"They're escaping," snapped Kaparis into Kane's earphones. "Back of the desk. Stop them. Now."

Finn and Delta ran to the hole in the desktop and slid down the power cables.

The hooded youth padded carefully into the kitchen. Eyes fixed on the computer. Finn and Delta disappeared into the darkness and dust beneath.

"Where the hell are the cavalry?" muttered Delta. "He must be a looter; he's coming for the PC..."

"Cables – he's going to want the cables," said Finn.

They scrambled up on the skirting board, Delta leading, powering ahead, perfectly balanced and aware, vaulting obstacles – cables, lumps of Blu-tack – with speed and ease. Though physically awkward and spiky in life, she was balletic in combat. *West Pole*, thought Finn. A switch had flicked and Delta was back in the game.

Kane approached the desk, cautious, constantly checking his hand-held scanner, but there was too much heat coming off the PC and the plugs to get a clear fix.

Delta pelted along the top of the skirting board, dust flying, Finn right behind. A massive hand reached round to pull out the printer and shake up their world.

CLUNKCHHHHHHHHHHHHHHHH!

Dust bloomed and light washed in. An exposed centimetre of grey cable disappeared into the wall at the end of the skirting where the white plastic electrical trunking ran short. It was tight, but Delta dived in and wriggled through the gap, turning to haul Finn after her.

Together they fell into an empty, dark space. When they switched on their headlamps, they found themselves in a huge narrow void, all plasterboard, and pipework and wiring running this way and that. They were inside a partition wall, literally under the skin of the building.

"What's happening out there?" said Finn.

"Something bad," said Delta.

She grabbed her pack and checked its lethal contents. Two grenades and the rest of the plastic explosive.

"What have you got?"

"Just three flares," said Finn. "But they'll be here any minute, won't they?"

They could feel the boy's presence, close now on the other side of the wall, and then they heard a voice.

"*Got footprints. Got thermal.*"

"Uh-oh..." said Delta.

"What? Got... what?" said Finn, with barely time to puzzle the words, before –

"Up!" Delta screamed as – *SLAM* – a massive finger crashed its way through the hole after them and started to rip at the plasterboard.

She grabbed a dangling grey cable and started to climb, Finn grabbing the one next to it, a heartbeat behind.

"Climb!"

The giant hand tore at the board below them.

You're Tarzan, Finn told himself as he pulled himself up the cable. *You're Tarzan, climbing a vine... Don't let go.*

Kane uncoiled half a metre of fibre-optic cable, screwed it into the end of his phone and poked its glowing head through the plasterboard. Twisting it, he caught an image of the two tiny figures clambering up the wires.

SLAM! A fist clattered against the plasterboard right beside Finn, releasing a shower of dust as he school-gymed it up the cable.

"Faster!" said Delta. Finn needed no urging.

SLAM SLAM SLAM! Like huge explosions.

Kane wasn't going to break through the plaster with his fists. He looked round the kitchen for something to use. Spotted a meat cleaver.

Delta and Finn were only a few nano-metres from the wood of the ceiling joists when – *SMASH!*

263

Finn was deafened and rocked as the leading edge of the cleaver smashed through the plaster beside him, like the prow of a ship through pack ice. He swung on the cables and choked on the dust.

SMASH! A second blow carved an open wound in the wall, quickly filled with the blinding light of the fibre-optic camera. Finn instinctively kicked at it as he swung.

"Yes…" said Kane, pulling out the camera to see for himself.

Finn saw Kane's massive eye now fill the hole. A dead, speckled eye… An eye that made him think of – *Spiro?*

Delta was descending now, biting the pin out of a grenade and releasing the catch. Five… four… three…

"Noob! Get out of the way!"

Delta dropped upside down from her cable and pitched the grenade at the giant eye – just like she'd been pitching baseballs since the age of three. The explosive fastball beat Kane's blink reflex by a whisker, getting caught behind the tear duct of the lower lid just as it went off – *BANG!*

"ARRRRRRRRGHGHHH!"

"Go!" Delta scrambled back up her cable, Finn still making his way up. As he reached the ceiling joists, he felt Delta's hands grab him and pull him over.

"AARRRRRRRRRGGHH!"

Kane reeled through the kitchen, clutching his stinging eye. Although no catastrophic damage had been done – the nano-blast could only impact in the way a sharp jab from the point of a compass might – it did have the power to hurt like all hell.

Delta and Finn scrambled over a large beam and dropped into centuries-old dirt somewhere beneath the first floor. They found themselves in a dark tunnel that ran the width of the house, its sides ancient oak floor joists, its roof equally ancient floorboards, the tunnel blocked by patches of brick at either end.

"Go!" said Delta, not letting Finn recover.

They scrambled through the knee-high soot and dirt between the oak joists.

"Arrrrrrrrrrrrrrrrrrrrrgghghh!" They could still hear Kane's anger shake the world below.

"He has Spiro's eyes!" Finn called as he caught Delta up.

"What?"

"Spiro, who tried to blow us up! This guy has the exact same markings…"

Delta slowed. "What do you mean markings?"

"They're speckled, like a pattern, like a tattoo or something, but you can only see it up close. Either they're evil twins or… Maybe it's the mark of whoever set this thing rolling, or…" said Finn, trying to make sense of something so strange.

Delta was way ahead.

"If he's working with whoever Spiro was working with then they know where the Scarlatti was released, and they were monitoring it…" said Delta.

"So they saw us attack?" said Finn.

"And they'd know we have to be close by. All they needed

to do was watch the local telecoms net…"

It was making horrible sense. Footfalls above replaced the racket from below as Kane switched his search.

"We're screwed," concluded Delta. "Go."

She started to run through the drifts of dirt again and Finn had to force himself to keep up.

"Where are we going?"

"He said 'got thermal' down there. If he's got a FLIR night sight – thermal image sight – then he can see through anything," said Delta.

RIIIIIIIIIIIIIIIIIP!!

"Is he pulling up the carpets?" said Finn.

"He can't pull the whole place apart," said Delta.

Above them, crazed by the pain in his weeping, stinging, bleeding eye, Kane roared and tore at the flooring, ripping through carpets and underlay. Raising hell.

When he was through to the wood, he started hacking away at the first floorboard he could.

Delta grabbed Finn and pulled him beneath a copper pipe that ran the length of the joist. She reached up and slapped it. It was warm. Thermal cover.

"What do we do?" asked Finn. "If they intercepted the message then no one's coming."

"We know nothing for sure," said Delta. "We've just got to sit tight."

They crouched beneath the hot pipe and waited. It was going to be a long night.

And with every fraction of a second that passed, Finn felt more and more certain.

"They're not coming. No one knows we're here."

THIRTY

Dr Cooper-Hastings, a dedicated, if highly strung scientist, had a single passion – opera. He had been to see one production at the Royal Opera House three times. The production featured the Russian soprano Olga Tieneto, of whom he was a particular fan.

After responding to criticism of her on an online opera fansite (as Cutmeibleedverdi72), Cooper-Hastings had been astonished to receive a message from *Olga herself*, thanking him for springing to her defence. A correspondence developed. Daily emails became phone calls that lasted hours. She poured her heart out. He fell in love. She was locked in a struggle with her Italian ex-husband over custody of her son. Cooper-Hastings took the boy out of his boarding school to attend a steam fair one weekend to save him from a paternal visit. He was a sullen, aggressive teen with strange, speckled eyes who seemed to know little about opera.

Cooper-Hastings lost the boy on the way home outside Aylesbury Aquatics. A car had pulled up and he was snatched. There was violence, then tearful calls from Olga begging him to do exactly what her husband said. The mafia were involved. Her life was in danger.

Hypnotised by terror – convinced the life of a child and the woman he loved were on the line – Cooper-Hastings went along with whatever the Italians demanded. When he almost faltered at the Scarlatti request, they played him Olga's 'Ebben? Ne Andrò Lontana' and he fell under her spell again.

One phone call to the real Olga Tieneto from the head of the Russian security service, the FSB[25], confirmed she had absolutely no idea who Cooper-Hastings was. The whole thing had been an elaborate set-up, no doubt concocted with the help of detailed observations of Cooper-Hastings' habits and character from his junior colleague – Dr Spiro.

All regarded Cooper-Hastings as a gargantuan fool... all save the suave men and women of Le Commando Hubert, who smoked and drank and listened intently, fully au fait with '*les maladies d'amour*'.

DAY THREE 03:37 (BST). Hook Hall, Surrey

"You touch Fatty and I swear, I swear I will kill you..."

---

[25] Trans. ФСБ, Федеральная служба безопасности Российской Федерации.

With these words, two hours and forty-six minutes after the rescue of Cooper-Hastings, Al had to remove himself from the command area at the centre of the control gallery and make his way over to where the RAF controllers were coordinating the sweep for the lost nano-crew. The repetitive, overlapping call signs were a poetry of sorts. A comfort.

"Come in, Messi, come in, Messi? This is Ronaldo, repeat, this is Ronaldo, over."

"Come in, Messi, come in, Messi? This is Ronaldo, repeat, this is Ronaldo, over."

Al needed to calm down. He feared death at the hands of his mother. He wanted to throttle Dr Cooper-Hastings. And he badly wanted to kill Commander King.

Firstly, news had come through that Grandma had somehow disappeared from her cruise ship and was en route from Oslo. He could sense her closing in and felt ten years old again. As children, he and Maria had once burnt down her favourite gazebo test-firing a rocket, then had to wait hours for her to come home from a sponsored walk. That had been bad enough. How on earth was he going to explain this?

Secondly, after all the effort and risk of life, after all the waiting and hoping, the Cooper-Hastings trail had died at sea, literally. After being revived, and following a brief period of interrogation, the blond German teenager 'Stefan' – the apparent leader – had suffered a sudden and fatal brain haemorrhage.[26] The guards onboard were

---

[26] A post-mortem revealed a tiny compressed air vessel planted in his brain that had been set off via sensors on his scalp. All he needed to do to end his life was scratch his head.

mercenaries hired for a single task. They knew about the irregular satphone calls to Stefan from persons unknown, but little of the security routine linked to the laptop.

Despite much fevered activity since, the whole G&T operation appeared to be getting nowhere. The rescue of Cooper-Hastings had stalled. The public evacuation had turned into a panic. And they were eating up, chewing through, time.

Then Commander King made things a whole lot worse. He had checked his watch. He had glanced round the global feeds. And he had made a decision.

"We have to get the Fat Doughnut to Felixstowe by 6am. Dismantle the Large Accelerator."

It had felt like surrender. Technicians down on the floor of the CFAC had looked at one another at first, unsure of what to do. One or two craned their heads to see if Al was present and at least aware of the order.

"I repeat," said King as Al walked in, "dismantle the Large Accelerator."

Al found he was still shaking with rage as, out of the corner of his eye, he saw King walk the entire length of the gallery to join him.

King stopped beside Al, checked his watch and, pretending to take in the view, spoke quietly so that no one else could hear them.

"I know what you're thinking."

"Believe me, you have absolutely no idea; you weren't there when we blew up the gazebo."

"You know full well at this point in time there is absolutely no other choice. Look around you at the global feeds. Presidents have been replaced by Generals who have been replaced by mere advisors. Power and influence are draining from the room and, if we are not seen to act, control of the operation will slip away. I need you at my side and I need you active and angry. What's more – they need to see it."

"Angry? You have *no idea...*"

"Good. You're only really effective when you're angry, have you noticed that?"

"You stuck-up, upper-class bloody wizard on a stick!" Al began to hiss back when –

"Sir! Dr Allenby!"

They realised an assistant had been shouting at them across the gallery for some time.

"The satphone on the yacht, sir! It's ringing!"

The bubble burst. "Halt all work on the accelerator!" ordered King.

He and Al raced back to the command area, listening to the satphone ring over the audio feed.

They retook their positions at the centre of the control gallery at 03:46 (BST) and ordered the satphone onboard the motor yacht in the Bay of Biscay be answered.

Onboard, the lead commando received the order, and attached the handset to Stefan's laptop. "*Trois. Deux. Un,*" he said, and picked up.

Li Jun jumped.

The alarm sounded shrill and hard. It was sunrise in Siberia, and for a moment she thought she was in the barracks asleep.

She snapped out of it. She had been given fresh blood and stimulants to maintain focus and they had made her edgy. She must fight to maintain self-control at all costs. She felt her fingers twitch as she zeroed in.

In his lair, Kaparis was tackling the championship downhill at Zermatt, his entire screen array devoted to the virtual reality experience as he shot down the piste, life-support apparatus bouncing on hydraulic rockers to mimic the sensation of movement and drag while he breathed an infusion of pine needles and powdered snow.

"Sir, we have a 109 breach of the Atlantic," Li Jun broke in.

Kaparis blinked and instantly the ski scene evaporated.

"Stefan and the yacht have been fatally compromised," reported Li Jun.

"Oh dear," Kaparis said, as his regular screen array refreshed. "Do you have an indication of what might have happened?"

"Not yet. But the response code has been poorly copied and Stefan's chip did not register."

"System integrity?"

"Secure. They will only be able to trace the last leg of the signal route."

The last leg of the signal route ran through various Russian companies and trusts used by Li Jun as a front and forming only the very outermost shell of her fiendishly complex cyber-security set-up.

"There is no chance of them tracing it back to here then?"

"None whatsoever."

"Good. I would hate our lives to depend on it."

"Of course, Master."

Kaparis flicked his gaze towards screens showing radar and traffic activity in the area of Hook Hall. Nothing seemed to be moving with any urgency, and it was nearly 4am.

"What a pity. They're not confining themselves to the task in hand," he remarked to Heywood.

His eyes went to the live feed from the house. Still Kane laboured. But Kaparis was confident he would succeed. Indeed, from the operation so far had come a rather delightful image of the boy Drake looking rather uncouth... The fight in the boy's eyes really was something special.

He shouldn't. He really shouldn't. But...

"Would it be amusing at some point, do you think, to drop them a little reminder?"

"...These apparently false directorships are in turn all allied to an organisation called Quadrock Investments, registered in Hong Kong."

Al paced. He was out of his depth in the world of corporate and financial subterfuge, but felt that if he kept pacing up and down like a caged tiger he could at least add a sense of purpose and momentum.

The commandos had tried to patch the satphone call into the laptop, but it had cut immediately – some digital response error must have been detected – but seconds later technicians reported that enough signal had been exchanged during the short connection for the call to be traced back as far as the telecoms account of a ghost company in Russia.

King got straight on to the FSB and Spetsnaz[27] Command in Moscow. Now they were up and running again. Onscreen, advisors were being replaced around the world by hurriedly woken Generals and Presidents.

All eyes were currently glued to a pair of forensic accountants, one from MI6 in the CFAC, Sonia, and one onscreen from the FSB in Moscow, Yuri. The lead from the yacht to the Russian front company had generated a blizzard of corporate intelligence and it was their job, together with some whiz-bang software, to pick a clear trail through it all as document after document flashed by onscreen. Nobody else could understand a word they were saying.

"…Wheelie trusts then channel back through the Macau-Lisbon exchanges…" said Sonia.

"…to Section 14 Luxemburgski clearing houses…" said Yuri, "which in turn own a third basket of legitimate companies…"

"…that all lead back again to Russia and the Novoskodorv network?"

"Yes, Novoskodorv, but in pool trusts."

"Oh dear," said Sonia.

"Problem?" said King.

---

27 Russian special forces.

"Very dark forest… May take many, many days to go through," said Yuri.

"What is he saying?" asked the US President.

"Basically, a system of ownership by multiple defunct companies not yet digitally re-registered. A paper-only kaleidoscope of ownership preferred by international criminal gangs, because, by the time you've traced each share to source, they're long gone," said Sonia.

"Time frame?"

"About a month."

"Great."

"Aha! Criminal gangs and one very, very shy investor!" said Yuri, suddenly excited, calling up a photocopy of a document with three signatures on it, then finding the same three again, and again on several more.

"Ah!" cried Sonia.

"The three stoogski!" said Yuri.

"The three stooges," explained Sonia. "Three false identities associated with one very private man – someone we all want to know a lot more about, the reclusive David Anthony Pytor Kaparis."

Sonia hit Return and a formal picture of young, able-bodied 'Dr D.A.P. Kaparis' flashed up onscreen. A tall, superior, almost perfectly chiselled young man.

Commander King felt himself draw closer to his enemy.

Al stopped pacing and his jaw dropped. "Stop!"

He couldn't quite believe it. He put on his glasses to take a closer look, to try and remember.

"I think… I think…" said Al.

"You know him?" asked King.

"I think my brother-in-law may have had something to do with this."

"Your brother-in-law?"

Thousands of miles away, Li Jun hit Return and threw a cyber curve ball west across the great Eurasian landmass at the speed of light.

…an attack so complex, ferocious and overwhelming that it not only blitzed the Hook Hall digital defences, but also caused a power surge that blew out the picture of the young D.A.P. Kaparis and sent sparks flying through the control gallery.

There were shouts and minor panic.

In Siberia, a direct AV feed blinked up on Kaparis's array from inside the CFAC – the same one the world leaders enjoyed of Al, King and co. It wouldn't last long. The Hook Hall defence system would soon repel such an open assault. But a few moments were enough.

Kaparis cut through the hubbub.

"Good morning, Dr Allenby. Good morning, Commander King."

THIRTY-ONE

The last Oslo to London flight, severely delayed because of the emergency, had seen Violet Allenby land at a deserted Heathrow Airport at 04:02 hours.

She had managed to get a short flight from Trondheim to Oslo, then, knitting and chatting the whole way, the connecting flight to London. As a result, two Australians would be coming to stay in June (an architecture student and a nurse, both charming) and she had promised a young 'science major' (shy) from Des Moines, Iowa, an internship at Al's lab. She'd also completed a three-colour sweater panel and slept for two hours.

Altogether she was relatively bright-eyed and well-rested for her homecoming and was appalled to find the airport in chaos and about to close due to an 'Evacuation Panic'.

"What on earth are you talking about?" she'd asked a flustered customs official.

"We have to clear out by dawn, because of the gas cloud."

"What 'gas cloud'?" she'd demanded, suspicions rising.

After explaining what had happened, staff asked if she had a way to get home, as many transport unions had refused to let their members travel anywhere near the restricted zone. When they learned she lived *inside* the zone, they advised her to run for her life.

"Nonsense," she had said, switching on her phone to harangue Al's voicemail for the umpteenth time.

"Just point me in the direction of whoever is in charge."

DAY THREE 04:05 (BST). Hook Hall, Surrey

The command gallery fell silent as Kaparis's weird, disembodied voice floated around the room, punctuated by the hum and hiss of the iron lung drawing air into his broken body.

"*As it seems you've shot my messenger, I thought it just as well I get in touch directly... I presume you are both still in post?*"

"It's him..." said Al. "It's always the quiet ones you have to look out for."

King thought, *Keep him talking* – the longer the line was open, the more chance there was of tracing something.

"Good morning... Dr Kaparis?" King said.

"*How clever! However did you discover my name?*" said Kaparis, pleased they'd made an effort.

"International ways and means. You have succeeded in uniting the world," King went on and stood over Sonia to take in the notes on her screen.

"David Anthony Pytor Kaparis. You were born Paris 1965. Left Cambridge University following a breakdown 1990. Zurich in financial services for a decade, specialising in new and ever more complex financial products. Circa 2000 you were paralysed – possibly as the result of a drugs overdose. You then disappeared without trace, around 10 billion dollars disappearing with you. It's rumoured you rigged the market in toxic US mortgage bonds in the noughties, cashing out at the peak and making yourself the world's first trillionaire."

"*I was crippled as a result of gross medical negligence. Please amend you records,*" Kaparis hissed.

"Of course. And do please tell us, Dr Kaparis, what is it exactly that you want?"

Kaparis realised his pulse rate had climbed, so took a moment.

"*I am hoping, Commander King, to improve the human condition, for which I require certain technologies. I have tried assassination, famine, financial chaos, but have experienced only diminishing returns – and everything takes so long.*"

"And for this you have to threaten Armageddon?"

"*Me? Remember, you are the ones who created the Scarlatti, this monster;*"

I'm just putting it to good use. It could be one of hundreds of vile organisms or nerve agents locked away in your collective vaults. You so-called Great Powers hold a gun to our heads every day."

"If allowed to flourish, it will kill billions. Can you really say it is safely under your control? You are forcing a nuclear response. If you do not give us the location of the nest site, the only way to ensure those nymphs don't hatch will be to scorch the earth and leave a blight upon it for generations to come."

"Only Surrey," Kaparis protested. *"A few garden centres and some mock-Tudor villas."*

"Half a million lives displaced and homes destroyed."

"More if you stretch the blast area as far as Bracknell."

King remained unamused.

"You must know you will never be allowed to get away with this."

"You misunderstand. I don't need anybody to allow anything," Kaparis explained. *"I am a higher form of being than you, just as you are a higher form of being than those who serve you. Look around you. You are better than them."*

"That's it!" said Al, who had been wracking his brains trying to remember the details, delighted to have got there, taking centre stage and wagging his finger up at the camera.

"I remember now! You had some mediocre theory about a master race and went loco! Am I right?" said Al, as if recalling someone who'd come third in an egg-and-spoon race.

Heywood saw Kaparis's heart rate leap off the scale at the word 'mediocre'.

"Some master race struggle for dominance, wasn't it?"

"*Race had nothing whatsoever to do with it!*"

"Supermen? Or super-duper people or something? And you got the statistics mixed up and were proved wrong by my brother-in-law, Ethan Drake. I was only a kid really, the details are kind of hazy," Al said, playing to the gallery, "but didn't you stalk him for a while and they had to call the police because you turned up on Christmas Day? Didn't they get some kind of court order against you? Maybe you were a little bit in love with Maria too? I think that was—"

"*I'll show you about the struggle for life!*" Kaparis snapped.

He ripped the still image of Finn from his array and cast it across cyberspace so that the image briefly appeared on every screen at the CFAC – Finn's face as he hung on the cable in the wall. Bleached by the white light. Defiant. And seeming to aim a kick towards the camera.

Jaws dropped.

Al's heart leapt, and was alarmed at the same time – Finn. Alive. Fighting?

"*And while I'd love to stay and chat...*" said Kaparis, trying to keep his voice steady and fighting a losing battle with lung capacity, "*... I just popped in to leave you a little reminder.*"

The CFAC feed on the Kaparis array was flickering out as the Hook Hall cyber-defence system started to reboot and fight back. At her keyboards, Li Jun fought to retain it.

"*We have the dear boy, as you can see. We have the Scarlattis too. If you want the location of either, I want the Fat Doughnut on that ship and under way at dawn, and the sequencing codes from Dr Allenby. Once I have them, you may have the location of the Scarlattis' nest site, and the unfortunate Infinity Drake.*

"*The first of the Scarlatti nymphs are reaching maturity now and, with the help of the morning sun, they should soon be ready for their final moult. They will then fly the nest and wreak havoc upon the world. Time is short, so don't waste any more of it trying to find me – you never will. And Allenby? If you want any chance of seeing your nephew again, I will have those sequencing codes... It would be a pity to unpack such a toy and not have the correct instructions.*"

Li Jun indicated she was about to lose contact.

"*Sweet dreams, Dr Allenby.*"

The gallery was in blackout for a few moments after the link to Kaparis was cut and the cyber-attack repelled. There were shouts. Slowly, screens blinked back to life.

Al slumped into a seat and stared. The picture of Finn remained onscreen.

"Could it be a fake?" King asked a technician. "They must have hours of CCTV of him from here."

But Al read the fight in Finn's eyes. He'd seen it before in the days after his mother had died.

"No. That's for real."

"What's your strategy now, Allenby?" General Jackman asked Al from the US.

Al didn't take his eyes off Finn.

"We cannot give that man anything. He's mad. He's powerful and irrational and quite mad."

"We have no choice. Give him the rig, then we'll go after him," said General Mount beside them in the gallery.

"How's he ever going to be able to pick it off that cargo ship? Let him have it, we'll follow then – boom – hit him hard," agreed General Jackman from the US.

King could see Al was barely listening and stepped in with his own analysis.

"Nothing Kaparis said detracted from the credibility of his threat. He's convinced, he's capable and he's a control freak. He'll be three steps ahead of anything we anticipate. But at some point, to pull this off, he has to take a risk. Until then... we play along and buy as much time as we can."

"He owns time right now," said the US President.

"What is he going to gain from the technology? A few little teeny people?" asked the French Conseiller Scientifique.

Al spoke up again. "Whatever he wants this technology for, it will be far, far worse than anything we can imagine. I tell you he's mad... You open Pandora's box – *you people made me open the damn box* – and this is what happens."

Al stood up. Action. *Just keep going.*

"They're alive. We find them before it's too late. That's all that matters."

"How, Herr Doktor?" demanded the German Chancellor. "The only way is if he gifts them to you. *Nein?* And to gift them to you he needs the Boldklub Doughnut and the codes."

Her English might lack finesse, but nothing could fault her logic. "Unless you have yet another Scarlatti hidden somewhere to smell out the others you have scattered about the place?" said the French Conseiller Scientifique sarcastically.

"There are no more Scarlattis," answered King, and added grimly, "yet."

A spark fired in Al's mind. A tiny spark, but a spark nonetheless. He fell into a trance as he tried to work through the possibilities... smell...

"No, not another Scarlatti," Al started, "but quantum vibration – if that's the basis of the sense of smell – then all we'd need was... although..."

King looked at him quizzically. And Al realised if he carried on thinking out loud people would start to think he'd gone crazy. *I've got to get out of here*, he thought.

Meanwhile the US President leant forward. "I want to make one thing absolutely clear. You can make whatever play you like. But if we run over that deadline and you don't act? We can't stand by and watch the world get wiped out. With regret, we will nuke you ourselves."

"*Oui*," agreed the French President. "The situation is impossible."

Wise heads nodded one by one by one around the world.

"Allenby, we need those codes," said the Prime Minister.

"I think I'll hold on to them a little longer if you don't mind," said Al, now looking round for an exit.

"Commander King?" said the Prime Minister, demanding some kind of public assurance.

King felt like he was trapped in a game of chess played against three powerful opponents: one quite mad, one a truculent genius and one a ticking bomb. Who knows what he might have done, had not a message buzzed in his ear. An urgent message from security at the main gate.

He made a snap decision. The best idea he'd had all night.

"Arrest Dr Allenby."

THIRTY-TWO

Kane squinted through his one good eye, like a cyclops.

He examined the lens of the glowing fibre-optic camera worm, and wiped a thumb over it, to remove the dirt as he did between each run, then fed it under the filthy boards again, scouring the joist gap with the all-seeing snake. Nothing. He picked up the thermal camera again and for the umpteenth time scanned the floor.

It had indeed been a long night and all around him the top floor of the house lay in chaos. He had lifted more than forty floorboards, ripping up carpets and crashing aside furniture and any other obstacle that stood in his way.

He knew they'd been hiding under the network of radiator pipes, disguised by the latent heat, but two hours – maybe more? – had passed now and the glow of the pipes had all but faded. He'd almost caught them twice already, but each time they'd managed to slip away into parallel joist gaps through old bore holes for pipes and wiring, and he'd been unable to shift furniture and associated junk fast enough to lift the next board along and so trap them.

So he'd changed tack and become systematic. He'd started lifting every third floorboard – checking the gaps between with the two cameras – moving systematically across the floor towards the end wall. And he was getting close now. He'd caught a flicker of a heat signature twice already and he knew he was driving them into his trap.

Beneath the floorboards, Delta waited with the bomb.

She and Finn had sweated and laboured for what felt like an age and were now covered in ancient soot and dirt from head to foot, their headlamps completing their coalminer look. They had run from the cover of one pipe to another to stay one step ahead in their bizarre game of Battleships with Kane, crouching and hiding a few minutes at a time, sometimes drifting into hope that he might stop or give up, before another long floorboard was wrenched up and the nightmare of chase and entrapment began again.

As the minutes, then the tens of minutes, then the hours wore on – it was hard to judge time in this exhausted state, in this black and filthy place – they realised the heating pipes would soon offer no cover at all.

Delta knew they were being driven towards the wall. The endgame was in sight. The situation was hopeless.

Finn knew it too.

"He's trying to trap us against the wall. We've got to take him out or we've got nowhere left to go," said Delta.

"How?"

"Got to take out that last eye."

So she'd taken the remaining C-4 plastic explosive out of the pack and moulded it into the size of a grapefruit. "Get grit, dirt, anything and work it in."

They scrabbled around in the soot for small pieces of stone, copper filings, anything that would act as shrapnel, and worked it into the explosive dough.

The blast would be small at macro level, only about as powerful as a firework, but still capable of serious damage. Delta's first thought was to try and make some kind of cannon to fire a projectile at the remaining eye, but the chances of being able to aim it with any accuracy were slim indeed. So she fell back on something much cruder. Make a dirt bomb and get it somewhere near his face, and when – however temporarily – he was blinded, make a run for it.

But how to get it near? He was on his feet most of the time and 150 times their size.

She had one plan and one plan only.

She set Finn running.

Straight down between the joists in the wide open spaces with no thermal cover at all.

* * *

Kane could hardly believe it. There was a heat signature clear as a bell.

He lined up his fibre-optic worm and shot it under the floorboards after the runner. There was the boy. Plain as day. As the camera worm caught up with him, he hopped across to the right-hand joist and dived through an ancient drill hole.

Quick as a flash, Kane jumped to where Finn had just been, hacked his hammer and meat cleaver into the floorboard and...

CRRRRRRRRRAAAAAAAAAAAAAAAAAAACK!

...prised it up.

But where he'd expected to see a nano-boy running – nothing. Where had he gone? Towards the wall? Back beneath him? He spun and pulled out the fibre-optic worm to search again, not bothering to glance at his phone screen as he did so.

As the worm shot past her, Delta jumped out of her hiding place and pitched the sticky bomb they'd made straight on to the end of the lens, having seen how he brought it up to his face to clean each time. *SPLAT.*

In Siberia, watching live via his array at a 0.44-second delay, Kaparis saw the fibre-optic camera feed black out as the bomb splatted against the lens.

"END OF LENS!" he snapped.

His message took 0.44 seconds to bounce back across Europe.

...and it took 0.88 seconds for Kane to pull out the end of the fibre-optic worm, glance down with his good eye, ready to bring his thumb across the lens, then hear Kaparis's warning... in the very same moment that Delta beneath the boards hit the detonator.

BANG!

Kane's head snapped back and he was knocked – as much in shock and reflex as by the blast – flat on his back across the floor.

His ears rang. His skin burnt. His hands shook... but he had closed his eyes and turned his face away in the 0.06 seconds available to him. The very nick of time. Kane cursed and shot straight back to the joist.

Realising she'd blown their last chance, Delta dived through the hole in the joist where Finn was hidden and screamed, "GO!"

DAY THREE 04:43 (BST). Hook Hall, Surrey

"Why you superior... perfidious... mendacious..."

Al kicked and screamed and fought like a tiger as he was dragged out.

"Seize the codes. Dismantle the Large Accelerator," King had ordered.

The Security Service guards were far bigger than him, picking him up like a rag doll and easily robbing him of the small blue memory stick containing the sequencing codes from his jacket pocket.

"I've had an idea! I've had another idea, you fools!" he shouted. But no one listened.

It felt a huge relief at last to physically struggle. To fight. To hit and be hit. It was (weren't men idiots?) fun, despite it all. He felt like he could fight and fight. He would fight to the end. He would find him. He would find Finn.

CLUNK. The cell door closed in the security block at the back of Hook Hall.

Al sat on his bunk. He thought of Finn. He held on to the lump of spharelite around his neck and scratched it.

Was this what the end of the world felt like?

King walked in.

"You!" Al snapped.

King pulled up a plastic seat opposite Al and studied him through the bars.

"I could get used to this," said King.

"Get on with it," said Al.

"Someone always has to look after you, don't they? Can't or won't hold down a job, can't or won't commit to anybody or anything, always waking up with a hangover and a desire to tinker with something new. Restless and irresponsible."

"Hey! Some of us need to get more out of life than a chauffeur-driven car and a civil-service pension!"

"If you must know, I meet the cost of my car and driver from my private income. Both have been with the family for years."

"This country needs a revolution."

"I had to establish that I was credible and still capable of controlling the mission. And I had to get you out of the way of your mother."

"My mother?"

"She's at the main gate."

Al swallowed a lump of emotion.

"You better get me out of here. I've got an idea. I'm going to find Finn."

"How?" said King.

"It's so stupid I don't want to say. I just know I've got to try, otherwise I'll go crazy and my heart will break and the world may as well end. I can't lose another..."

King wondered what that meant, but didn't press him.

"You have to satisfy yourself that you have done everything you possibly can to look for him," stated King.

"That's right."

"Will you need anything?"

"Six hours."

"I'll give you three."

Al couldn't quite believe it.

"But you have to give me the sequencing codes."

"Your goons took them already."

"I imagine there's at least one piece missing from that particular jigsaw."

Al smiled. You had to hand it to King, you couldn't kid a kidder.

"I don't think the Fat Doughnut rig matters, it's the codes he wants," said King.

"True. You could get most of the parts off eBay; it might take a year or so, but you could put something together," agreed Al.

"You know that, and I know that," said King, "but the trouble is I think he knows that too. It's why he chose to send the picture of the boy as extra leverage against you. I think that much we've just learned."

Al scraped at the spharelite again to make it glow. Studied it a moment.

"You know what I have learned?" said Al. "As soon as you create something special, it becomes corrupted. As soon as someone sees it, it's out of your control, you're done for. If we hand these codes over to that madman? One burnt county might seem like a walk in the park. Why do we ever allow ourselves to think these things? Nuclear weapons, biological weapons, codes – why can't we just leave the genie in the bottle? Why?"

"I have no answer. I am not God."

"But you are the King."

"And I have to try and remain in control. You can go off on whatever wild goose chase you want. But I have to have those codes."

Al had to admit that he loved the way King's mind worked.

Three minutes later, King was smuggling Al out of the rear gate. The De Tomaso Mangusta had been brought down. World leaders, senior staff and Grandma – who had now barked her way through as far as the Security Chief's office – were clueless.

Al climbed in, felt the seat cup round him and smelt the leather. He turned the key and started the engine. He closed his eyes for a moment. Home.

King took out a scrap of paper and a pen.

"Codes."

Al explained. "I hold the key equation as a mnemonic, in a snatch of poetry. Come here."

King was obliged to bend his head down to Al, as he whispered:

"But at my back I always hear
Time's wingèd chariot hurrying near,
And yonder all before us lie
Deserts of vast eternity—
where B is acceleration and E opens and closes brackets,
and where all other vowels are disregarded."

King gave him both eyebrows.

"It's Andrew Marvell. Except the last bit."

"I know who it is."

"Trust me, it's in there. Just find yourself a couple of cryptanalysts with a romantic bent and you've got it. I promise."

Al gunned the engine and offered King his hand. King shook it. Al put his foot down.

The beast roared.

PART
FOUR

PART
FOUR

THIRTY-THREE

CRRRRRRRRAAAAAAAAAAAAAAAAAACK!

Light was appearing everywhere now. They were still being driven towards the wall, but Kane was pulling up every board and drawing out the process.

Delta couldn't figure out why, until she noticed that, not only had he abandoned his splat-bombed fibre-optic worm, he'd stopped pausing to use his thermal camera too. The blast may not have taken out Kane's good eye, but it looked like he'd fallen back and smashed the camera in the process and now had to rely on brute strength and logic alone.

CRRRRRRRRRAAAAAAAAAAAAAAAAAAACK!

299

"Run!" said Delta.

"Running!" replied Finn.

DAY THREE 05:24 (BST). Siberia

With the pictures from the fibre-optic worm gone, Kaparis had to make do with a cloudy feed from the integrated camera on Kane's phone, and the floorboard sound effects. The rest he filled in himself with stock images of revenge from his blood-curdling imagination.

Heywood had prepared a bottle of Krug '95 and cued up the Haydn Trumpet Concerto in E flat major to try and calm him down after the unfortunate exchange with Dr Allenby. But with resentment and rage and sour memories still riddling through him, Kaparis could only feel one thing.

Kill Kill Kill…

CRRRRRRRRRAAAAAAAAAAAAAAAAAACK!

Another board splintered up above them. They were running at the wall now. There was no way forward. It was a dead end. Or so they thought. But, when they reached the wall, they noticed – just under where one of the joists had been trimmed to fit the wall – a shadow in the brickwork. A gap?

CRRRRRRRRRAAAAAAAAAAAAAAAAAAACK!

They had no choice. The last board was up. For a split second the demon stood over them. Kane in all his myopic glory.

Delta shoved Finn down into the gap and dived in after him.

A heel the size of a house came at the wall – STAMP!

The collapse of old masonry caught Delta's trailing leg – "Arrgh!" – as she struggled and just made it through.

Finn pulled Delta through into the darkness after him. She was in pain. They were trapped inside some nightmare tunnel, no more than a fracture in the brickwork. The way back had been blocked by Kane's stamp. They had no choice but to squeeze and struggle on through the tiny space, crawling through ancient mortar that had long ago turned to dust. They began to choke as it kicked up.

Then suddenly Finn felt the tunnel give way – Delta had to grab his shoulders to stop him falling down and forward.

As the dust cleared and their choking stopped, they found themselves on a ledge above a sheer drop where all around was blackened brick. Slowly, their headlamps picked out more detail, and they realised they were in an old chimney. The fireplace below that it had once served had been blocked somehow and a series of copper pipes now rose up the shaft, as if from an organ.

It was a bleak spot, but to get at them here Kane would have to demolish the house.

"These pipes must be running to a cylinder up in the attic. If we get up there, we can reach the eaves in the roof and climb down," Delta said.

Two power cables dangled alongside the pipes invitingly. Delta looked at her ankle. It hadn't broken, but it had been caught and twisted and was badly hurt.

"You'll never make it. We'll go down the pipes, not up, and see where they lead," said Finn.

There was a clatter from below. Down the shaft they glimpsed a patch of light. Something poked through it, then the hole was sealed again and the light blotted out.

"What's he doing?" asked Finn.

Hissssssssssssss...

Delta looked at him.

"Gas."

Hissssssss...

Kane held the hose and waited. He'd detached the gas line from the back of the large cooker and stuck it through the hole he'd smashed in the plasterboard covering the old fireplace, sealing it with a wet tea towel.

Hissssssssssssss...

Finn grabbed hold of a dangling cable.

"We've got to go up!"

"Wait!" said Delta. She lashed a safety line between them, so that they were connected by six nano-metres or so of dangling titanium.

"Now," she said.

Hisssssssssssss...

They jumped into the cables and began to shin up. Finn fast, but Delta struggled to keep up, pained by the injured ankle.

"Climb!" Finn pulled harder, trying to tug her up after him.

She felt it and made extra effort, hoisting herself up through the pain.

Hisssssssssssssss...

Finn tried to drag her on. But Delta suddenly realised something, and stopped. She smelt the air. Nothing.

Finn felt the line drag. "Go!"

"Stop! Give me one of the flares."

"What? Climb!"

"We're in the country. It's tank gas. We have it at the cabin."

"What?"

"At our cabin in the woods – you have to buy the gas in tanks. It's heavier than air, so it doesn't rise quickly, which makes it dangerous, because it pools if it leaks. They must have it here otherwise we'd smell it already. It's not rising. He'd have to fill most of the shaft for it to reach us. How long's that going to take?"

"You want to stay and find out?"

"Release the line and get far enough away – I'm going to fire down."

Finn digested the crazy consequences.

"What if you get caught in the flames?"

"I'll worry about that. You get clear."

Finn took the white flare out. He looked down at Delta. Pain was etched on her face. Memories flooded back. By the time he got another couple of macro-metres up the shaft the gas would surely reach her. Death.

"Give it to me and go, Noob," she said, reaching up. "It's just a game."

They were still lashed together by the line.

"Not the kind that good boys play."

He aimed down the shaft.

"FINN! NO!" called Delta.

He pulled the tab.

The flare lit and the shaft flashed white as it shot down into the column of gas below.

WHOOOOOOOOOF!

My bad, thought Finn as –

Up – a fireball raced and twisted towards them, beaten to it by a shockwave.

Up – hitting them like thunder and sending them up the shaft like bullets from an upturned gun.

Up – with dust and dirt and ancient soot.

Up – till they began to slow and the energy pushing was spent and gravity began to claim them and their stomachs turned a top-of-the-rollercoaster turn and they began to fall again.

Down.

Blind.

Finn tried to reach out in the sooty blackness, but grasped at nothing, and then – with a terrible jolt – the line bit, like a crocodile's bite, into his guts and stopped him dead.

THIRTY-FOUR

DAY THREE 05:58 (BST). Langmere,
Bucks

Christabel Coles, vicar of the Church of St James and St John,
Langmere, hated packing.

It wasn't just about getting the suitcases down from the attic or
having to find the right number of pants. No, Christabel – an
intelligent Englishwoman in the prime of her life – suffered from
Wearing the Wrong Thing. It was why she had chosen a job with
a uniform.

Wearing the Wrong Thing was born of physical embarrassment
and social confusion. She would always end up wearing a ballgown
to a football match, or a boiler suit to a garden party.

What would happen if the Queen wanted to meet some refugees? was her current concern.

They were bound to pick her: she was a vicar, as well as acting transport steward for three elderly parishioners (a minibus was due any minute to collect the ancient evacuees, which is why she was up so early). All she had that was remotely suitable was a floral print skirt that according to her sister made her "bum look like a sofa". She had just tried it on. It was true.

She'd buy something new, but she only had £17 in her bank account and was always poor. She would have to be made a bishop before she'd be given a clothing allowance – which would of course only mean more blessed outings to see the Queen.

"Stop!" she told herself out loud.

She sat on the edge of her bed and took deep breaths. Why was everything in her life much more difficult than her relationship with God?

YAP! she heard outside.

Then there was the blessed dog, of course. What on earth was she going to say to her sister? She had promised only to bring one suitcase. Perhaps she could claim it was a stray?

YAP YAP YAP YAP!

The majestic roar of an Italian sports car joined the barking, before screeching to a halt.

Christabel realised who it was and hurried out.

"Get in the back of the car!" Al yelled.

Goodness, how masterful! thought Christabel.

But Yo-yo got there first, leaping a metre in the air to hit the rear seat with another delighted *YAP!*, turning cartwheels, looking for Finn, tail drumming the upholstery.

Oh glory! He meant the dog...

"Christabel..."

He seemed stunned by her skirt and sudden appearance; she had to distract him.

"What have you done with Finn?"

"Oh... he's..." said Al, leaving the rest to a circular arm movement, and her imagination.

"Having a good... evacuation?"

"Ah... Tiring," Al said.

"Great that you're taking the dog though. You're just in time, I was about to leave for my sister's. Let me get his food and basket for you," Christabel said, backing inside so as not to present her floral rear end.

"No! I can't keep him!" said Al. "I just need him to try something. I'll bring him back after."

"But we've got to evacuate or we'll all be gassed, haven't you heard?"

"Trust me, it's much worse than that, but please don't leave till I get back," Al begged her.

Had the man lost his mind?

"I'm sorry, but I really can't, I have to..."

"Please, Christabel... I'll buy you some new clothes..."

DAY THREE 06:00 (BST). *Oceania Express*, Felixstowe, Suffolk

As the sun rolled up the sky in the east, fresh from Siberia and the great eastern steppe, two shipping containers carrying the four sections of Al's Fat Doughnut Accelerator had made their way – slung beneath twin Chinook[28] transport helicopters – across Suffolk to the port of Felixstowe.

The container ship *Oceania Express* had been fuelled and readied for embarkation.

The dockyard was almost empty, but in the CFAC, and all around the world, eyes watched intently. Every conceivable electronic tagging, tracking and intelligence-gathering bug would be crawling over the ship and its precious payload. Submarines full of Special Forces were streaming under the North Sea to track it from below, and far above similar units circled at high altitude in stealth aircraft ready to strike.

The Chinooks gently deposited the two Fat Doughnut containers on to the deck of the *Oceania Express* and withdrew.

As soon as they did so, the Danish Captain of the *Express* reported the ship's computer system had gone rogue. A pre-recorded announcement ordered all crew to disembark or face death. An electromagnetic pulse knocked out most of the tracking and surveillance gizmos while all-spectrum signal jammers drowned out the rest.

Within ten minutes, entirely crewless, the *Oceania Express* was steaming east into open sea.

[28] Boeing CH-47 Chinook, twin-engine, tandem rotor, heavy-lift helicopter.

"Well. Where is he?"

"I'm afraid I can't say."

"Don't be so ridiculous. You either know or you don't know," said Violet Allenby.

Commander King, struck by her logic, didn't quite know how to respond.

Grandma had reached Hook Hall by getting her airport taxi driver (Alan, thirty-nine, recently divorced but coping) to track down the centre of operations through rumours circulating on something called The Twitter. She had then used Al's name and that of the Crown Prince of Japan to badger, hector and harangue her way through various levels of security until, finally, she'd managed to get three minutes in an anteroom with the gentleman in the lovely coat, the so-called 'Commander': a slippery customer doing everything he could to avoid a straight answer. She was getting nowhere. She needed specific information. She needed hard facts. It was time for the gloves to come off.

She narrowed her steel-blue eyes, pursed her lips and gave him her hardest lie-detector stare.

King felt she was peeling away his flesh to look deep into his soul. He had negotiated with hardened killers, global terrorists and genocidal maniacs in his time. This was worse.

"Do. You. Know. Where. He. Is?"

"Not… in the building."

"And my grandson?" she asked.

"Once again, I'm afraid I—"

"Are they at least together?"

"I don't know."

"Rubbish!"

King broke the stare and held up his hands.

"All I can say is your son is engaged in vital work of global importance and—"

"My son is Up To No Good and I intend to get to the bottom of it!"

"Believe me, Mrs Allenby, I know your son well and I appreciate your frustration," he tried.

"You have no idea!"

She shot up. King stood in turn (impeccable manners).

There was a brief stand-off (what a woman).

Then she tried to go. He tried to stop her.

"Mrs Allenby! There is one thing I wanted to ask you," King said. "Before Al left, he was adamant that he would not 'lose another one'. Do you have any idea what he might have meant?"

Grandma's heart skipped a beat and her mind went back to much darker days and a sudden call to Cambridge because her daughter had collapsed. In grief.

"I think… I think Al's referring to my son-in-law. Al was working as one of Ethan's lab assistants when Ethan had his accident and disappeared. I'm afraid Al was very young and rather blames himself."

"I'm sorry," said King.

"And that, sir, is *a straight answer*. Good morning."

As she left, King couldn't help but blurt out, "We're tracking his car! He's going round in circles between here and Wellington. Stopping and starting. Should be back mid-morning."

She turned in the doorway and gave him the approval of those same steel-blue eyes, now containing the love of the world.

"Now doesn't that feel better?" Grandma said.

It did, King wanted to say. Yes it did. Then the eyes narrowed again and skewered him.

"Be warned. If anything has happened to my grandson, I *will* be back."

She walked. He let her.

Bloody hell.

Arriving in Langmere a short time later, Grandma found the village totally deserted and thought it quite pathetic.

Sanctuary was only to be found in the church where Christabel was loading parishioners on to a minibus, and she at least was able to fill Grandma in on Al's repossession of Yo-yo.

Getting home, Grandma dumped her bag in the hall, and put on her walking shoes and waxed jacket. She pocketed a baked doggy snack of her own invention and around her neck she hung a dog whistle and a ziplock cellophane pocket containing an Ordnance Survey map of the Surrey/Berkshire borders.

Then she went out to the garage and climbed aboard her 50cc moped (an old Honda abandoned as impractical by her daughter in 1990). She depressed the starter button, turned the throttle and set off.

At seventeen miles per hour.

Where exactly she was setting off to, she didn't know. She only had a vague search area west of Wellington and could easily have waited at Hook Hall, but the thought of doing nothing when she hadn't heard from either Al or Finn for more than eighteen hours was simply too much to bear.

She put the whistle in her mouth and blew.

WHEEEEEEEEEEEEEEEEE.

THIRTY-FIVE

Finn coughed and choked and spat. The convulsions didn't help the pain of where the titanium line had tried to cut him in two.

He could hear Delta coughing close by and through the black fog could make out the beam of her headlamp. As the soot began to clear, he saw above him the line that they dangled from – hooked over a nail on the side of a giant wooden platform. Pipework ran all the way up the chimney shaft where it connected up to what looked like a petrochemical plant at this scale, but what was in fact the back of a hot-water cylinder.

He realised they'd been blown right to the top of the open shaft and were in the roof space.

Still unable to speak, he grabbed the nearest handholds and began to climb the last few nano-metres to the nail. Delta, coughing, hobbled up the shaft behind him.

They scrambled on to the platform and unhooked themselves. They were in the attic, out of the shaft.

"If your cabin in the woods is going to be this much fun, I'm definitely coming to America," said Finn.

Delta grabbed him. "That was *my call* down there," she said, turning on him. "You need to learn how to be a little kid! You could have been killed."

"So could you," said Finn. "I've watched someone die. I'm not going to do it again."

"Shall I tell you something kids never realise about grown-ups? *They care about you ten thousand times more than they care about themselves.*"

"Can you smell smoke?" said Finn.

They looked down.

Smoke was rising up the chimney shaft.

The blast had ripped off Kane's hood and blown him flat on his back, covering him in flames. He had slapped and rolled wildly. By the time he'd put himself out, part of the kitchen was already on fire.

He blinked burnt, lashless eyes that stung with rage and every kind of injury and he wanted only one thing.

The furniture banked up against the old fireplace was really beginning to catch now.

Flames reflected in Kane's battered good eye. If the gas blast had not already destroyed the nano-warriors then the fire surely would. The wooden units were beginning to burn. He kicked them, urging them on. The fiercer the fire, the quicker the death.

The Master would not be pleased. It was not clean, but at least it was done.

"The eaves!" said Delta.

In the darkness of the attic, a thin strip of dawn light emerged where the edge of the roof timbers met the top of the walls – the eave gap that allowed the roof and the whole building to breathe.

Behind them, out of the shaft, the smoke began to pour.

"We have to climb down or find some way to lower ourselves," said Finn, trying not to choke.

They jumped off the platform and made their way across the accumulated junk in the attic, Finn trying not to think about how vulnerable they would be once outside again – out of weapons, ammo, food and water.

Delta winced at the pain in her ankle, then bent down to pick something up. It was a strip of polystyrene, broken pieces of which lay scattered around the platform. Some kind of packaging.

"Got it."

"What?" said Finn, turning round, "A piece of polystyrene?"

Delta studied its long curved edge.

"No. It's an aerofoil – and when you move it through air it produces an aerodynamic force perpendicular to the direction of motion. The basis of all flight."

She started breaking it up, shaping it.

"A *wing*?" said Finn.

"Sixteen... seventeen... eighteen... nineteen... OK! That's twenty!" Kelly called from the combustion end of the jet engine.

"Er... Move to position two then!" Stubbs instructed from the cab, glasses askew, scraps of paper everywhere, old mind on a million things at once as he fiddled with the controls.

Kelly jumped down. In 'position one' he had pumped air into the Apache engine mounted on the back of the toy jeep. In 'position two' he was to grab the line wound round the jet's turbine shaft and – on command – pull it like hell.

In the cab with Stubbs were the innards of the toy jeep's remote-control unit, remodelled into a power lever and steering wheel. It was all the wrong scale, plus there were no proper brakes (just a crude friction system that involved hauling on a stick) but he had created, not just a mammoth, foreshortened, jet-powered dragster, but a masterpiece.

The fuel in the ignition chamber was under pressure. It had to be lit as the turbines spun to create the mutually efficient cycle of 'burn and turn' on which all such devices rely.

There was only one way to see if it worked, and that was to utter the three most exciting words in the Stubbs lexicon.

"Ready... Steady... GO!"

Nothing happened.

"Go…?" Stubbs repeated. Still nothing. What was Kelly doing?

"Go, goddamn and blast you, Kelly!" Stubbs shouted.

Eventually he leant out of the cab to see what was going on. Kelly was staring up the garden towards the house.

"Fire…" he said, pointing.

Kelly grabbed the line and began to pull like hell.

"Hey! Not yet, wai—"

Stubbs jumped back to the controls as the turbines began to spin. He heard the line run out – whacking clear of the jeep – and pressed the ignition.

BANG!

With a jolt and a spout of flames, the fuel in the compression chamber ignited, and slowly, falteringly, as Stubbs adjusted the throttle, the jet came screaming to life.

Kelly leapt into the cab.

"GO!"

Stubbs was flabbergasted. They couldn't possibly move to 'forward motion' until at least the first page of testing was over. But Kelly was looking at the black smoke now billowing from the house.

"Stubbs, we have to go… NOW!" and he grabbed the power level and pulled it back.

With a scream, the jet produced 6,000 nano-lbs of thrust and shot the jeep out of the shed and up the garden – achieving the equivalent of 0 to 60mph in 1.22 seconds.

Out in the countryside, as the breeze pushed through the taller grasses and the sun kissed all it surveyed, Al stood at the top of a field and did his best impression of Dr Dolittle.

"Where is he, boy? Where's Finn?"

Yo-yo's super-advanced canine olfactory senses were Al's last desperate hope – if Yo-yo couldn't pick out some pheromone, some tiny spark, some subatomic resonance of Finn out of the air then nothing could.

Yo-yo barked. Yes. He liked Finn. Yes. Bark. Wait. So? Nothing.

Al sighed and dragged him back to the car.

Yo-yo whimpered. Why weren't they going for a walk? This wasn't walking. This was a whole morning full of stopping and driving and stopping and driving. What was there for Al to misunderstand? You walk along, you occasionally throw things, you pick up crap and put it in a bag. What was it with all the talking?

Yo-yo had a point. Al had driven to six different locations in a loose five-mile arc southwest of the centre of the original release area, clinging desperately to the 'loamy soil' theory put forward by one of his teams earlier following examination of the nest site clip. It was not science. It was emotional. And it wasn't working.

Al would take the dog into the middle of a field, wait to see if it would pick up some tiny marker of Finn out of the infinite air, get disappointed when he didn't, then drag him back to the car.

Al was about to turn the key in the ignition again when Yo-yo suddenly snapped his head up and became very still.

"What is it, Yo-yo?"

Yo-yo hopped out, pulling back the way they had just come.

Watching the dog carefully, Al let him pull him back across the meadow which rolled down towards an area of woodland.

"Where is he? Can you smell him?" Al whispered. Yo-yo gave a snuffle and pulled forward with more urgency. He barked twice. Facing down the hill.

Al let out the lead. Yo-yo was really on to something, he could tell. He leant down and let the dog off the lead, then bounded off down the meadow after him.

Yo-yo barked and barked again. *Yes...*

Then a pair of squirrels broke cover beneath a fallen oak.

"NO! NO! YO-YO!!"

Yo-yo chased the fluffy rodents with evident joy. He chased them round the dead tree. Then he chased them round the meadow. Then he chased them over the wall and into the wood.

Eventually Al stopped calling. He had dared to think the nightmare might be over. Now he realised it had only just begun.

Time had been kind. Temperature hadn't.

Yet.

The core of the Beta had remained cool, even wrapped in the carcass of a cat. Its insides had spent the night forging proteins, refitting and renewing, leaking scar gum over its damaged wings, building reserves of venom and energy. It had even allowed itself to sleep.

But now... now it could taste the scent again. Danger... the scent was distant but distinct, and sparked fury inside its nervous system.

It needed to wake. To move. To sharpen its instinct. Its purpose.

The nymphs needed it. The swarm. They had spent the night wriggling and feeding. Growing. Several had now developed full wings and were hardening ahead of their final moult. Once they were all ready to moult, the Beta could leave. But until then it must wait. And tend them. And feed them.

The night had done its work. All it needed was the temperature to rise across the day and it would be able to fly... or for a shaft of sunlight to find a way, low between two oaks, to hit it directly, a shaft of pure energy radiated across 93 million miles...

The Beta opened its wings and basked.

THIRTY-SIX

Finn and Delta stood in the gutter. Icarus and Daedalus.

Smoke was beginning to pour out of the eaves around them.

Delta had snapped and shaped the polystyrene so that they both
had the equivalent of a small hang-glider on their back – a single
piece of wing. Finn was attached to his through the straps of his
backpack, Delta from a harness rigged out of the titanium line.

They scrambled up the far slope of the half-pipe gutter and held
on to the edge to stop themselves being lifted by the breeze.

"Just centre your weight and counter whatever the wing is doing
as you fall so you achieve some kind of balance. The faster the wing

is moving, the more control you'll have," Delta instructed. "Even if you lose control and just spin, you should drift to the ground like a falling leaf. Close your eyes and brace yourself and I'll try and follow you down."

Finn peered over the edge. Through the smoke was the bucolic garden, laid out in the morning sunshine. But the drop was endless. His stomach turned and he felt he was looking over the edge of the abyss. There was just no way he was ever going to be able to—

WHOOSH!

Before he'd even had time to process the thought, a gust of wind caught him and he suddenly found himself tumbling, upside down and airborne.

"No no no no..."

The initial thrust had sent the jeep speeding halfway up the garden before it went spinning in a wide arc across the damp grass. Kelly had only just managed to slow it down by hauling on the brake.

"Don't touch anything else!" yelled Stubbs.

"We just need a little less gas," said Kelly, ignoring him.

He gave a touch on the power lever and the jet punched them forward again, Stubbs just managing to control the steering wheel this time, and taking them back in a straight line up towards the house, which they were already approaching.

"Now we're dancing!" said Kelly.

"Contact!" cried Stubbs.

Kelly looked up. The teenager was emerging from the house, backing away, watching the house burn.

Finn's world was a kaleidoscope of sky and ground, sky and ground.

He must stop it.

He must stop the spin.

"Fight it," Delta had said.

He looked back and saw his wing's whiteness against the spinning horizon. He hauled his shoulder straps to try and centre himself and level out the wing. Instantly the wing reacted and lifted him. For a moment he reached some kind of equilibrium and he found himself gliding beautifully – straight towards an upstairs window.

"Pull right!" he heard Delta call from somewhere.

Finn hauled his right strap and spun again, faster this time. Again he hauled on the straps and regained control, floating in the right direction at last, but also, impossibly, upwards, on a thermal rising from the fire.

Sparks and cinders rose from the roof with him. Far below he could just make out the other scrap of polystyrene – Delta.

He held his straps tight and leant towards her. The wing reacted and flip-flapped out of the thermal. Gaining control as he fell, Finn managed to hold the wing steady again and arrowed downward.

Delta watched him drop to within thirty nano-metres of her before he pulled out of the dive and awkwardly steadied himself. He was getting it. She circled directly beneath him, tracking him. Bringing him in. Then she heard a familiar jet-engine scream and from the corner of her eye saw a burst of flame.

Below, the toy jeep was fizzing up the garden path, spitting a corona of pure fire from its afterburner.

Stubbs... headed straight for Kane.

The polystyrene wing was no $150-million Raptor, but Delta dropped her shoulder and took it into a perfect dive.

Kane backed away from the smoking building, leaving nothing to chance, scanning window ledges with digital optics from the drop.

Two scraps of polystyrene flapping out of the smoke and ash went unnoticed.

A screaming, flaring toy jeep did not.

"Go right up!" yelled Kelly as Stubbs guided them along the path. "He's seen us!"

Stubbs cut the fuel so they could coast right to the spot.

"DO NOT BE ALARMED, YOUNG MAN!" Kelly started to shout, leaning out of the cab.

But just before they reached him, a sheet of white polystyrene suddenly blocked their view as Delta THUMPED and speed-rolled off the bonnet, wing shattering as it broke her fall.

"STOP!" she yelled.

"BRAKES!" screamed Stubbs. Kelly slammed the appropriate stick.

Delta looked up. Hundreds of nano-metres above them Kane raised a giant foot. Delta sprang back up at the jeep and threw herself across the bonnet.

"GO! ENEMY! GO!"

Stubbs hit the gas – *WHOOSHHSHSH!* – and the jeep shot forward, the G-force nearly pulling Delta's arms from their sockets.

SLAM! Kane's stamping foot missed them by millimetres.

Stubbs kept the gas on until they were all the way round the house and heading for the road.

"NO!" shouted Delta. "Finn… we've got to go back!"

Stubbs braked. Without ceremony, Delta clambered through the open windscreen, shoved Stubbs along the plastic bench and took the controls.

"Welcome home," said Kelly. "Where's the kid?"

"Back at the house," said Delta.

She turned the jeep into a screaming 180-degree spin on the gravel driveway and, seeing Kane coming round the corner, charged straight at him, Kelly popping up through a hole in the roof of the cab where they'd mounted the Minimi.

DRRRRRRT! DRRRRRRT! DRRRRRT!

The tiny bullets couldn't pierce Kane's skin, but they could surprise and sting.

They snapped at his face, and he kicked out viciously and hit air as the jeep shot past him.

Finn drifted. Delta had disappeared. So had the jeep.

Hell.

He had tried to follow her down and instead flipped in a gust and again caught a thermal from the fire.

He had righted out of it. But what to do? Land? Hide?

The breeze dragged him left. If he didn't get low enough, he would sail over the garden wall and fall into the field beyond.

Land, Finn thought. *Leave the wing on the ground as a marker and get away.*

He tried to angle down and right when suddenly he heard the jeep again – just as the wind shifted. He overcompensated. He flipped upside down. The wall was now hurtling towards him.

The jeep, the wall, the wind raced to see who would get the better of him.

The wall was going to win.

Fight the wing. Resist.

He pulled on the straps and swung his body round. For a moment he experienced deceleration and lift and flipped round the right way up. But he was going so fast the impact would still kill him. He pulled hard on the straps and swung right up. Just enough to stop himself dead. Then he dropped – *THUMP* – right on top of the wall.

The impact ripped his backpack straps through the flimsy polystyrene, snapping the wing clear. He lay still. Winded. Groaning.

When he looked up, the jeep was flying down the garden beneath him. Kane was running and taking fire—

DRTRTRTRTRT! DRTRTRTRTRTRTRT!

But Kane kept on. Not towards the jeep. Towards Finn.

He had seen the second wing come down. He was closing fast. Burnt, stung cyclops, face a rictus of cruel intent.

Finn started to scramble along the top of the wall in a useless attempt to escape. But Kane didn't reach him. Something else did.

Finn heard:

OOOOOOOOOOOOOOOOOOOOOOOOOOOOOOOOOOOOOOOOOOOO OOOO!

Then all was oblivion.

It extended its wings. It felt strong. It felt a rush of hormone. Its triple stings flexed and venom seeped from them.

Its muscles twitched. The wings rose and SMASHED and slapped – but did not shatter – as it twisted to find the angle, to find lift…

Wwk…zzk…zkwkw…kwkzzz….wkzzkzkwkwkwkzzz…wkzz…kzz-kzkwkwkwkzzzwkzzkzkw…wkwkwkzzzwkzzkzkwkwkwkzzz kzkwkw-kwkzzz…

It rose resplendent over the waking nest site. Its reds, blacks and yellows alive. The nymphs were largely still below as they began to moult, to work their growing bodies out of their own exoskeletons for the final time.

And again on the breeze, stronger than ever, it tasted the scent of danger.

Kill…

But not yet. Resist… for the swarm, it must resist.

THIRTY-SEVEN

Finn woke and felt a desperate, impossible desire to breathe.

He sensed blackness, wetness, hotness... a squeezing and pumping... he felt a *rata-tata-tata-tata* heartbeat... he felt he was blacking out and throwing up at the same time and, just as he did, the wetness squeezed hard as rock and snapped at him, sending him slick and sudden and newborn into – light! Air!

His lungs gasped open and he fell headlong into an extraordinary sound.

*()()()()!!!OOOOOOOOOOOOOO!!()()()()!!!OOOO!)()()()!!!OOOOO!!!-
()()()()!!!OOOOOO!!!!*

Red.

Screaming, mile-wide red.

Falling from one wet tunnel into another.

Into the mouth of a chick.

Regurgitated – along with a bucket or so of digestive juice and yuk.

In the split second that the oxygen hit his brain and he determined all this, Finn felt the chick's beak snap shut and the red-black envelop him once more, dragging and sucking him down again.

He was going to drown in bird guts, dissolve in stomach acid.

No no no no... He kicked and scratched and mauled and swam and fought the pressing gut... and must have struck a nerve or hit a reflex, for he felt the world tighten around him again as he was vomited out.

"ARRRRGGGH!"

He slipped from the cluster of scything beaks and sonic hell.

()()()()!!!OOOOOOOOOOOOOOO!!()()()()!!!OOOO!)()()()!!!OOOOO!!!-()()()()!!!OOOOO!!!!

He wriggled between them, into the heat and muck and fluff of the nest. Into the mire. Into the straw and sticks and twigs.

()()()()!!!OOOOOOOOOOOOOOO!!()()()()!!!OOOO!)()()()!!!OOOOO!!!-()()()()!!!OOOO!!!

And he was all but crying when he finally forced his way down, down between the twigs, down far enough to where flies and fleas wriggled free from the beaks, down in the guts of the nest.

The mother bird dashed back with another protein fix for the chicks who increased their crazed *()()()()!!!OOOOOOOOOOOOOOO!!()()()()!!!OOOO!)()()()!!!OOOOO!!!()()()()!!!()()()()!!!*

And Finn saw she was a starling and, as he looked out, he saw she had brought him high, high into a tree at the edge of the wood.

The smoking roof of the house was not far, a few seconds' flight time for a starling, but to Finn... as good as a million miles.

Game over.

Al stared up at the clouds playing British Bulldog across the sky.

It was beautiful. But he knew the brief feeling of wonder would pass, that like the sky it was just a trick of physics, that what lay beyond was infinite, a lifetime of hoping Finn would be waiting somewhere, smiling, just around the corner.

Which of course he never would.

Kids were kids. He should have just wrapped him up in sixteen tonnes of cotton wool like his mother had. The anxiety she emitted was a real thing, not a mad thing. She knew kids were too small, too delicate, too dumb... too loved. They were kids.

He had everything, and now he had nothing but the clouds. His sister was up there somewhere. "I'm so sorry..." he told her. And to her long-lost husband: "Ethan, wherever the hell you are, I need you now."

Finn swayed in the nest and contemplated the end.

He could fight the chicks for the regurgitated food their mother brought, but he didn't fancy his chances. He could simply drop to the forest floor, and risk breaking back and legs, for what? An endless journey into the unknown?

The black button face of a small beetle pushed through to inspect him.

A full stop.

He had lost it all now. Had too much XP. Was sick on it. Always having to stay one step ahead of... what? Grief? And fear maybe. But not any more. Not now he'd reached the end of something. If what he could do was what he was then he was at an end. All he would have to do was wriggle a little further through the lattice of twigs and grasses, close his eyes and let himself go.

Experimentally, he shifted. His hands felt fresh, free air. Free fall...

Trust yourself.

The end of the fall might contain his parents. Her. Him. Them. Which meant, although he was not a master of death like Kelly, nor could he ignore it like Delta, he was not afraid of it.

It was a thought that surprised him. Struck him like a revelation.

"I am not afraid of death," he said aloud.

He smiled. He felt giddy. His body relaxed and he slipped further through the nest until he was dangling out, arms extended in the fresh treetop air, senses open, drinking every last drop of life.

Yap.

I am not afraid of death, so I need never be afraid of life, he thought. He was in pain. He was starving. Thirsty. Exhausted. But... *I am not afraid of life*. This was something that he had learned... this was something about who he was, or would have been.

Be yourself.

And a sense of wonder, of life to be enjoyed, to be run at, to be savoured, gripped him. The sound of the birds and the fragments of sky, the scent of lemon balm somewhere in the fabric of the nest – all seemed fantastic. An endless journey into the unknown. A miracle. His every instinct and nerve ending screaming – *LIVE!*

LIVE! screamed Al; *LIVE!* screamed Grandma; *LIVE!* his mother said; *LIVE!* his father said.

Live, thought Finn.

Just keep going.

Yap.

THIRTY-EIGHT

*Y*AP!

Finn heard the sound, and everything he'd just thought, everything he'd just felt, came together in one essential, primal –

"*YO-YO!*"

His eyes popped and his head snapped over to look down...

...where far below Yo-yo's mind spun, followed closely by his whirling body.

First he thought he remembered Finn, then he thought he could smell Finn, somewhere on the edge of the wood, then he could definitely smell Finn, and now he could hear him.

"YO-YOOOO!!"

FinnFinnFinnFinn!!

WOOF WOOF WOOF BOW-WOW-WOW!

()()()()!!!OOOOOOOOOOOOOO!!()()()()!!!OOOO!)()()()!!!OOOOO!!!-()()()()!!!OOOO!! went the baby birds in response.

"Oh, you idiot, you beautiful idiot…" said Finn. "STAY, YO-YO!"

Fiiiiiiiiiiiiiiiiiiiiiiiiiiiiiiiiiiiin!!!!Finn!Finn!!!Finn!

WOOF WOOF WOOF BOW–WOW-WOW!

"STAY! GOOD DOG!"

Finn wriggled through the nest until most of his torso hung beneath it. Arching his back, he could see a hazardous route along the twigs, down the branches – ultimately to the trunk. But it would take many hours, demand far more energy that he had left, and leave him wide open to bird and insect attack.

Or he could drop. He looked down again.

BOW-WOW-WOW

Only to see Yo-yo bound off after a glimpse of fluffy grey squirrel.

"NO! YO-YO!"

The tiny voice cleaved Yo-yo's instincts in two and sent him skittering to a confused halt.

"COME BACK, YO-YO!" Finn shouted, killing his throat. "GET BACK HERE NOW!"

Yo-yo abandoned the squirrel and returned.

"LIE DOWN, YO-YO! LIE DOWN!"

The dog lay down. Finn wriggled further out of the nest till he was left clinging to its underside. This was crazy, he told himself. This was totally crazy.

He climbed round the nest until he was level with a twig sprouting a fresh growth of three bright green leaves, each the size of an umbrella. If he could break off the stem, the leaves would slow his descent and, if he got really lucky, he might hit the forest litter at a force that didn't actually kill him. And if he got even luckier than that...

Just keep going.

With a last look down and a "STAY BOY!", he swung himself over and grabbed the soft green stem with both hands. It bent... then, after an age, he felt the base tear neatly from the twig, and he was suddenly and rapidly falling.

"*ARRRRGGGHHHHHHHH!!*"

The leaves flapped but offered little drag. Only one thing could save him now.

"HERE, BOY! HERE, BOY!"

Yo-yo *just* had time to spring excitedly off his haunches towards the sound. Finn hit the warm fur and felt firm flesh envelop him – *WHUMP* – knocking the wind out of him and bouncing him straight back up in the air to somersault once more... before landing again and coming to a halt by *just* clinging to the furthest tendril of Yo-yo's mane.

Yo-yo spun, madly barking – *BOWOWOWOWOWOWWOWOW!* – wanting to find Finn and love him and roll around and *BOWOWOWOWWOWOWOWOW!*

Finn had to hang on for dear life. "SIT! Yo-yo, SIT! Easy, boy. Easy now..."

Yo-yo's few coherent brain cells galloped through a line of dog reasoning: Finn. Where's Finn. Nowhere. Somewhere. Some sound.

Some smell. Some Finn. Is some Finn the Finn-ness of Finn? Yes.
Finn! BOWOWOWOWOW!

"SIT!" Finn all but begged.

Yo-yo sat. Absolutely still. One happy idiot.

Grandma puttered and whooped along the back lanes of Berkshire.
Whooped, because the automatic clutch of the Honda repeatedly
engaged and disengaged according to the patches of remaining wear
on the plates, causing sudden bursts of very high revs.

She couldn't admit that she had lost Al and Finn, because that
would be to Admit Defeat.

And a mother's love never failed.

It was in the small print.

Even if you did find yourself weeping into your helmet with the
stress of it all every ten minutes.

So, when she finally did find an abandoned De Tomaso Mangusta
(not that she actually knew or cared what it was called), it was with
a sense of great relief and no little self-justification.

It didn't take her long to find him.

When Al was small, and through his troubled teens (never had a
boy engaged in so many imaginary love affairs), he would go and
lie in the cornfield behind the house (scaring her witless imagining
combine-harvester accidents). She would go and lie down beside him
to jolly him along or just to listen, as lying in fields feeling sorry

for yourself was the type of romantic thing everyone should do in childhood. If not at thirty-two.

She approached him across the meadow.

"Well, well, what a lovely day. Bit breezy, but lovely. Oh, it's good to be back."

"I've lost him," said Al. "I've lost another."

"Don't be silly!" Grandma said and, with old lady difficulty, managed to lower herself beside him. They both stared at the sky.

"Do you think you'll *ever* settle down with a nice young wom—"

"Do you really have to ask that now?"

"Well, I didn't meet Daddy till I was twenty-seven and that was considered very old in those days. Isn't that cornflower blue just magical? Christabel and that man, King Rat or whatever he's called, gave me the gist. Finn's run off and you've gone looking for him with Yo-yo, hoping to pick up the scent no doubt. Well, that is admirable. But you are not to worry. Whatever you may think of Finn, he is in fact the most resourceful, most intelligent, most robust…"

"Mum, it's not quite that sim—"

"I'm talking! Most brilliant boy, and he's bound to pull through – and sensitive, did I say sensitive?"

"Mum…"

"And may I remind you that in this family the tradition is not to just lie there and do nothing, but to try and try again, to reach for the stars every day, no matter what! We did not crawl out of the primordial slime by wallowing in it. No. We love and we hope and we do."

Long used to such perorations, Al had switched off.

"I've even lost the damn dog…"

"Nonsense."

She chivvied herself to her feet and, for want of anything better to do, Al got up with her. When she had steadied herself, she took the dog whistle from around her neck and blew hard on it. They looked down the meadow. Nothing seemed to stir.

"I don't think that…"

"Well, of course you don't. You're not a dog. Let's try further down the hill."

"It really isn't all that simple, Mum…"

"Come along, you can tell me all about it on the way."

And she yomped off through the long grass like some kind of mad old lady guided missile, putting the dog whistle in her mouth.

WHEEEEEEEEEEEEEEEEEEE.

THIRTY-NINE

Finn hugged the warm, smelly clutch of mane in his arms and felt the dog's drumming heartbeat beneath his feet.

He looked back up at the tree he'd just dropped from. Unbelievable.

He tried to take in Yo-yo's size. His great tail was thwacking the ground behind them. He was like some rodeo dinosaur. A mountain of magic carpet in need of a shampoo. If Finn could hold on, he could rejoin the fray. He could find his friends. He could fight.

To get more support he wriggled his legs under Yo-yo's leather collar. Automatically the dog's swing-bridge-sized rear leg scratched at him.

"STOP! DON'T SCRATCH, YO-YO!"

Yo-yo's hind leg froze in mid-air. Finn sat back more on the worn rim of the collar, holding on to the fur like reins. The hind leg dropped.

Finn tried. "OK, let's walk." He held on as they sprang up.

"Good dog! Back to the road, boy! Back to the house!"

Yo-yo barked, happy, but just trotted round in a big circle. Then sat again. Finn realised the dog had no idea where he was.

How was he supposed to guide him? Dogs didn't follow directions. They followed things – scents, owners, cars. He'd have to wait for something or someone to pass, but there were no cars – they were in the middle of an evacuated nowhere – how were they ever—

VROOOOOOOOOOOOOM!

The jeep shot past on a road concealed above them at the edge of the wood – its jet at screaming pitch and travelling at twenty-five macro-miles per hour – loud and clear.

The Apache? thought Finn. *But that's imposs—* Before he could finish the thought though, Yo-yo had exploded off after it.

Finn clung on.

Back in the garage of the burning house Kane had found what he was looking for.

He straddled the family's quad bike – fat, fun and 400cc – slammed a Vehicle Override Key into its ignition (the VOK was every Tyro's favourite bit of kit and worked on everything from cycle locks to Ferraris) and turned.

The quad rasped to life. Kane stood on the foot plates and revved. The quad shot out of the garage and ripped down the gravel drive.

Out on the road, the jeep whizzed along at breakneck speed.

Kelly looked back out of the cab. The quad with the Cyclops aboard rocketed up the road towards them.

"He's gaining!" he yelled above the scream of the jet and jumped up to man the Minimi.

The quad came right alongside and Kane raised a boot. Kelly aimed at his helmetless head.

DRTRTRTRRTTRTRTRT!

Kane cursed as tiny bullets stung his scalp. He fell back and lined the quad up to run them down. Then hit the gas. As he did so, Delta hauled on the brake – *SCREEEEEEECH!* – and for a moment the crew found themselves and their jeep shooting underneath the four giant rubber wheels of the braking quad bike – *WHOOM!* – but the jeep stopped first and the quad went shooting by, Kane riding the brakes, skidding all the way, skewing to an eventual halt.

Delta hit full power again before he could right himself on the road, and the jeep shot past him, briefly leaving the ground as it hit a rise in the road.

"Fetch!"

Running parallel to the vehicles streaking past on the road above,

Yo-yo stretched his body in hopeless, delighted pursuit, Finn clinging on to his expanding, contracting, galloping back.

"Good boy, Yo-yo. Get the jeep…"

"We've got to lose this sucker!" said Delta, Kane roaring up behind them again in no time.

Ahead of them a track led off the road into the woods. She took it.

As they flew past, Kelly noticed a sign – MBT TRAIL. He barely had time to mentally process the abbreviation into 'Mountain Bike Trail' before they hit the jump…

…describing a perfect arc over the first ditch and landing with a spine-bending thump on the run up to a half-pipe.

Stubbs looked back to check that the mounts holding the jet still held.

"It wasn't designed for this!"

"Don't worry. I was," said Delta.

"WAAAAAAAAAAH!" Stubbs cried – discovering hidden emotional depths – as Delta took the jeep at 90 degrees round a section of high-speed banking before levelling out to hit a ramp – *WHUMP* – that saw them soar over an open canyon of dirt – *WHAM* – landing on its far distant side.

"Badass…" Delta said through gritted teeth, loving every second.

Kelly simply threw up.

They looked back to see Kane, a few macro-metres behind them on the quad, racing towards the jump.

Kane gave it full power and was approaching the corner at the required angle…

…just as Yo-yo appeared.

WOOF WOOF WOOF BOW-WOW-WOW!

Kane's balance was thrown (he HATED dogs) and the bike left the ramp 0.68 degrees askew, hitting the ground all wrong and leaving him – *SMACK!* – somersaulting over the top of the quad and into a 100-year-old elm.

As the crew wondered what had just happened, Stubbs saw the trail curve ahead. "There's a gap in the banking, we can get out there!"

The jeep's jet sang as it hit the gap and its wheels left the earth…

…just making it over, landing on two wheels instead of four, before – *SLAM* – coming back down to safety.

"Where the hell did that dog come from?" said Kelly.

"Man's best friend," said Delta, "or maybe not…" as, looking back, she saw it bounding towards them.

"Shoot it," said Stubbs. "It probably wants to eat us."

"OVER HERE!" Finn yelled from Yo-yo's collar. "GUYS! IT'S ME!"

He saw the Minimi swing round.

"Wait, Yo-yo! Stop!"

DRDRRTT!

Yo-yo yelped and backed away as the tiny bullets stung his chest.

"STOP FIRING!" called Finn, useless now as the jeep sped on. "COME BACK!"

DAY THREE 07:52 (BST). Hook Hall, Surrey

The fire crew that had entered the kitchen at Lanyard House to douse the heart of the flames immediately noticed material stacked up bonfire-style against the cooker.

They reported signs of arson to the authorities who in turn reported these suspicious findings to Hook Hall, as instructed.

It was almost certainly nothing. Looters probably. *But*, King thought, *I must dot every i. Cross every t.*

Time was running out. Further discussions at Hook Hall and in secret session at the United Nations in New York determined that if his fears were true and Kaparis didn't keep his side of the bargain and give up the location of the nest site then the nuclear response, no matter how terrible, must be a joint act between all nations. A briefing would take place at 09:00 hours to prepare all parties for the possibility. Then, with preparations all in place, if the location of the site had still not been discovered or divulged by 12:00 hours, the Prime Minister of the UK would ask the UK Joint Chiefs to carry out the order.

A series of five-megaton hydrogen bombs would be detonated in a ten-mile radius around the original release site producing fifty megatons of explosive force, creating fifty square miles of 'total destruction' and a much wider area of 'severe damage'. The blasts would be felt across the continent.

"Get men down there. Search the entire area," snapped King.

There were eleven nymphs. Seven were already starting their final moult. The rest were close behind.

It had done its duty to the swarm, and the energy from the rising sun would soon do the rest.

The scent of danger was too strong to resist now. Its instinct, its fury was too strong.

KILL...

It flexed and forced and drove towards the danger, towards a chaos of sound at the north end of the woods.

Wkwkwkzzzwkzzkzkwkwkwkzzz kzkwkwkwkzzz...

FORTY

Sandy Dale Golf Club was founded in 1900 as a private golf club for '200 Gentlemen Members' paying an annual subscription of five guineas. Over the subsequent 114 years, it had become one of the most prestigious and beautiful courses in the world. Patronised by Open champions, celebrities and billionaires alike, it was famed for its luxurious grand old clubhouse and its manicured greens and fairways.

The jeep flew out of the wood and landed on the elegant seventeenth green at the nano-equivalent of 110mph.

Not expecting the sudden change of terrain – and certainly not expecting automatic overnight sprinklers to have left a skid-pad sheen of water across the entire course – Delta hit the brakes hard. Water shot up in a perfect unbroken blue sheet as she slid towards the infamous Long Bunker.

Immediately behind, undeterred by the bullets and spurred on by Finn, came Yo-yo, still happily giving chase, then forgetting everything for a moment to stop and bite a spurting sprinkler head, soaking its nano-passenger – "No, Yo-yo! Catch the car!"

He sprang up again with a *Yap!* to chase the jeep which had brushed the Long Bunker's lip and was throwing up rainbow arcs of water this way and that as it snaked its screaming way off the sodden green and on up the eighteenth fairway, mist rising in the dawn.

The eighteenth fairway ended at the last hole and the colonnaded grand old clubhouse.

The jeep jumped as it hit the lip of the green and landed on the far side of the final flag, wheeling round as it hit the clubhouse terrace.

Yo-yo, tiring now, bounded up after it, tongue hanging out.

The jeep screamed and circled the clubhouse terrace, looking for a way in. At the rear of the building Delta spotted a service door with a cat flap. She briefly calculated its height, compared it to the distance from the lip of the terrace and swung off the flagstones.

"What are you doing?" asked Stubbs.

She turned back towards the door and hit the gas.

"Oh great..." muttered Kelly.

The jeep hit the edge of the terrace and leapt the fifteen centimetres or so it needed to hit the cat flap – *WHACK!* – with enough force to lift it and let them through, landing safely on the other side and...

...coming face to face with a set of large double doors.

"Great. Now what?" asked Stubbs.

Just then, Yo-yo squeezed and barked and dragged his chaotic limbs through the cat flap after them.

"Oh great... Man's best friend's back." Stubbs climbed up to man the Minimi.

"Don't waste the ammo and don't hurt it!" shouted Delta. "Just yell at it, take command of it!"

They turned to the cathedral-sized dog now sitting panting before them.

"GET THE HELL OUT OF HERE! SCRAM!" screamed Kelly, the others joining in.

"NO! IT'S ME!" they heard a tiny voice reply.

Delta couldn't believe her ears – she looked up at the colossal dog and said, "Finn? FINN!"

"HERE! I'M HERE!" Finn started shouting down, waving madly from the collar.

Delta whooped. Actually whooped.

"I don't believe it! FINN?!" Kelly shouted up.

"KELLY?!" Finn grinned and saw the soldier grinning back up at him. "YOU'RE ALIVE!"

"DAMN RIGHT! WHERE DID YOU GET THIS THING?" shouted Kelly.

"IT'S MY DOG! CHRISTABEL MUST HAV—"

But their relief at making contact was cut short as outside they heard the quad approaching. Finn saw the double doors and realised the problem.

"Go, Yo-yo! Through the door! What's in there, boy? What's in there?" He felt Yo-yo rise beneath him and obligingly barge through the swing doors, the jeep scooting through after him.

Both emerged into a large empty ballroom, Yo-yo's claws skating across the sprung wooden dance floor.

"Look, a phone!" yelled Delta, pointing to a handset on a wall at the far end of the room.

The quad reached the eighteenth green and took off as it hit the lip of the colonnaded terrace, Kane powering it straight into the large French windows of the lounge bar – *SMASH!*

A sign above the door bar warned MEMBERS ONLY.

In Siberia, Li Jun had already found architectural blueprints of the clubhouse on a building contractor's server.

"The telecoms line runs in cable housing under the false ceiling of the main service corridor."

"Got it," replied Kane, already there, punching up through a ceiling tile and firing through the cable housing.

In the ballroom, they heard the sound of smashing glass, and the shot, and watched the LED on the phone extension go out as they reached it.

"He's shot out the line," said Kelly.

Kane burst through the double doors, bleeding from the smashed glass. He saw them and his mouth contorted into a smile. He threw the lock on the double doors.

"Ah, we're trapped," said Stubbs, helpful as ever, as they took in the evil teen.

Kane picked up a chair and walked to the centre of the dance floor.

There was only one other way out, at the opposite end of the ballroom, which they could see through glass panels led into a large central kitchen.

"You are got!" Kane shouted, voice ricocheting round the empty ballroom.

"What do we do? Rush him?" asked Delta.

"I'm thinking..." said Kelly, options spinning through his mind.

Yo-yo issued a growl that ended in a whimper.

"Don't be afraid, Yo-yo," said Finn.

Then Kane heard a tapping at the window. He turned. He saw it. He smiled. He walked to window and let it fly in.

...kzzwkzzkzkwkwkwkzzzwwkwwkzzwkzzkzkwkwkwWKKKKZZZZZ...
Kill.

"OK, be afraid," said Finn.

FORTY-ONE

Small Security Service teams had dispersed across the area surrounding Lanyard House after deep tyre marks were found in the gravel drive, but none had so far found any trace of an off-road vehicle, or indeed any sign of life.

One two-man team sped through the scattered, prosperous Sandy Heath neighbourhood towards Wellington when they approached the grandiose sign for the Sandy Dale Golf Club – Members Only.

"Up there?"

"OK, but we're not staying to play a round."

The car swung out to take the sharp right into the entrance with barely a touch on the brakes at 55mph, briefly lifting two wheels off the ground.

Ahead of them they could see the clubhouse rising out of the heather. They would reach it in nine seconds and get a clear view of the smashed lounge bar windows and of the quad bike lodged therein. Another three seconds and they'd see the mess made of the eighteenth green, and the drama now taking place in the ballroom.

But just as they were approaching the green...

"*All cars – motorbike and car on traffic camera at intersection B237 and A38 three minutes ago.*"

The driver hit the brakes and spun back round.

The trap was set.

Wkzzwkzzkzkwkwkwkzzzwwkwwkzzwkzzkzkwkwkw...

The Scarlatti circled the ballroom ceiling, sifting the danger, picking out the individual scents.

Yo-yo and the jeep shifted nervously on the dance floor, ready to bolt, eyes and Minimi trained on the beast above.

Kane retreated to block the kitchen doors, and enjoy the spectacle from the far end like an emperor watching the climax of his games.

The Scarlatti circled the ceiling for a final time then plunged down from the mirrorball at the jeep in a death-dive, tail curled, stings flexing and pointing.

Wkzzwkzzkzkwkwkwkzzzwwkwwkzzwkzzkzkwkwkw!

"GAS!" shouted Delta. The jet spluttered, then the jeep shot forward. The diving Scarlatti missed by millimetres. The jeep pulled clear across the polished floor. The Scarlatti levelled in pursuit.

Kelly braced himself against the Minimi on the roof of the jeep.

DTRTRTRTRTRTRTRRTRTRTRTRTRTRT!

The Scarlatti felt the first couple of impacts and wheeled away. Adapting. It had learned it could not take many hits on already damaged wings.

DRRRRT! DRRRRT! DRRRRT!

Kelly missed, as the Scarlatti dodged and swung back and forth around the speeding jeep, inviting further bursts of fire, trying to gauge the angle of its enemy's sting.

With a screech, Delta spun the jeep back the way it came. The Scarlatti arced round after it, chasing it back down the ballroom in a dance of death.

Yo-yo paced, held fast by Finn, desperate to bite the flying thing, to snap it out of the air like a ball.

Wkzzwkzzkzkwkwkwkzzzwwkwwkzzwkzzkzkwkwkw!

"Low on fuel. Low on ammo," Stubbs reported to Delta.

"Where have I heard that before?"

Kill kill kill...

The dancers turned.

The tiny jet screamed.

The Scarlatti, frustrated by the jeep's evasions, sensed an easier prey.

Finn saw the beast wheel away in a long elliptical line and head straight towards them. He gripped two handfuls of dog fur. The

Scarlatti skimmed the dance floor at speed, growing in size and momentum as it zeroed in. Finn felt his heart beat faster, faster, faster...

But Finn was not afraid. Finn knew this game. This was British Bulldog by any other name.

As late as he dared, he yelled, "Run, Yo-yo! Get the jeep! Run away!"

Yo-yo barked in protest, but sprang up, dodging the venomous imp like a toreador.

The Scarlatti overshot and – *WHACK!* – bounced off the end wall before it could turn. It struggled in a frenzy of brain-bleeding pure fury for a couple of seconds, fizzing like a lethal puck across the dance floor.

It was as Yo-yo shot skittering down the ballroom after the jeep – which had turned too, heading back towards Kane and the kitchen end – that Finn saw it.

Just left of the double doors to the kitchen that Kane was guarding was a serving hatch. Just like at home. Its doors were closed. But surely they wouldn't be locked?

There was only one way to find out.

"Go, Yo-yo! Go!" Finn said. "Who's at the hatch? DINNER!"

An override synapse fired in Yo-yo's brain – he saw only Grandma's hatch and everything turned dog food.

"Jump, boy! Jump!"

Like no jockey ever rode a horse at the Grand National, Finn clutched the dog's neck and urged him on. And like no horse ever leapt those famous fences, Yo-yo sprang like Pegasus for the serving hatch.[29]

And, to Kane's disbelief, they sailed right past him, burst open the hatch doors and crashed skidding into the kitchen, scattering crockery like some mental dog bomb.

Kane kicked through the double doors and snatched up a knife from the scattering steel.

"YO-YO!" screamed Finn.

From deep within his wolfish past, Yo-yo reacted, springing past the flashing blade to sink his blunt teeth hard into Kane's armpit, one canine tooth penetrating the muscle deep enough to nick Kane's median nerve.

Kane fell back against the double doors. His hand opened. The knife dropped to the floor. So did Finn – spinning from Yo-yo's collar and bouncing off Kane's gut to land on the kitchen floor as Kane and Yo-yo struggled, a cacophonous nightmare of growls and screams and flailing limbs the size of buses, one blow from which would kill Finn in an instant. He ran for cover, any kind of cover, but – *WHAM!* – down came a paw and – *WHACK!* – down came an arm.

As man and dog fought on the floor, the door to the ballroom was kicked open creating a momentary gap. Delta went for it.

The jeep shot through – hitting Kane's hand which acted as a ramp and sent them leaping over the battling pair before the doors could swing shut again. They narrowly missed Finn as they landed.

---

[29] See citation (ii) Appendix A, PDSA Dickin Medal for Animal Gallantry, 1st Class.

"Brake!" screamed Delta and she spun the jeep, executing a tight figure of eight in order to pick Finn up – Kelly leaning out of the cab with an arm like steel to snatch him off the floor – and spin back out again, away from the fight.

"RUN, YO-YO! CHASE THE JEEP!" Finn screamed back at the dog.

Yo-yo left off Kane immediately, and bounded through the kitchen doors after them, chasing them through canyons of stainless steel as they led the way out through the lounge bar double doors, smashed wide open by Kane.

Kane was still flailing on the kitchen floor... they were getting away... they were getting away...

The Scarlatti sensed his pain. An attack on the swarm.

It buzzed and whacked against the kitchen doors in frenzy again, until Kane kicked them open to let it through.

Wkzzwkzzkzkwkwkwkzzzwwkwwkzzwkzzkzkwkwkw...

Kill...

The Scarlatti flew arrow-straight after them, out through the kitchen, through the lounge bar and its smashed French doors. Zeroing in on them as they raced round the terrace.

Yo-yo saw it and barked. The beast responded and headed straight for him.

Finn screamed, "NO, YO-YO! RUN!"

But Yo-yo couldn't hear. Didn't want to hear.

SNAP!

He leapt up and his jaws tried to bite it from the air.

"NOOOO!" Finn screamed.

Both beasts wheeled, Yo-yo growling and snapping at the Scarlatti as he bounded away from it towards the woods, the Scarlatti in hot pursuit, coming in at crazed trajectories, trying to get an angle to dive, Yo-yo in a world of his own, in a whirligig conflict that Finn could only despair of as they disappeared through dense brambles into the woods and out of sight.

"We've got to stop them!" Finn shouted. He felt the blood drain out of him and panic flow in.

"YO-YO!" he called. "YO-YO!"

In the woods Yo-yo snapped and snapped again at the flying thing, still dodging its stings, but he only had so much energy left... he would have to lie down soon... he would have to submit and sleep... let the thing bite him... they would give him a treat today surely... biscuits he thought... biscuits...

...then he heard something, felt something, passing into his very soul.

Home, he thought. *Home...*

Λ

FORTY-TWO

Finn looked desperately into the woods as they shot round the perimeter of the eighteenth green.

"Where is he? Where did he go?"

There was no sign. Finn suddenly found he couldn't deal with anything and his head filled with tears. Not Yo-yo. All of a sudden he wanted to go home, he really badly wanted to go home. It had been fun, it had been extraordinary, it had been wild, but not Yo-yo, nothing was worth losing Yo-yo.

Kelly said, "He's chasing him down. He's wearing it out for us. Come on, kid. He'll be OK."

Delta grabbed Finn's shoulder. "Hey! He's a warrior! He'll be back! What did I tell you about Kelly?" she demanded.

"You said he'd be back..." Finn said, deciding to hold on to it, to believe it, if only to stop himself crying. "You said he'd be back... and he came back."

"There you go then," said Delta.

"How much fuel have we got left?" Kelly asked Stubbs.

Stubbs checked the plastic bottle of fuel Kelly had filled overnight. "Five minutes at the most."

"Which way?" said Delta.

"There's a town on the horizon, at the bottom of the course," said Kelly, pointing back down the eighteenth fairway.

"Wellington... I think that's Wellington," said Finn. "I recognise the spires."

There was still no sign of the Scarlatti or Yo-yo.

"And if we head cross-country and run out of fuel before we hit a road...?" Stubbs started.

"If we run out of fuel, we're screwed either way," said Kelly.

Delta hit what was left of the gas.

Kane could just hear the jeep screaming away as he finally got the quad to sputter back to life. The engine fired intermittently – which, together with the escape of the jeep and the dog bites, made him even more psychotic.

He kicked the quad round, scattering shattered glass, and it stuttered back out on to the terrace. As he yanked at the spark plug leads to get the quad engine to behave, the Scarlatti emerged from the undergrowth on the far side of the eighteenth green and flew erratically towards him.

It all but flopped into his lap – a black-red rat, struggling, disoriented and fatigued. Kane picked it up gently, let it taste him. He could see how weak it had become. Its weakness, its need, calmed him. True and faithful, Kane opened his shirt and placed it on his chest. Let it jab and sink its barbed mouthparts into his skin. Let it attach itself and feed on his blood. On his dark life force.

The voice of Li Jun reported in his ear, "*Target heading northeast, towards the B237.*"

Kane revved the quad.

FORTY-THREE

The ghost ship *Oceania Express* had travelled at full speed northeast of Felixstowe and arrived at a point ninety miles into the North Sea. It was nearer the coast of the Netherlands than that of the UK, and almost dead centre of the network of military formations that stood ready to board it or attack anyone who came near.

It now slowed. Why? *For effect*, thought King.

Pure theatre.

Kaparis must know that they would have deduced the whole thing was a red herring and that what he really wanted were the sequencing codes. So why all this? Why bother with this whole charade?

The display of power: the first instinct of the insecure and idiotic throughout the ages.

He was showing off, enjoying himself as the world danced to his tune.

How depressing to be brought so low by such a person, King thought. He had rarely felt so hopeless. In Central London a room full of 'cryptanalysts with a romantic bent' waited to hear Al's cryptic mnemonic key. Should King let them in on the secret scrap of poetry?

Uncertainty was all. Uncertainty and fear.

And, as everyone else waited for, indeed demanded, action, King decided he wasn't ready to give in. Not just now. Not just yet.

Not to him.

In Siberia, Kaparis watched similar images of the container ship, and examined similar maps, showing the extraordinary disposition of forces. He had rarely felt so satisfied.

He actually managed a laugh. Which alarmed Heywood.

"Li Jun, would you be so good as to find me a secure line to Commander King?"

"Yes, Master."

SPPPS SSH CHUKCHUKCHUK... SCHHHHUP... UPH...

"Come on... Come on..." said Finn.

The jeep was slowing.

SSH CHUKCHUKCHUK SSSSF UPH...

They still hadn't hit the road.

Kelly and Finn were either side of the plastic fuel bottle, tilting every last drop of liquid into the fuel line.

"She's dying," Stubbs lamented.

"Burn, baby! Burn!" Delta urged, slamming the power lever back and forth.

The jet was running dry.

A final *CHSSSSS* sent the jeep over a last rise before it stopped altogether.

Silence. They came over the top of the rise and their momentum took them downhill – towards a road.

"There it is!" yelled Delta.

"Make it make it make it make it..." Finn repeated as all four of them willed themselves heavier in order to generate momentum.

Down the slope they rolled – under a wooden fence, and up, just enough to clear the lip of ground that banked the road, rolling forward on to the asphalt of the B237.

Slowly, oh so slowly, they rolled a few centimetres further to come to a halt on a white line in the middle of the road.

It could not have been emptier. The houses they could see were far ahead, big buildings set back from the road. They may as well have been on the dark side of the moon.

They weren't going to make it. Not in the jeep. Maybe not for hours. Maybe not at all. In the distance, they heard the quad spluttering down the course behind them.

"We need to get out of here," Delta said.

"We'd better abandon ship," said Kelly.

All four grabbed what they could and leapt down on to the white line.

"Ow!"

"Argh…"

"Ooh, nasty…"

From the cries of pain, Finn realised he was the only member of the crew not carrying an injury, or over sixty. He was looking round to see if there was anywhere they might hide when –

"What the…?"

Coming down the road towards them on an old BMX, knapsack on his back, was a kid.

"It's a kid!"

"On his own?"

"It's a KID!" said Kelly, heart swelling.

"No… it's not…" said Finn, recognising the mop of brown hair, the thick glasses, the awkward shrunken body and outsize limbs.

"It's bloody Hudson!"

DAY THREE 08:47 (BST). Hook Hall, Surrey

Over the line from Kaparis, King heard the sounds of a choir singing a sentimental dirge.

> "*Go to the dreamless bed, where grief reposes*
> *The book of toil is read, The long day closes...*"

"*Ah, 'The Long Day Closes', Commander King. Do you know it? It's a great favourite of mine. The sequencing codes, please, as per our agreement,*" said Kaparis.

"I don't remember an agreement. I remember a threat," said King.

"*If you will, as per our threat.*"

From screens around the CFAC, King could feel the eyes of the world upon him.

If he failed to act, he would be exposed to nuclear attack from historic allies as an alternative to releasing Armageddon in insect form. If he surrendered, he would hand over a technology with unimaginable potential to a lunatic trillionaire terrorist.

Just another day at the office. King nodded at an underling.

"The code is being sent to the nominated site now. The root equation will follow," said King.

While Kaparis waited for Li Jun to confirm its safe arrival, he made chit-chat.

"*Do you admire the works of Gilbert and Sullivan, Commander? I find the operettas insufferable, but the melodic structure of the songs prefigures much of modern 'pop music'.*"

"I'm no musicologist."

"*Oh, do loosen up.*"

Said the world's greatest psychopath.

Li Jun confirmed the data transfer.

"*We have the majority of the code, thank you so much,*" said Kaparis. "*All that remains now is for you to provide the key equation.*"

"Is that all?" asked King. "What is it that you *really* want? Fame? Love? More billions? There are better ways to spend your vast wealth. Ending global poverty, eliminating AIDS, malaria – even war."

"*Oh, I quite enjoy a war. The equation, please. And where is Dr Allenby at the moment?*"

"Dr Allenby is under arrest. We have only just managed to extract the missing equation; it's held in his own mnemonic code. I will release it the moment we've had time to break it."

"*The mnemonic, Commander. This is no time for games. We'll soon know if it's genuine. I suspect my people are far better than your poorly paid 'public servants'. Otherwise, I'm afraid, matters must stand as they are... ad infinitum.*

"*The long day closes, Commander. And this, the last tick of the clock...*"

FORTY-FOUR

Hudson stopped pedalling and freewheeled.

He'd seen the toy jeep on the road as he came down the hill. *Curious*, he thought, stopping for a look. He could hear a motorbike somewhere. If it was the police, he should at least be seen to *try* and get away.

Hudson did everything for effect. He didn't really have bowel problems, or problems making friends, or migraine headaches. He could poo on any toilet he liked. But his mum and dad were locked in a brutal divorce and being awkward was his way of getting back at them.

Some hope, he thought, and pedalled on towards the—

Whisshsshshshshshshshsh!

An arrow of blue light and smoke shot up from the toy jeep and struck him neatly in the middle of the chest. Startled, he skidded and beat at it as it fizzed and smoked and tried to burn a hole in his jumper, the bike falling away beneath him with a clatter.

He thought he heard something. He looked down at the toy. He *could* hear something. He could hear his name...

"HUDSON! HUDSON! HUDSON, DON'T FREAK OUT!" Finn shouted as Hudson's massive face bent to stare in terror.

"HUDSON, IT'S ME! FINN! INFINITY DRAKE! FINN!"

"Uh??!" Hudson said.

"DON'T FREAK OUT. LONG STORY. I CAN EXPLAIN, BUT NOT RIGHT NOW! RIGHT NOW YOU'VE GOT TO PICK US UP AND GET US AWAY!"

Hudson looked like he was about to cry.

DAY THREE 08:52 (BST). Hook Hall, Surrey

"What is it to be, Commander?"

King stalled to the last.

"Even with these codes, the engineering challenges are such that it is very unlikely you will be able to repeat the experiment, and even less likely you will have time to do so before we track you down..."

"There are a million places I can go, way beyond the reach of a few Western governments. I have people everywhere, even if they don't know it

yet. All I have to do is pay. The world is my oyster, yours is a clam, full of rules to obey and principles to fall short of."

There was a pause. Both men glanced at their array of screens. Gods on Olympus.

King felt the Presidents and Generals and force commanders watching. Ready to make deadly decisions of their own.

Kaparis had prepared meticulously. Played his hand perfectly.

Did this mean they were beaten? No. Not yet. Wounded? Yes.

There would be other battles, thought King. Other days. Kaparis had been identified and his vanity was so vast it would only be a matter of time before he was traced and destroyed. King would probably be out of a job, but he would see to it personally anyway.

Convinced he had very serious problems and that he'd somehow managed to contract a major mental illness, Hudson pedalled home. He turned into his driveway.

Hudson prayed repeatedly and continuously and silently that none of this was really happening, that he was well, and he silently promised God he would never ever fake an illness or a behavioural quirk again, that he would go back to being normal, the most normal, most average, most unremarkable middle-class boy in Berkshire (and that was up against some pretty stiff competition).

He unlocked his door. The home phone was ringing as they got into the hall. He knew it would be his parents. What should he do?

With shaking hands, he opened his backpack. The tiny people were still there. Tiny Finn Drake was still there.

"DON'T ANSWER!" yelled Finn, looking up into frightened eyes the size of swimming pools.

Hudson made an involuntary warble noise.

"CUT THEM OFF! DIAL 999! TELL THEM YOU NEED TO BE PUT THROUGH TO COMMANDER KING! TELL THEM IT'S AN EMERGENCY! AND SAY THE WORD SCARLATTI!"

"Sca—?"

"OR BOLDKLUB! AND THEN LIFT US UP AND PUT ME UP ON YOUR SHOULDER SO I CAN SPEAK!"

Hudson picked up the phone long enough to hear his mother squawk then put it down again. He loved his parents dearly, and they didn't deserve what he was putting them through, not one tenth of it. He wanted to cry.

"YOU'RE GOING TO SAVE US, HUDSON, YOU'RE GOING TO SAVE THE WORLD!"

He dialled 999.

FORTY-FIVE

As the American President shifted in his seat, ready to command his own people to take over, King finally spoke.

"The mnemonic for the equation is this:

'But at my back I always hear

Time's wingèd chariot hurrying near...'"

Kaparis glowed. *Bravo, Allenby.* He loved a puzzle. And he LOVED seventeenth-century literature.

He told himself he would crack it in seconds as he mouthed along.

"And yonder all before us lie..."

"And yonder all before us lie..."

"…Deserts of vast eternity."

"…*Deserts of vast eternity… Ah, don't you just adore the metaphysical poets?*"

"The key to which is…" said King, swallowing his urge to verbally let rip, "… where B is acceleration and E opens—"

"SIR!" A technician brutally interrupted. King raised an eyebrow. This had better be good.

"It's him."

"Allenby?" For a fraction of a second King wondered – dared to hope – that Al had somehow…

"No. Drake, sir. Infinity Drake," whispered the technician.

King's mind spun. Was he quite mad? Had the tension got to him?

"*Where B is acceleration and E opens… What, Commander?*" prompted Kaparis.

"One moment please, caller…" said King, and jabbed hold.

This had better be *really* good.

"Drake?"

"Commander King?" said a tiny voice.

"What the…"

King had been so fixed in the language and thought patterns of command, he couldn't quite…

"We're at Hudson's! QUICK! We got the nest location and we got one of them! But…"

"*Infinity Drake?*" King repeated in disbelief.

"Yeah, I got caught up with the crew, Spiro…"

"We know…"

"Another bad guy is here now though, and he's coming through the door! He's here now! Just get here as fast as you c—"

"Units are on their way."

They heard a smashing of glass, then – *drrrrrrrrrrrrrrrrr* – the line went dead.

"Trace that call! Get a team in there, NOW!" called King.

Demands were coming in from the screens around the world.

"What is going on?"

"Can you confirm that was Drake?"

"That *kid*? Can you be sure?"

"I believe I can," said King, and looked down at the call unit linked to Kaparis. Still waiting on hold.

It was his turn to take a risk.

"Run, Hudson!"

Hudson watched in terror as Kane – a bleeding, burnt fiend – reached through the broken glass of the door panel to undo the lock.

"RUN!"

Hudson dropped his backpack and turned and ran through the house.

Kelly, Stubbs and Delta crashed into a mountain of sweet wrappers, cans, comics and a fleece.

Finn rode on Hudson's shoulder. *At least he's easier to control than Yo-yo*, thought Finn, and held on tight.

Deep in the Siberian permafrost, Kaparis listened, appalled, to the Hook Hall 'hold muzak'.

Vangelis.

Insult to injury.

Not only was it an astonishingly poor recording, it also speeded up and slowed as the signal oscillated around the world to give the impression that it was being performed by an orchestra of drunkards.

Staff were busying themselves around him.

Li Jun had picked up a spike in activity from the open-channel emergency radio traffic she could still access. A 999 call had been followed by an open-channel request for a 'Boldklub' rapid-response team.

Kaparis had already ordered the evacuation of the bunker.

The screen array above and around him was blinking out. The chamber was becoming dark.

What a lot of effort for a single equation.

What little reward.

Vangelis.

"Lock it! Lock the door, Hudson!"

Hudson threw the latch on the door and started to back down the cellar steps. The tiny voice jabbered at his ear all the way.

"Barricade it! Don't just lock it. They're on their way, we just have to hold out. He's already injured, he won't get through that easily. Find a weapon or—"

"Shut up!" said Hudson. "This is not... natural," was all he could manage.

"Sorry, Hudson. My bad. I know it seems mad. I can explain. Just not now," said the voice.

The cellar was old and musty and lit by a single bare bulb. There was a workbench covered in junk and wine racks.

From above they could hear the sound of Kane searching. Coming down the stairs. He found the cellar door – locked. He kicked at it. *BANG!*

DAY THREE 08:58 (BST). Hook Hall, Surrey

King came back on the line.

"My apologies for the interruption..." King started.

Kaparis could sense a thousand years of superior breeding and sound judgement were back. The bile rose in his gut. One of the few bodily functions he still retained.

"The key is: where B is acceleration and E opens –" King plucked some disinformation out of the air – "n to the power of three atmospheres per—"

"*There will be other days, Commander,*" Kaparis interrupted immediately.

King elected to remain silent.

"*This hasn't even started.*"

Kaparis cut the line dead.

BANG!

Hudson could see the door shudder at the top of the steps.

He looked around in terror. There seemed to be plenty of junk on the workbench, but no obvious tools to use in self-defence.

"Bottles, you can use the bottles," Finn suggested quietly, as Hudson crouched, terrified, in the corner.

"There's a way out through the coal hatch... we could hide there," Hudson whispered.

SMASH!

Kane had smashed a big hole in one of the small panels at the top of the door. Through it he could just see Hudson's terrified face, lit by the single light bulb. He reached inside his shirt and detached the semi-dormant Scarlatti from his chest. Pulling hard to tear out the barbed mouthparts. Blood spurted out of the wound as the Beta Scarlatti gave up its hold.

It was angry to be ripped awake in this way and struck its wings.

WKKKDSKDDWKKK!

FORTY-SIX

Finn heard the noise and his blood ran cold. And suddenly he knew what Kane would do.

"Put me on the workbench! Just get to the hatch and run, Hudson!" he called in Hudson's ear.

The beast was coming through the hole in the cellar door. Still groggy, it dropped at first, rat-like, to the top step. But, refuelled by Kane's blood, and with the air thick with Finn's scent, it soon struck its damaged wings together and took off.

Wkzzwkzzkzkwkwkwkzzzwwkwwk...

Hudson ran to the coal hatch. But, unlikely hero – unlikely human being – that he was, he wasn't tall enough to reach up and throw the bolts that locked it in place.

"CHAIR!" Finn yelled at him from the workbench.

Whether he heard him or not, Hudson grabbed a rickety old stool.

Wkzzwkzzkzkwkwkwkzzzwwkwwk...

Hudson froze when he saw it in the half-light. Finn had seen him do it before in school. Finn had done it himself the day before in the woods.

Wkzzwkzzkzkwkwkwkzzzwwkwwk...

"JUST RUN, HUDSON! GET OUT OF HERE!" Finn shouted.

Hudson reacted. Jumped on the stool. Threw back the heavy bolts on the hatch and punched it straight up.

Finn saw blue sky. Felt fresh air. For a second.

Hudson jumped up and swung wildly from the lip of the opening as he tried to haul himself up and out.

The Scarlatti circled the single bare bulb, getting a fix on Finn.

What do I do? thought Finn.

He did not know.

But I am not afraid of life, he thought. *I am not afraid of death.*

He saw the beast curl as it prepared to dive. He ran for cover, any cover, as it drew out its stings and arrowed towards him.

Among towers of old magazines, random tools and an unfinished model aircraft lay the gaping mouth of a bone-china vase, lying on its side, its neck neatly broken, waiting for repair beside an exhausted tube of superglue.

Finn felt the breath of the Scarlatti on his neck and dived head first through into the body of the vase. As he hit the inside of the ice-white cave, the whole thing jolted and spun 180 degrees, as the beast bashed against it in frustration. Finn scrambled up, thinking, hoping, calculating that the Scarlatti couldn't possibly make it through the same broken aperture after him.

But instead of sanctuary, he had dived into a trap.

The gap was tight, but the Scarlatti already had its head inside the broken neck of the vase and was wriggling and crawling the rest of itself through, blotting out the light, its wings ever louder as they echoed round the glazed tomb.

WKKKDSKDDWKKK!

Finn watched the head, twice his own size, squirm and writhe, its mouthparts, still slick with Kane's blood, flicking and extending towards him. He was a sitting duck.

But so was the beast, Finn realised, and it was getting no closer. Its anger was in the way. The more the beast struggled, the more it flicked and flexed its outsize wings, so that each millimetre of progress was countered, and the angrier it got. If it had relaxed, for just one moment, it would be in... but its rage was holding it back.

Stay mad, was Finn's only thought. *Just keep being mad.*

In a flash, Finn ran straight at its Easter Island head and – springing hard on one of its mandibles – vaulted up the creature's terrible face, grabbing one of its antennae where, like a thick tree root, it entered the top of its iron skull.

The beast writhed in outrage and its wings clattered – *WKKKDSKDDWKKK!*

Finn clung on. The beast instinctively withdrew, leaving a crawlable gap between its head and the top edge of the broken vase. *Get out,* thought Finn – and nothing else. *Get out! Get out!!*

He let go of the antenna and clawed his way out down the back of the monster's neck, its scaled head giving way to a flexible coating of thick barbed-wire hair at the top of its back. But, as he clawed his way down, he found himself trapped once more – this time rendered deaf and blind – stuck directly between the creature's beating, cacophonous wings.

WKKKDSKDDWKKK!

Before Finn could wriggle away, he was enveloped by light suddenly, then had the sensation of falling first downward then rapidly upward.

WKKKDSKDDWKKK!

It was a fraction of a moment before he realised what was happening – they were airborne.

Finn watched the items on the workbench rapidly shrink beneath him... then everything was thrown into a blur as the Scarlatti careered and crazed around the cellar, taking Finn on a nightmare rollercoaster ride.

The noise was incredible. The wings were incredible. The sense of unleashing unstoppable power was overwhelming. He was inside the maelstrom.

The beast spun and twisted and corkscrewed crazily to try and get at him, to try and throw him off. Finn clung on, still facing backwards. He threw a hand round to cling on to another clump of back wire, as soon as gravity and momentum allowed, so that he could pivot round and lie askew on the creature's back, at least facing forward.

WKKKDSKDDWKKK!

Which was worse. Much worse. He suffered wave after wave of

sheer terror as they near-missed then near-missed again – wall, door frame, ceiling, floor. He knew the rodeo must end, inevitably they would slam into something, and at this incredible speed he would not survive.

WKKKDSKDDWKKK!

It was surely just a matter of moments. They had only been airborne a few seconds, but it felt a lifetime. It must end. Finn dragged himself up the twisting creature's fuselage until he was again at its neck. It must end.

WKKKDSKDDWKKK!

He snatched hard at, grabbed at, wrenched at the Scarlatti's left antenna. Its fury reached its zenith and it bucked and spun and fizzed…

WKKKDSKDDWKKKWKKKDSKDDWKKK!

…veering wildly off course. This was it, thought Finn, as he closed his eyes and spun and clung. This was the very edge of life. And then at tremendous speed…

POP!

…they struck the single dangling light bulb.

Dust and glass and sound filled time, space and Finn's lungs in the same instant as the bulb imploded.

He had the sensation of falling, still clinging to the beast, and then – *BOOOF!* – being blasted off it, as they bounced off a pile of magazines on the workbench, both the Scarlatti's body and the direction of the pile's collapse breaking Finn's fall until he came to a stop at the foot of the slope.

Then he saw the Scarlatti. There it lay. Centimetres away. Twitching in shock itself. One set of wings sliced through by the shattered bulb, now hanging from its body by a gangrenous thread.

A thousand optical cells burnt into Finn.

Finn thought, *Kill.*

And in that instant – using its good wing as a crutch – the Scarlatti flicked forward.

SLAM!

Finn flew back into darkness, for a moment unconscious – as much from exhaustion as from the impact – as much from the challenge that was somehow always there. Why him? he'd thought when his mum had died. Why did these things have to happen to him? All he knew was that he must be strong enough to survive. Consciousness snapped back.

The Scarlatti's head again filled his view. Ink-black, feelers first, dipping its antennae towards him, tasting his fear, savouring the moment. It was across him. It crushed him as it wriggled round, and he felt the stab of the barbed-wire hairs that covered it.

But at his back he also felt... a rod. He twisted as the beast turned to bring up its stings, and grabbed the rod. It was a single thin nail. A panel pin, dropped by cold fingers months before during the home manufacture of a botched Christmas gift... a compliment of the season.

To Finn it was a metre-long spike. Excalibur.

He pointed it at the massive writhing Scarlatti, right on him now and so close Finn could feel the plates of its thorax slide. As it brought its three gleaming, twitching stings round to finish him off,

Finn jammed the spike in the tiniest space between the plates – hard.

The Scarlatti reflexively clamped the spike with its chest plates – but the nail held. The plates bit too hard and their ligaments buckled beneath. The beast became rigid.

Fear...

And Finn – with all the might and anger and sadness and fight at his disposal – *heaved* upward on the spike and drove it deep, deep into the insect's soft core, with everything he had... up into the vital organs, up until he felt the final kick and struggle, up into the heart of death itself.

Its insides burst beneath its armour and its glistening mouthparts gaped in infinite, silent agony.

And then... nothing.

A terrible stillness.

And Finn. The noise of his lungs and the thump of his heart. Just Finn.

Outside, Kane – attuned to the Scarlatti in every cell of his being – inhaled a few microns of the Beta's death musk... smelt death... felt the end of the swarm.

Feeling pain. Feeling grief. He collapsed in the hallway and vomited.

At the coal hatch Hudson still struggled, but his head and shoulders were already out. He braced his right leg ready for the final push and launched himself up and over the edge.

As he did so, Kane staggered out of the house and appeared over him. A nightmare of burnt skin and bitter rage. An extendable metal cosh flicked open in his hand. *THUK*.

"WATCH OUT!" Finn yelled, hopeless.

Kane raised his arm to bring the cosh down hard on the boy's soft skull. The boy could not move, could not bring a hand up to deflect the blow.

Kane would club him unconscious, or better still... Kill... Kill... He savoured the moment.

He shouldn't have.

Yo-yo arrived.

Yo-yo had first heard the high-pitched whistle when snapping at the Scarlatti. Though distant, it lit up the one part of his small brain loaded with even more significance than 'Finn' or even 'food' – *Grandma!* Six minutes later, he had seen her on her moped and bit her tyres with joy. She had nearly crashed. He had been instructed. "Find Finn, where's Finn?" Which was the easiest thing in the world. He just followed his nose.

With perfect timing, he sank his teeth deep, deep into Kane's raised arm, hitting exactly the same point he'd hit before, already wounded, infected and heavily inflamed, causing an off-the-scale magnification of pain.

"ARRRRRRRRRRGHHHHHHH!"

Kane reeled back. Hudson rolled away across the driveway – almost into the path of the swerving moped.

Grandma – arriving at exactly twelve miles an hour, losing control of 1064 kilograms of metal and momentum – *BEEEEEEEEEEEEEP!* –

fractionally avoiding Hudson but crashing with a sickening force –
WHUMP! – into Kane.

"OH!" she shrieked, as she toppled slowly to the tarmac. "Oh,
my dear boy! I'm so terribly sorry! Oh, that was my fault! Stop it,
Yo-yo! What on earth are you doing? Oh, you poor thing! ARE
YOU ALL RIGHT? Stop biting, Yo-yo! Bad dog!"

Helicopters were landing nearby, as King's men finally closed in.

"Don't just lie there!" she implored the prone Hudson. "I think
he's unconscious! Al! Help! I've crushed a youth!"

Al drew up in the Mangusta.

"WHAT ON EARTH HAS HAPPENED TO YOUR FACE?"
Grandma bellowed at Kane.

"What is he, deaf? Stop yelling," Al said, as he came over from
the car.

Hudson got to his feet and looked at the man who'd got out of
the incredible car to crouch over Kane. He reached towards him,
gripped his arm. Al turned. Saw the wide-eyed fear in Hudson's eyes.
Saw he was pointing, wordlessly, desperately, inside.

"They… there are these little peop—" he managed.

Al followed his pointing arm to the open cellar. He made a wish.

"DO YOU KNOW YOUR BLOOD GROUP? NOD ONCE
FOR TYPE A, TWICE FOR TYPE B, THREE TIMES FOR…"

FORTY-SEVEN

*T*HUMP. THUMP. THUMP.

Three huge explosions deep in its hull ripped through the gut of the *Oceania Express* and caused it to reel and spasm with a mighty rending of metal. Immediately it fell on to one side.

Within two minutes, 110,000 tonnes of steel and oil had slipped remorselessly under, sucking acres of ocean in after it, churning and spinning the surface waters.

Both containers floated briefly, before sinking below the waterline.

The explosive charges had been planted below the waterline three months before. It was an act of spite and fury. But also a demonstration to any doubters, Kaparis thought.

He had arrived. He would not rest. He would be back. And he had been able to get at least part of the Boldklub sequencing codes, he was convinced of that at least.

Even as he was being rolled through his now dormant bunker, Kaparis ordered, "Have work start on that mnemonic. Search through everything Allenby has ever produced and look for precedence, a crossword puzzle he set for a school magazine, anything. We will see how his mind works and crack him. And tell Switzerland to redouble work on the accelerator and delve into the rest of the equations. We can adjust the alignment to suit…"

His voice died away as Heywood pushed him down the concrete corridor to the fully primed escape vehicle.

Super-organism: organism consisting of many organisms where behaviour is selfless and division of labour specialised and where many act in concert to achieve a collective goal beyond the capabilities of individuals; e.g. ants' nest, coral reef, human society.

It all started with an innocuous question – why does grass grow in clumps? There were many boring explanations, but brilliant young David Kaparis had come up with a startling new one.

Grass clumps were super-organisms formed to serve the selfish instincts of a 'super-few' individual blades of grass. These 'super-few' sucked in the best nutrients, etc. from the weaker, dying grasses around them, constantly strengthening their own position.

The implication was that all super-organisms did the same – ants' nests, coral reefs, human society. They were merely support structures for the 'super-few'. Taken further, super-organisms could become more efficient if these super-few were identified and super-served.

He was irritated when the university and his fellow students attacked his theory. So he set out to prove it. Over nine months, he grew and measured millions of individual grass stems to identify those which exceeded the normal range of hydroponic gel consumption.

The research was tedious, but as the data started to come in it clearly showed that 0.06 per cent of the grass was greedier and more acquisitive than the rest. There could be no question.

Why Does Grass Grow In Clumps?
A General Theory on the Development of Super-organisms
A lecture by D.A.P. Kaparis
St Stephen's Hall, 10am, Wed 4th May 1993

The hall was full. His voice rang true; his theory was simple and elegant. He imagined Maria Allenby, the most beautiful and talented student of their generation, would immediately join him, not only in his future work, but in their lives together.

At the climax of the lecture there was silence…

…and then came the crunch of an apple. And the first question. From

Ethan Drake, a scruffy young man with chaotic hair and round glasses sitting next to – of all people – Maria Allenby. He said with his mouth still full of apple *that he thought there was "a mistake in the mathematics".*

Pointing at the blackboard, he explained. "Your equation doesn't balance. You've got $X2Y+3Xyz$ when it should surely be $X2Y+3xyZ$. No? Which would spread the bell curve and put your 0.06 per cent back in normal range. So no super-sorts at all, just lots of nobodies trying their best to get on, variously happy or sad, subject to chance and occasionally bumping into one another."

Silence.

"Unless I've got the wrong end of the stick," he'd added, before casually abandoning his apple and walking out of the hall to find something more interesting to do.

Maria Allenby watched him go, her face a picture of amusement and admiration. They had sat by each other for the first time that day… quite by chance.

It had mattered. That. For some time.

Until one lonely Christmas in a jail cell, Kaparis had suddenly realised. If there was no 'magic' in the data then the magic must be inside himself. He had proved he was one of the few simply by coming up with the theory.

The rest of his life had been a rather more successful experiment.

At Hook Hall there was no immediate burst of applause.

No sudden release of tension or crowning moment for those

huddled over their monitors at the CFAC, or linked in around the world.

Just a checking and rechecking of facts and information as it flowed in. And a growing sense of fatigue for, as the tension drifted, King and others became dizzily aware of the sleep they'd missed out on, the food, the need to fall unconscious.

King fought it, naturally. He wasn't going to miss this.

Slowly but surely, his bets were coming in.

The Kaparis operative captured at the Hudson house by Violet Allenby died in custody of a massive brain haemorrhage – just like the other Kaparis teen, Stefan. (His death was concealed from Mrs Allenby.)

After some confusion, the remarkable survival of the crew, and of Infinity Drake, was confirmed.

News came through that the nest site in Willard's Copse had been located – verifying Infinity Drake's narrative – and totally destroyed by the biohazard team. The entire wood was destroyed by fire over the next four hours. Perhaps even more unfortunately, the Hudson house where the body of the Beta Scarlatti had been found was extensively disinfected – rendering it uninhabitable and unusable for at least six months.

The tension in the CFAC only really broke when Dr Allenby walked in carrying a case of wine from Hudson's cellar, followed by his confused mother, Hudson and a Security Service Officer carrying an unfinished Airfix model of a Heinkel He 111 on a cushion. It contained Infinity Drake and the crew members in various states of exhaustion.

The Heinkel was placed on its cushion at the centre of the command gallery and Finn, Delta, Kelly and Stubbs staggered out of the plastic fuselage for all to see.

"For God's sake, don't try and shoot it down," Al warned the RAF liaison officer.

Laughter like a wave had broken across the gallery. Laughter that turned to applause and rang round the world. A very un-British foot-stamping endorsement of the strategy, actions and decisions of Dr Al Allenby and Commander James Clayton-King.

King ignored it, leaning on his knuckles and refusing to get carried away. Thinking forward.

They had been to the very brink. They had looked over the edge. They had returned. How much of the sequencing code had he given away? What possible consequences would there be? Would divers be able to locate the Fat Doughnut containers? What damage would seawater do to its components? They had not caught or stopped the perpetrator. Not even begun to understand him.

An official announcement was made that the 'poison gas crisis' was over and the evacuation order was officially rescinded. The population was urged to return home over the next forty-eight hours in an orderly fashion.

Eleven days of comment, criticism, panel-show satire and general opprobrium would follow before the affair was blown off the front pages by a romance between a princess and a footballer.

When the central node of all the Kaparis communications had finally been identified three days later, elite Spetsnaz forces moved on the Siberian bunker.

They found nothing but smoking ruins.

Fourteen metres above, an injured Arctic fox, alarmed by the explosions and stung by the smell of burning, had dragged himself out of his lair on the day of the blasts.

Half a mile away, he was found by another, a young male. A son of his from two summers past, set now to claim a territory of his own.

Instinct dictated that the young fox must kill his father. But his heart wanted to lick his wounds and warm him. The young male could not decide. The old male could not tell him he would love him either way.

They stared at each other on the ice.

FORTY-EIGHT

"To see a World in a Grain of Sand
And a Heaven in a Wild Flower
Hold Infinity in the palm of your hand
And Eternity in an hour..."

"Hold infinity in the palm of your hand." *At least someone's having a laugh*, thought Finn.

The worst thing was the poetry. It was Miss Jones's English class and she always did 'voices' and 'feeling'. It was mentally embarrassing.

"A *Rrrobin Rrredbreast* in a Cage
Puts all Heaven in a *Rrrage*..." she trilled.

It was a hot day near the end of summer term. Part of the deal with Grandma of staying in the CFAC with the others was that he had to attend school and lead as normal a life as possible – a tough call given that he was 9mm tall. So he attended remotely, watching the lessons unfold onscreen via a camera hidden on Hudson's lapel.

Unbelievable. Here he was in one of the most advanced laboratories in the world, surrounded by the world's finest scientific minds and shedloads of equipment, and he was grinding through poetry. Poetry!

"He who shall hurt the little Wren
Shall never be belov'd by Men."

At least this one was zoological. He drifted off to think what he would do this afternoon (he was excused games).

He could go down to the collection. 'The Collection: Live!' as he liked to call it – his very own bestiary in an adapted aquarium where he spent a lot of free time playing with, and only occasionally fighting off, some of his favourite bugs. He was even trying to teach the beetles to perform tricks.

He wondered what the others might be doing and looked out of the 'classroom' window. Delta was flying about the quarters in one of the nano-microlights the USAF had specially constructed for her. Kelly was out front doing push-ups. Stubbs must be down in the CFAC with Al and the team, helping to reconstruct the Fat Doughnut Accelerator which was being slowly dried out and rebuilt. The latest estimate to completion was twelve days, but Al had recently revised this to a less precise, "Yeah, twelve-ish..."

Maybe Finn would take a trip down to see how they were getting on. He'd take the train. A four-track Z-gauge rail network ran round the entire CFAC and each crew member had a personal locomotive to ride on top of (Z gauge being 1:220 in scale). Delta and Kelly just had engines to get from A to B, but Finn had added an open trailer to carry stuff and a couple of unusual carriages for show. Stubbs had gone to town and ordered a bespoke Flying Scotsman Express that boasted fourteen luxury carriages, a buffet car, realistic fake steam puffer and pulled into his very own 'snow-effect' highland railway station, where he would often pass the time of day chatting to the plastic passengers waiting on the platform. *What did they talk about?* Finn wondered.

He yawned and might have dozed off, but the next line snapped him out of his reverie.

"The wanton Boy that kills the Fly
Shall feel the Spider's enmity."

A shiver shot down his spine in unhappy remembrance – but then happily the bell went.

"Thank God that's over," said Finn, waking up a bit.

Hudson, who had been accused too many times of talking to himself 'like a weirdo', waited till he was safely out of the classroom crush before responding, "I hate her. She's so rubbish. I'm going to get some lunch. Over and out."

Hudson was often busy at lunch now that he'd become 'normal' again. He'd come over some evenings and at weekends to mess about too, but Finn's closest friends right now – whether he liked it or not – were Stubbs, Kelly and Delta.

They were quartered in a glass cube, two macro-metres square, in Lab One. It was actually an isolation unit from Biohazard Defence, but served just as well as a controlled environment for four miniature musketeers. At first they had been given a doll's house to live in. It looked absolutely perfect, but was full of sharp edges, hard plastic and static electricity – besides which it was way, way too twee for Delta.

Other vessels were tried, mainly variations on the cardboard box, but it was Grandma who had hit upon the solution one Sunday afternoon in her potting shed. Plant-fibre seed trays: a grid of forty five-centimetre-square cells laid in rows of eight by five with a translucent plastic cover. Two had been fixed back to back to form a kind of tower block. Each crew member had a five-cell apartment to themselves with bigger communal knocked-through cells on the lower levels. The fibre meant they were easy to climb through, soft to the touch and easy to push through and remodel – with wiring and plumbing, etc. particularly easy to install.

A hand-painted sign read THE SONS OF SCARLATTI, for that's what they'd christened themselves in the days after their rescue, when they'd learned they were going to be stuck with each other for a while longer yet.

At dinner one night (they lived mainly on distilled sugar water and a disgusting refined soya pulp which they could absorb about 30 per cent of), they realised they were all, one way or another, orphans, so Kelly had proposed, "The beast brought us together, the struggle against it made us. Let's call ourselves 'The Sons of Scarlatti'." Naturally this had started a fight, but Delta had later compromised by adding a second sign declaring: INCLUDING THE ONE AND ONLY DAUGHTER OF SCARLATTI. It all sort of made sense – though Al and the team called them 'Snow White and the three dwarfs'.

Maybe he'd take a trip down and hang out with Al. Maybe he'd watch a movie. Though one of Finn's favourite things to do at lunchtime – if she was awake yet and not too flustered about a test or anything – was to play transatlantic Rummikub with Carla, the infuriating and addictive game she and Delta had introduced him to on their first meeting.

Because Delta would regularly text, call or Skype her sister, a miniature fake 'barrack room' had been built by model makers to fool Carla into believing they were regular-sized when onscreen. Through this, Delta got in touch as normal with Carla, claiming to be on some long boring mission in Europe. Finn was introduced in passing as 'just some English kid from the base'.

"'Just some English kid'?" Finn complained after. "Not 'co-warrior' or 'Top-secret Special Agent' or even 'my friend'?"

"Keep it simple," said Delta. "If she starts cross-examining us, we're toast."

Carla, amused that her spiky big sister had made a new pal, asked, "And does he play, your young friend?"

"Play what?" asked Finn.

It had become an addiction, and their App sessions could sometimes last hours.

He liked Carla. They got on. She was as sparky as her big sister, laughed way more, and she was as interested in art and life as Finn was in science and technology. He didn't get what she was on about all the time, but he enjoyed trying to catch up – and he hoped he'd taught her a thing or two about the physical world in turn.

He went into the 'barrack room' set and skipped across the inbuilt touch pad to see if she was online. The wall-sized screen before him lit up (five centimetres square) and Carla was indeed online, hurrying about her room and getting ready for school.

"Hey," said Finn.

"Hey, you on a break?" she asked.

"You want a game?"

"I haven't got time. I missed the bus yesterday and I have a test. Do you know much about Brazil?"

"Great footballers."

"Oh great, that's a pass."

"We had *poetry…*"

"Which one?"

"I dunno. But it was sort of about me, it was about 'infinity something something'."

"'To see a World in a Grain of Sand/And a Heaven in a Wild Flower/ Hold Infinity in the palm of your hand/And Eternity in an hour…'?"

"That's it! How did you know that?"

"My God! How could you not know? William Blake! How can you call yourself an Englishman and not know who William Blake is? In fact, how dare you! He was every kind of genius. You guys

398

don't even deserve to speak English…" She tailed off, looking for a calculator as Al walked into Lab One and called.

"Gotta go. My uncle's here," said Finn.

"When am I going to meet him? You know Delta talks about him *a lot*." She rolled her eyes in an exasperated kind of way.

"Yuk," Finn agreed.

"Gotta go!" Carla called, heading out with her bag.

Finn came out of the block to see Al towering above the isolation unit, carrying a fiendishly complicated chunk of metal dotted with microelectronics.

"Hey. What is it?" Finn asked.

"I call this 'a sherbet whizz', but that's not important right now. What's important is Grandma's coming this afternoon. I forgot to tell you – we've got to go to the opera."

"What?"

"It's a local am-dram production in the village hall, you're going to *love* it."

"No way!"

"Yes way. If I have to go, you have to go," said Al, wandering off with the whizzer.

Kelly laughed from the bench press in his outdoor gym.

Just what I need, thought Finn, a couple of hours on Grandma's shoulders listening to *opera* interspersed with deafening chat with other old ladies concerning the medical peculiarities of people they once knew, or know now, or who were distantly related to people they didn't know particularly well, or Prince Philip.

And he thought the poetry was bad. Finn had to admit that sometimes... he missed having to save the world.

Still, he couldn't live in the past. *Just keep going.* Next week was the end of term. Carla was going on tour with her orchestra, but when she returned Delta and Finn would join her at their cabin in the woods (after dinner at the White House with everyone, including Grandma, which they were going to spring on Carla as a surprise), then there was the whole long holiday to look forward to.

He watched Delta circle above. He took in the giant figure of Al lolloping off out of the lab. Maybe he'd just lie down and wonder at the wonder of it all until Grandma got here.

Only twelve days left. Then his whole life ahead of him.

He couldn't wait to be big.

Having spent some time in a French jail, then a mental institution, then intensive care – Spiro turned up in the desert of northern Niger at point 104024e 234982n.

He could see nothing but sand.

Somewhere beneath his feet, and at four other sites across the world, the finest minds that money could buy laboured over the snatch of poetry scratched out by Andrew Marvell some 400 years before.

And a lung breathed in...

And breathed out...

INFINITY DRAKE — FINN FOR SHORT — IS STILL... WELL... SHORT.

Only 9mm tall, in fact. But before Uncle Al can figure out
how to return him to normal size a new threat materialises
that sends the gang to the other side of the world.

After stealing Al's shrinking secrets, evil villain, Kaparis,
has devised a crazy, ruthless plan. To create an army of
self-replicating nano-bots – a hardware virus that will
spread from the massive computer factories South of
Shanghai across the world – giving him total control of
global technology and communications.

Once again Finn is thrown into the action and finds himself
on an impossible mission and in a race against time: to save
himself and to stop the bot infection...

...BEFORE IT CONQUERS MANKIND, ONE SCREEN AT A TIME.

COMING SOON

INFINITELY MORE...

www.infinitydrake.com